SINGLE
VERSION

SINGLE VERSION

a novel

Scott T. Barsotti

Published by Quill, an imprint of Inkshares, Inc.,
San Francisco, California
www.inkshares.com

Cover design and illustration by Susie Kirkwood

ISBN: 9781942645139
e-ISBN: 9781942645146
Library of Congress Control Number: 2016935543

First edition

Printed in the United States of America

For Erin
viewfloor21.wordpress.com

PROLOGUE

The large cockroach skittering, scuttling across my desk doesn't faze anyone. Except me. No one else even looks at it; I just catch it out of the corner of my eye. People got used to this far too quickly. It wasn't too long ago that a cockroach, any cockroach, let alone one this big, running across a desk, would have resulted in screams, shouts, and directives to *kill*. Not anymore. Cypermethrin and other similar poisons no longer have an effect on them, and that was always my preferred method. Even if you could still spray something on a roach and kill it—which you can't—there isn't much point in doing so.

Which is not to say I never kill them. I do. Sometimes, you have to.

My client and her parents sit across from me, listening to everything I have to say. Read this book. Get this unpaid internship. Sure, go to college. Why not? No one cares about the roach. Oop, there's another one. My client's mother looks at the second roach and tilts her head. She says, "Mm," then brushes it aside with a flick of her wrist. The cockroach ends up on its back and can't right itself. My client's mother watches it as it kicks its legs skyward in vain. And for just a moment, she smiles.

PART I

*After certain shifts in the
United States and world*

*Prior to my visit to Forest Grove
Cemetery, Plain City, Ohio*

ONE

I've never done drugs, and over time that has a cumulative effect. To remain as you are while the world goes mad isn't sanity. I've often wondered what it's like to do acid, meth, heroin, always been curious about the altered state, but never followed through on any of that. Came across plenty of drugs in my life but always found some reason, some excuse, not to try them. I had class in the morning. I was anticipating a job interview. I'd just read about three teenagers in Tennessee who took a bad hit of something and died within hours, slow, painful drawn-out cramps and seizures blood vomit no thanks.

Drunk and sleep deprived are the only altered states I'm aware of. So when things start to get a little iffy, I have very little to compare it to, even though I feel like this is something I should be able to do. Like when you have trouble describing the flavor of something that isn't really quite like anything else, but still you feel like you can describe it, surely you have the words, and it should be easy, only you can't, and you don't, and it isn't.

This morning, I wake up to a cramp in my left calf. Not as bad as others I've had, but still, it's enough to wake me up. I bolt straight up in bed, and my hands reach for the knotted muscle, my eyes pressed closed, teeth grinding through the pain. My calf feels for a few seconds like it is going to tear itself to shreds and never be the same again, gorily burst from my pajama leg (I picture a werewolf). At last the pain begins to subside, and I half laugh at the immensity of the relief. I swing my legs over the side of the bed and try to put weight on my left leg, but there's no strength in it. When this happens, it's usually an hour before I can walk without a limp. Sometimes I can't walk at all, like now. I pick up my phone and text my boss.

late today had cramp again sorry

I change "sorry" to "c'est la vie" at the last second, thinking that French is better than an apology.

I take the Maw-Gard away from my mouth and wipe the sweat from my lips and chin. A gross way to wake up, but better than the alternative. There was a time when you didn't have to wear a mask to sleep, when people didn't die by cockroach-crawling-in-mouth, choking on them in the middle of the night. A simpler time.

I listen to the news. They're talking about drone strikes. In Pakistan, I assume, considering recent events, though it's entirely possible these drone strikes are elsewhere.

Once I can walk confidently, I go to the kitchen. My cat, Larry, needs to be fed, and I fill his bowl. He's not one of those cats that rations, not one of those you can leave alone for a weekend with a supply of food. He eats every bowl you put in front of him immediately, like he's never seen food before in his life, and fuck is he starving, he may never see food again. Larry was an alley cat, so at one time in his life this was true. He didn't know. Find food, eat it. I once just kept putting food in front of him to see how much he would eat. I thought it was hilarious when he scarfed down the second bowl. I thought it was crazy when he tore through the third. When he got half-way through the fourth, I felt sad and had to end the experiment. When I took the bowl away he looked up at me with huge pupils, heartbroken, and mewed in despair. He may never see food again.

A cockroach flits by Larry as he eats. He looks up from his bowl for just a moment, acknowledges the roach, goes back to eating. When Larry was younger, he would have attacked the roach, impaled it with an expert claw, but now he's like me where those things are concerned: at a certain point you just have to ignore them. I still hate them, just as I always have. Phobias die hard. But if I tried to kill every roach I saw, I literally wouldn't be living my life. It would just be kill kill kill. Kill. Again, kill.

Breathe, kill.

And besides, they're strong. It takes too much energy to kill one, let alone all of them.

There's another one clinging to my coffee mug. I choke back the desire to cry. I hate them.

On the podcast they're talking about drones again. Or still. I'm only half listening, and I've heard them say "-istan" a few times. It could be Pak-, but it could also be Turkmen- or Uzbek-. Afghan- always a possibility. I swear these people are all mumbling. Warfwarfistan.

In separate tabs I pull up the Weather Channel and the *Chicago Tribune*. Sunny today. Murders last night. Several headlines catch my eye: one about a local veteran coming home and meeting his baby daughter for the first time (the daughter's name was Trouble, because people name their kids things like that), another about the rise in violence in the West Loop, another about some sort of huge coyote or panther or wild boar or dog that was on the loose in Rogers Park. One headline reads "PLEASE STAY HOME SHOOTINGS" in my periphery, but when I look at it straight, it really says "Bears survive insane shootout." The Bears won their Monday-night game by a score of 44–42 on a last-second field goal from 51 yards out. The lead changed six times in the fourth quarter, and there were nine turnovers total in the game. They call that "insane." Because language doesn't matter.

I don't have any client meetings today, so there isn't any real reason for me to look nice, and for that reason alone I dress nicely. No tie, but the rest is there. When I get to the office, my colleagues will say, "You look nice." I'll smile, say thanks, even though I don't really like being complimented. Larry waits by the front door and stretches, yawns. There's a siren in the neighborhood.

News. I hear one more story before I walk out the door. Mexican police had a shootout with drug cartels. Like an actual shootout, like what that word really means, with guns and aiming and blood. Not with footballs and limits and rules. Eleven *federales* and eight civilians were killed. No mention of the word "insane."

***

I step outside and pause in the middle of my building's front walk. A plane flies overhead on its way to O'Hare, much lower than they usually are this far east. I walk to the train and spot a few dead rodents on the way. Squirrels, mostly. They're crawling with roaches, which scatter when I pass.

I walk halfway down the platform before leaning out to see if the train is coming. It is. As it approaches, I back away from the edge. There was that guy in the news who slipped in a puddle of coffee and fell in front of the train (he had done everything right until then). Or there was the video of the Chinese woman whose baby stroller was blown onto the tracks by a strong wind, right as a train pulled in. According to the story, the baby lived, but you really can't trust anything you read online, and the incident certainly must have scarred the mother and the train operator permanently, so who really "lived" through that? I turn my shoulders perpendicular to the tracks, so if I slip suddenly or lose consciousness I won't fall onto them. I don't want to end up on the news.

There are only a few people in the car. A mother is talking to her young daughter. Taking her to school. There are two men who stare silently. I am a third man, staring silently. Nineteen roaches on the car—that I can spot. The mother and daughter get off two stops later. I didn't think there was a school near that stop, but that's also not necessarily the kind of thing I'd notice. The train fills up as we approach Belmont station, where several lines connect. At Belmont, two police officers get on. One of them, a stout white woman with a long braid, makes eye contact with me, and I nod. She nods back. Her partner, a broad-necked Latino with greying hair despite his young age, turns toward me. One of his eyes is red, full of blood. He looks right at me. I nod. He coughs and winces.

Even though I don't trust the police, I do like it when there are cops on the train. People behave themselves. And in any case, the police make me way less anxious than CURE sentries do. (Last week I was on the train and this man came through "selling" knives, but really he was *brandishing* knives. Six sentries showed up on the car, and he put all his knives away and sat down like a punished child. Who called them? How did they converge so quickly? They were just waiting at the station, the timing was impeccable, even improbable. When the knife guy got off the train, the sentries followed him, which filled me with unease, like I knew this was not going to end well for him, or maybe he would just disappear. But then again, he was pointing knives in people's faces, my face, so I wasn't all that concerned.) Many people change trains at Fullerton, but the cops don't. And I don't. I decide to take the Brown Line all the way down. A man on the other side of the train keeps eyeing the cops. He's got that look, like he really wants to be ranting and swearing and screaming, he wants to be the person on the train who does that today, but he can't with them here. The police are oblivious to his glances. But I notice. I see his need.

A homeless man sleeps across from me. He has roaches on his hands and hat.

I get off the train at the Grand station and stroll in the direction of my office. I stop into a 7-Eleven for a cup of tea. When I ask if they have any honey, the cashier looks at me with a twisted face and says, "Honey? In tea?"

"Uh . . . yes?"

He shakes his head. "No honey. Sugar and stevia." Pointing to somewhere in the store, he adds, "You can buy a bottle of honey," followed by an exaggerated *blech*, sticking his tongue out, squinting. He brushes a cockroach off the counter and laughs to himself. Half of his right hand is cybernetic. When he brushes the roach away, it is with a heavy metallic scrape.

When I get to work, my colleagues are not busy. They're watching a video online. They look up at me and smile, but don't say anything, just keep watching the video. My boss gestures for me to come watch, too. The video is of a group of boys in Guatemala pushing a giant tractor tire over a hill and watching it roll. It gathers speed going down the steep incline until it finally hits a bump toward the bottom and flies up into the air, getting some very impressive hang time, and then splashes down into a lake below. The boys all cheer when it hits the water, and the video ends. In its simplicity, the video is joyous. My boss says to me, "We're trying to figure out if it's real."

My colleague Sheila, always quick with compliments, says, "You look nice today."

"Oh, thank you." I'm transfixed by the video.
The tire.
The hill.
It does look real.
But it probably isn't.

***

My job isn't all that exciting, so I'm not really going to get into it, but basically I'm an educational advisor . . . sort of. In a manner of speaking, I'm a consultant . . . kinda. A career coach . . . maybe. People come to me, come to us, when they're trying to decide what they should do. Their new direction in life. College, grad school, trade school, vocational, culinary, seminary, or, of course, nothing. Lots of measurements: personality surveys, interest surveys, skill assessments, ability tests, values and goals inventories. Why do you want to be a lawyer? What classes did you like in school? Do you know what "PhD" stands for? Is this your decision or your parents'? Would you rather be rich or fulfilled? What are your passions? Do you comprehend the level of debt you'll be taking on? Why do you want to be an anesthesiologist?

In short: my job is to tell people where they can learn what they want to learn, where they can get the degree or the distinction they wish to possess, which programs are the best, and how they should prepare. What people want from me, however, is something else. What people want is for me to make choices for them. Plan the next decade of their lives. Solve their relationship problems. Or their financial problems. Tell them school doesn't cost money. Tell them that they can probably do what they want to do without a degree. Tell them that their child does, in fact, love them. ADHD is to blame. Everything happens for a reason.

Today the schedule is empty. Just me and my four colleagues, but no clients and no phone calls. I ask if someone unplugged the phone, and no one responds, which makes me wonder if they even heard me, if perhaps my voice never reached their ears. If the vibrations were weak. Or if I spoke only in my head.

Business here is not great. Actually, business here is downright bad. As a firm that gives career advice, our services lose much of their value when there are no careers to be had. Millions and millions of jobs become automated every year, technology disrupts entire industries, 3-D printers handle all manufacturing, and driverless cars are the norm, negating the need for human labor and skill. And yet, still, everyone is expected to have a job. People who don't have jobs are called lazy; meanwhile, they can't give their time away. Many of our clients come in for theoreticals, best-of-all-possible-worlds affirmation. Even if you love what you do, there's a thrill in the confirmation that you would have been bad at something else. So you may not have made the right choice, but you didn't make the worst choice.

My boss asks me to make a bank deposit. We often have no deposit, virtually all our clients pay by credit card or transfer, never cash. But this week, we have a paper check, which is like seeing a praying mantis. I walk down Hubbard Street toward the bank. Right outside the door to our office is a bird in a losing battle against a swarm of roaches. The bird has an injured wing and can't fly. The roaches crawl all over it, tasting the oil from its feathers with their feet. The bird chirps in a panic, shaking its head and its good wing. The most I can do to help is to step on a couple of the roaches who are away from the mess.

Crack.

Crack. That's the best I can do.

I don't have the heart to kill the bird, to just end this. If I try to pick it up and move it, the roaches will get on me, and roaches have a way of following the pack. If one moves, two move, if two move, eight move, if eight move, ninety move, and so on. It's best to avoid them when there are so many, or else you'll be finding them in your pockets for days. In your hair.

I walk past a group of businessmen, all white, about the same height and weight, all with holstered guns. They stand outside their building (someone's building) and smoke vaporizers, laughing. One of them is telling a story about a home invader he shot dead. As he tells the story, he unholsters his gun and waves it around.

"And I say to him, 'See anything you like?' and he looks at me—"

"Muslim?"

"Asian, man."

"Asian?"

"Yeah, fuckin' *Asian*, like Korean maybe, and I say, 'See anything you like?' and he gets this look on his face—"

"Do it, show them the face!"

They all laugh, a revolting sound, but then they abruptly quiet down. None of them fail to assess me as I skirt past. A couple of them snicker, maybe because my hair is longer than they think it should be. Maybe because I'm unarmed and by myself and smaller than they are. Maybe because I'm here. Any number of reasons. There's a big laugh from behind me, but before I can worry too much about it, our ears are all pierced by a shrill tone: the unmistakable cry that precedes a police warning.

"PUT YOUR FIREARM IN ITS HOLSTER."

A deep pause. I don't have a firearm, so the officer can't be talking to me. And the police issue this warning only when a firearm is being pointed at someone.

"Put your firearm in its holster."

"OK, OK!" says one of the businessmen, and they all mutter to themselves, pocketing their vapes and heading back into their building. I peek over my shoulder. I see that one of them has two shotguns strapped to his back, like swords. As I notice this, I take a few steps farther down Hubbard without watching where I'm going, and run right into a homeless woman. For a person who's hungry and alone, she's quite sturdy. Running into her is like running into a tree, and I almost fall. She talks and talks and talks, to herself it seems. Or maybe she has an earpiece.

Just inside the doors to the bank is a security checkpoint, run by two large men bearing new-wave assault rifles. "Arm cannons," people call them. They both wear sunglasses, but I can feel their eyes on me. I toss my wallet and phone into a tray. I remove my belt and shoes. I step through the detectors. On the other side is a gigantic man wearing body armor, all of him is weapons, and on his hands are blue sanitary gloves. He holds up one blue hand, indicating that I should wait. An orange light comes on, announcing that I am unarmed. The guard gestures for me to come with him. We step behind a screen, and I'm instructed to remove my outer shirt and pants. There's great suspicion toward unarmed people, which I'm aware of; I'm far more likely than others to be searched when I go anywhere, security forces always figure I must be hiding something, I must have some sort of polymer weapon, something made on a 3-D printer, some powder, some explosive, some secret. The sentries of CURE are particularly edgy about the unarmed, but lucky for me our bank is one of the few left that doesn't contract CURE for security. The guard takes only a cursory glance at my underarms, my butt, and he's satisfied.

"All good. Personal banking is up the escalator to the left, business to the right."

I get my clothes back on and go up. At the top I see rows of tellers and bankers standing around talking to each other or to clients or on their phones. All of them are armed. Whenever I come in here, I'm always amazed by the utter lack of roaches. Some businesses are better than others at managing roaches, but Allies Bank is better than most. I see only a few crawling in the corners, underneath some ledges around the branch. (They're always there, you just have to know how to see them. Or hear them.) I do a quick scan of the business tellers, and I notice that one of them, a young white woman, probably twenty-four or twenty-five, has only a single gun. A small revolver. That doesn't mean anything, but I choose to believe that it means she's wearing a gun only because her employer requires it, and that she chose the least boastful model available. I wonder if it's even loaded—who am I kidding? Of course it is—as I step up and say hello. She smiles. She's cute, very nice, friendly eyes, and her smile is sincere. She smells nice, too, like a thunderstorm. I hand her my check and deposit slip; she marvels at the paper check and reminds me that we can and should deposit remotely. She takes a step back to retrieve a needed form, and when she does, I can see she has a second small handgun strapped to her ankle.

TWO

CURE is the largest corporate entity in the United States. CURE stands for the Coalition of United Response Engineers. They're not a coalition so much as a massive, privately owned paramilitary organization; and surely no one—not even anyone who works for CURE—knows what a "response engineer" is supposed to be. They are ready for war, replete with armored vehicles, chemical weapons, rocket launchers; if it was made for a combat theater, CURE has it, and in surplus. Their slogan for years was "Building Security," which is pretty shaky ground for claiming to be any sort of engineer. Last year they changed their slogan to "Building Liberty." Because language doesn't matter.

At the end of a very slow week, I finally have a client. A young man with his parents. He's off the charts on artistic ability tests, he's introverted, and his personality measures all point toward something creative and unconventional. I try to push him toward visual art, but his parents object, as they should. There is no art culture anymore. Very few colleges even offer fine art as a major, although there are still some dedicated art schools out there. When I suggest art, I'm encouraged to see his eyes light up, just a flicker. I dig a little deeper and find that he paints, likes photography, and can draw very well; he has an interest in graphics and filmmaking.

His father was a lawyer with a ceramics hobby. Was.

His mother was a speech-language pathologist and a former actor. Was. Former.

I ask my client to write down some ideas for potential careers. I pass him a sheet of paper. His parents fidget; his mother wrings her thin hands, her dry skin makes a brushing sound. The young man has a smile on his face as he writes for about thirty seconds. He passes the paper back over to me. Everything he has written has to do with CURE, except the last line, which reads "hedge funds."

His parents smile at me, expectantly.

***

There are homeless men on each corner of the Grand and State intersection. They sing their pleas.

"Have a blessed day. Have a safe night."

"Help me out today, today. Help me out if you can."

"C'anyone help me getta sandwich today, c'anyone help?"

"Spare something, anything. Spare something, anything."

There's a craft to it, like they must get together and role-play, share best practices. Each chants or singsongs for help in such a way that the cadence sticks with you, you find yourself repeating it during your commute.

Have a blessed day. Have a safe night.

Have a blessed day. Have a safe night.

His sound stays in your head, you picture him, hear his vocal quality, you can see his face. This is no accident. It's a tactic. A slow burn on your sympathy.

"Spare something, anything. Spare something, anything."

18

As I walk past these four men, I notice that they're all unarmed.

"Help me out today, today. Help me out if you can."

A shrill tone.

"MOVE OUT OF THE STREET."

I stare at nothing in particular.

"MOVE OUT OF THE STREET."

I feel a hand on my back, and I'm pushed to the sidewalk. Without realizing it, I had stopped in the middle of the intersection. A Chicago police officer has swooped in from behind and pushed me out of the street. Kind of him, actually, as it's not really his job to keep me from getting hit by a car. I probably wouldn't have, as it's mostly driverless cars downtown, and those don't (often) hit people, but still.

I thank the police officer, an older black man, for helping me. He puts a grandfatheresque finger on my sternum and gives a quick, hard poke with his fingertip. It's the first time anyone's touched me in weeks.

All around me, the buzz of drones. Messenger drones, most likely, considering the sound. Yeah, probably messenger drones. But while I hear them in all directions, I can't see any of them, and that always makes me uneasy. Hopefully messenger drones.

I enter the subway station at Grand and State, pass the security checkpoint, and head down to the mezzanine level. The entire floor is an advertisement for a health insurance provider. The picture is that of an elderly couple laughing, and the tagline is "Set Yourself Free." I walk across the ad and find, down in one corner, a box of fine print. The first phrase is "Restrictions may apply."

I walk down the stairs to the platform, and there's an ad plastered all over the opposite side of the tunnel. It's for a soft drink. The tagline is "Be You." Behind me I see other ads, the same insurance provider that was advertised upstairs. "Set Yourself Free." I stare at the ground. There are ads there for a debt-relief agency. "Free Yourself." I look at the ceiling. A phone provider. "Be Free." A train pulls in going the other direction. All across it, a car ad. "That's Freedom for You."

I close my eyes and hear, on the southbound platform, a busker playing guitar. He's good.

There's nothing to see here . . . nothing to see . . .

Move it along now . . . there's nothing to see . . .

I feel a tickle on my hand. I know, without even opening my eyes, that it's a roach, and I'd rather not look at it, so I just flick my wrist to get rid of it.

"Hey!"

I open my eyes to a flutter of fabric. A woman standing near me flails her arms.

"You just put that roach in my hair, fuckhead!"

I apologize, but she doesn't care. She continues to hurl insults at me until I walk away from her. Best to walk away. With women, it's always hard to tell where their weapons might be.

I walk to the end of the platform.

Be You.

Be Free.

A train hurtles into the station. It's mostly empty.

I step onto the train and it's cold aboard. I feel an instant numbness in my fingertips, and my toes feel bathed in ice. I'm underdressed. C'est la vie.

I sit and pull out a book. High fantasy novel, sword and sorcery, the kind they don't write anymore. At Clark and Division, a man sits across from me, wearing a lot of clothing that's dirty and far too big. Or maybe it's that he's too small. He sniffs in an exaggerated way, several times in succession. He coughs. He coughs again, louder. He wants me to look at him, so he keeps making abrupt noises. In this sense, the book is strategic. I am actually reading it, but it gives me a fixed point to focus on, in order to avoid looking up. I don't know what this guy would want with me (not that he needs to want anything), but he keeps at it, keeps writhing, making loud, throaty noises. He jerks his foot up off the floor, almost like he aims to kick the book out of my hands. In that moment I'm weak, I flinch, and he sees it.

"Hey."

I say nothing.

"Hey, I read that book. *Pssht.* I . . . read . . . that . . . book."

I catch myself shifting uncomfortably. Nonchalant, not too quickly, not too slowly, I put my right hand under my jacket, enough to raise some doubt as to whether or not I'm carrying. He calls my bluff.

"You ain't got nothin' under there. I seen you before."

This catches me off guard. It's rare anyone recognizes me. I look up at him. I recognize him, too, but I'm not sure from where. I look right into his eyes. One of his eyes is not like the other. It almost looks like a snake's eye. Or maybe a fish's. His normal eye twinkles and a grin spills across his face. The train stops at North and Clybourn, and he acts casual. No one exits the train; one old woman gets on. She has a huge browning bandage on her cheek.

"Listen. You live off the Brown Line, right? Albany Park? Ish? Nice area. Nice area. I got some friends up there. You should drop in on us sometime."

He reaches into his pocket and pulls out a crumpled business card.

JV
Unarmed Citizens
IXS

"I'm gonna tell you something. It's all you need to know. Kedzie. Kedzie Brown."

I look at the card. Kedzie Brown? He senses my confusion.

"That's all you need to know. Till next week. Next week it won't do shit for you."

The doors open at Fullerton, and he's gone. I look down at the old woman with the bandaged cheek. She has her hands cupped near her face, and she appears to be whispering into them. I watch her, all the way up to Belmont station. Whispering into her hands. Once or twice she holds her hands closer to her ear and laughs. At Belmont, the doors open, and I get off to wait for the Brown Line train. As I exit the train, out of the corner of my eye I see the old woman lower her hands to the floor of the car. A large roach crawls from her hands, out the door, down the side of the train, and disappears underneath. The woman laughs and looks around.

According to the schedule, the Brown Line is supposed to operate every six to eight minutes at rush hour, but the train takes thirty-five minutes to arrive. In the meantime, six other Red Lines come through, but the platform remains uncrowded because not many people take the train anymore, not since last year's bombing on the Blue Line. A bombing that still was never proved to be a bombing. An elevated train sitting at the Damen Blue Line station inexplicably exploded, killing over four hundred people on the train and on the street. There were investigations, obviously (supposedly? allegedly?), and it was determined to be a bombing, but there was no evidence to support that conclusion other than it being a convenient explanation for a sudden explosion. More people began taking driverless cars to work, or working from home.

I'm freezing by the time the Brown Line pulls up. It stops, and the operator gets off the train. She leaves the doors open, which won't help me get any warmer. I get on and sit with my book. I open it up, but I'm not reading. Instead, I try to remember why I live here, in such a place as Chicago. I'm originally from Columbus, Ohio, which only barely exists as a city anymore itself. All my relatives have left Columbus and are now living in small towns around central Ohio; my parents moved to a place called Plain City. Whenever I talk to them, they talk about how worried they are about me, living in the city, "that city," how scary it is here, how unpredictable. But it's just as dangerous where they are, maybe even more so. Violent clashes in small towns don't make national news, but they happen all the time. The city is dangerous, but there's a larger percentage of unarmed persons, so I have a sense of belonging here, or potential belonging at least, that I wouldn't have in rural Ohio. More of my people here. My mother would not tolerate me leaving the house unarmed in Plain City.

More random crime happens in the cities, but more calculated crime happens outside them. Not sure which is worse.

If I listen carefully, I can hear a woman screaming. But not from the street. It seems to be coming from the sky, but I can't locate the source. I look up from my book, and I realize that it's gotten dark. I'm still at Belmont. I have no idea how long I've been sitting here. There's no one on the train with me. I step off the train and walk up the platform to the front car. It's empty. The operator never came back, or her replacement never showed. Halfway down the platform a middle-aged white man with glasses is screaming obscenities in a gravelly voice. As he screams he swings his limbs, and there's something disturbing about the way he moves. I can't be certain, but I believe I hear the sound of jackhammering. Pounding.

I walk down into the station, hoping to find a customer service rep, but there's no one in the kiosk. I don't suppose there ever is.

I look out to the street and there's a constant stream of pedestrians going in both directions. Most of them are on the sidewalks, but many are in the road. A few driverless cars crawl through. I want to stick to main arteries, so I'll take Belmont to Lincoln, take that up north, then Wilson over into Albany Park. All told, it'll be about four miles, which my legs and feet can take, no problem, but long walks take a toll on my nerves. These neighborhoods are all constantly changing. You never know which streets, which blocks, which buildings, are shady. Usually, keeping to main roads is the better bet, more people but also better behavior, less of an X factor. No one wants a firefight. Also, the police monitor most of the major intersections. Get away from the crowd and you're more likely to run into CURE sentries who are working a block or searching for someone. Or, worse, you may run into a couple of sentries who are bored.

As I walk along Belmont, everyone is polite and quiet. I keep my head down. No eye contact, fewer ads, it's more peaceful this way, although looking at the ground means seeing more roaches dashing around stepping feet, riding on hems. For every live one there are two dead ones, crushed into the concrete, and the only difference is that the live ones are *fast*, almost unbelievably speedy, like they're on six tiny ice skates. I reach the six-point intersection of Belmont, Lincoln, and Ashland. I turn north onto Lincoln, but as I'm crossing Ashland, something happens. A young woman walks right into the middle of the intersection, pulls out a gun, and starts pointing it at all sides. The pedestrians all slow to a halt and watch her. She doesn't say anything, but in the silence I hear an odd sort of whimper. She points her gun north, northwest . . . south, southeast . . . east, west . . . all around. I recognize her: the teller from the bank.

A shrill sound.

"PUT YOUR FIREARM IN ITS HOLSTER."

She whimpers, her arm starts to slacken.

"PUT YOUR FIREARM IN ITS HOLSTER."

A shot rings out, I believe from the west. The woman stumbles and clutches at her neck. She points her gun at the sky and fires twice. She falls. The pedestrians erupt in applause. It's unclear whether she was shot by the Chicago police or by a fellow commuter, but at this point, it doesn't matter. She lies in the street, and everyone resumes moving, a tad quicker than before. Except me—I pause and try to remember her name. I want to remember her name. I try to remember a nametag, a placard, a business card, anything.

I walk up Lincoln through North Center. At the corner of Montrose and Lincoln, a pack of young men offer me protection. Twenty dollars per mile, they'll walk with me. (Some people have metal detectors in their eyes; they can just look at you and know.) I'm rattled by the teller's death, so I take them up on it. A teenage boy, sixteen or seventeen, hops forward and bumps my fist. He walks with me north on Lincoln, hand on his weapon.

"Where to, homes?"

"Albany Park."

"My mom's is over there, like Kimball and Ainslie, you know?"

"Sure, that's over there."

"Buncha Arabs, you know? Fuckin' Persians and shit."

"What's your name?"

"Des."

"Des, thanks for walking with me."

"Your money, homes."

"Yeah."

Des and I turn west on Wilson and walk toward my neighborhood. Most of the houses have darkened windows, but a few have people standing in them, watching us pass. Des is friendly in his way, talks a lot about his family, growing up in this area and watching it change. Talks about stories his mother told him; the neighborhood used to be full of young families. The churches functioned as churches. People used to canoe down the river, he says, "And that's crazy, like, not about to get in that shit. Can't even swim."

When we reach the bridge, I'm thankful he's with me; we pass some characters who would have created a problem for me, but with Des they give passage with no issues. We reach Kedzie, and bells ring just off to the north, red lights flash, and the candy cane gates close. Now that I'm almost home, the Brown Line is running again. The northbound train I was sitting on an hour and a half ago creeps across Kedzie into the station. I'd be upset, but then, who knows if I would have survived the ride. You just never know; any choice you make that doesn't get you killed was a pretty decent one—or at the very least, one you shouldn't regret. Tonight, I got some exercise and got to hang out with Des. There's your silver lining.

"You got cash, right?"

"Some. You don't take credit?"

Des holds up a mobile device, suggesting that he does take credit. "Been dickin' around with me, though. Won't connect."

"Yeah."

"They say they gonna fix it, but—" He clicks his teeth.

"Who's they?"

Des can't help but smile a little. He's still young.

"You got cash, right?"

"Like I said, I have some."

"How much you got?"

"I got twenty."

"Bullshit."

"That's what I got."

"Fare's forty. Twenty a mile."

"Fourteen blocks isn't two miles."

"You fuckin' with me?"

"Cash—I only got twenty. Take credit, you'll get it all."

Des shuts up, just shakes his head, his jaw tightens. On the final block, we walk past the old high school. Des points his gun at the now-abandoned school building. He fires once. Under the echo of the blast, I hear a tinkling of glass.

"Can you not fire your weapon, please?"

I can hear the sound of thousands of legs. Skitter-scuttling. Scattering. Disperse.

Des puts his gun away without a word. All of a sudden, as if by magic, his credit app stops dickin' with him and connects; I hand him a credit card. He taps it to his mobile device twice in quick succession, and the payment is approved. "Thanks, Des." He nods and walks away, back the way we came, checking his shoulders as he goes.

I travel the last half a block on my own. In the distance I hear light pops. Could be guns. Could be fireworks. Could be someone watching a movie. Playing a video game. I hold my key-card and stand outside my door just another moment. I hear a whirring, mechanical sound in the sky. It's a strange sound that seems to have layers to it, a shrieking and whooshing. I look up and see a passenger jet flying overhead toward O'Hare. It's really quite low. Then another follows, far too closely. I let out a heavy sigh and enter my building. I'm saddened to see that an ad has been put up in the space where the mailboxes used to be. A fast-food chain: "Because You're You!" A cockroach crawls across an image of a cheeseburger.

Inside my apartment, Larry waits. As soon as I walk in and turn on the light, he's right there. Dependable Larry. He's a good cat.

I think the teller's name was Anne.

***

I spend most of my night watching viral videos. I sign on to a well-trafficked forum where videos are shared and discussed, criticized and picked apart. Tonight I'm spending a lot of time on so-called ghost videos. They have titles like:

SPRITIT *COT* ON TAPE (REAL!!!!)

and

gosht in my parent house scurry nsfw

and

SEROUSILY REAL POULTTRAGIST!!!!!! o_O

Most of them are obvious fakes. Editing tricks, lighting tricks, clever angles, some are just actors in makeup. The footage is usually shaky and grainy, so you can't ever get a clear look at whatever it is that the video is supposedly showing you. There are scared voices and swearing. Everything is very typical. There is one I come across, though, that has been largely overlooked. The hits are very low compared with every other video, probably because the actual watching of the video itself is very boring. In it, a group of teenagers breaks into this old sanatorium in Poland, and the reason they're there in the first place is because they heard it was haunted and were dared to spend the night. There are specific rooms in the sanatorium they are meant to seek out, to catch the experience on video as proof of their exploration and their general balls. So the video begins with them finding a way into the place and setting up shop in one of the offices. At first they walk around a little in the daylight, just running around, messing with shit, laughing, being kids. Then the sun starts to set, and their movements through the building slow. They take their time, inspect shadows. When night falls, they wander around with flashlights, which is already pretty spooky on its own, but the moment that gets me happens about a third of the way through the video, when they reach the patients' quarters. They walk into several rooms in succession, and each is empty save some debris. In one room there's an old desk. In another, there's a broken chair lying on its side. They inspect the chair, film it from all angles. Two legs are broken, and another looks splintered and ruined. While filming the chair, one of the boys in the hallway calls them all to attention, and they hurry out to look at what he's looking at. Some sort of brown liquid on the floor. They talk about whatever it is, and something of an argument breaks out. Probably about what the brown liquid is or isn't (the argument is in Polish, and there are no subtitles). One of the boys gets some of the brown liquid (more like goo, actually; it's viscous) on his fingers and tries to get one of the others to smell it (or maybe eat it), chuckling all the time. And that's when it happens. The moment that gets me. The kid holding the camera moves one room farther down the hallway to continue the exploration, and in that room there is quite clearly, quite obviously, quite no fucking around, a bed—and not just a bed, but an occupied bed. In that bed in that room in that sanatorium, there is what appears to be a person under bedding spotted and slick with filth. An arm hangs over the side of the bed, and he looks like he may be dead. The arm is so skinny, it seems like he must be a dummy or a doll. But then it moves. Not on camera, but it moves: one second the camera catches the hand fully open, it moves away and back a moment later, and the fingers are splayed differently—the thumb is tucked into the palm. But the teenagers don't react. They don't freak out. They don't lower their voices. They don't investigate. In fact, they don't even seem to see it. The thumb, the person, maybe not even the bed. The camera catches him for only a few seconds when they first enter the room, and again for another glimpse as they film around the interior. And then they walk out. The video continues. They go farther into the bowels of the sanatorium, film some rooms, some showers, some instruments, some evocative corners that are genuinely creepy. They scare themselves a few times, they hear some noises in the darkness, but all the while you're watching it and thinking about that figure in the bed. And the broken chair, which, for some unknown reason, fills me with dread when I look at it. Toward the end of the video, they walk back the way they came, toward the office, and on their way back they come through the same hall of patients' quarters where they saw (or captured) the person in the bed. And then the coup de grâce: A clever filmmaker would give you just a peek at the bed on the way back through, maybe show that it isn't there, or that it's there but it's empty now, just to bring the set piece full circle. But they do no such thing. They walk right past the door of the room without hesitation, as though there was nothing noteworthy in there. Nothing whatsoever. They get back to the office without incident, and the video continues for another ninety seconds or so before just ending with no particular ceremony or closure of any kind.

Why would people fake something like this? That's the question I always have to ask myself. What's the point? Just to show they could? Just to try to trick you? Trick everyone? All the forums are preoccupied with more overt videos, where the ghost in question could be easily observed, where contact is made. Objects fly across the room. An apparition, orbs of light. Shorter encounters, cut to the chase. Fake. Fake. Fake, everyone says. *Fake!* The comment boards light up, the debate ends before it starts and devolves into insults, death threats. It's a fake. It's a fake.

But the comment boards for the sanatorium video are nearly empty. Just fifty-two comments at the moment, and most of them are centered on how the video "isnt scary" or "is looooong" or "is dum." No mention of how the boys don't react, no mention of how anticlimactic it is, no mention of how the video doesn't seem to be trying to manipulate us in any way. There's no tipping of the hand, no wink at the camera. I make a comment of my own. I could make my case, spend a few hundred or thousand words on why it might be genuine, but others would just flame it. Instead, I keep it simple:

"Pretty convincing."

Before going to bed, I watch one more video. It's the one my coworkers were watching, of the boys in Guatemala pushing the tire down the hill. People on the forums get very pseudoscientific in their explanations of why it must be fake. The particulars of how vulcanized rubber bounces. The speed of the tire isn't consistent. The line it follows is too straight given the unevenness of the slope. The signature of the splash isn't quite right for the size of the tire. People go to great lengths to not believe in something.

***

I wake up in the middle of the night, once again, with a cramp in my leg. I rub my leg, remove my Maw-Gard, drink some water, take two aspirin. My neighbors are yelling. Or someone is yelling outside. Or both. Larry is in bed with me, which is rare; he's usually up and around at night, looking out a window or running through the apartment. He's sound asleep, though, right here next to me. I put my hand on him, and he stirs but doesn't wake up. The moonlight paints a bar on my wall, changing the color of the paint to something that it isn't; a dull beige in the day, it's now a crisp silver. In that shaft of light, I see one small dark shape.

A cockroach.

Its antennae wave, but otherwise it remains still. They always say that if you see one cockroach in your home, it means there are hundreds, maybe thousands more. If there are a thousand cockroaches for every one we see, then the earth might as well be made out of them. They're everywhere. They've stopped hiding, they don't shrink from the light anymore. They're stronger than they ever were, resistant to poisons, able to multiply at a faster rate. Their predators are dwindling or have moved on to other sources of sustenance. We're told that, one day, birds, centipedes, beetles, lizards, and toads all stopped eating cockroaches. Wouldn't go near them. Biologists, entomologists were baffled. Animals that once fed on roaches were now turning up their noses, turning their backs, even cowering. And I understand. I do. I wouldn't want to eat them. But they're everywhere, they live everywhere and get in everywhere. Not only here in the city or in the US, but everywhere. Countless. Worldwide. And yet each one is an individual. I wonder if they can tell each other apart. They now live for years and years. Long enough to have generations. Family trees. Kingdoms.

The roach falls off the wall, out of the moonlight. I turn on my lamp. I have a hammer sitting on my bedside table, which I pick up. I see the roach near the wall on its back, unable to right itself. Its legs kick like crazy, trying to find something to grab on to, something with which to remedy its situation—anything would do. A balled-up receipt. A sock. My hand. But there's nothing. It's fallen onto a section of open floor between my bed and the wall, and it's stranded. Eventually it will give up trying to right itself and will instead curl up and play dead, waiting for someone to come along with a wad of tissues or a dustpan, patient, patient. They are calculating, smart, resilient, resourceful. They don't need weapons; they have numbers. They don't need to hunt; the whole world is their pantry. They don't need protection or drama or money or joy. They are perfect. They are, in their way, serene. Superior.

I try to take a step, but the cramp in my leg makes me crumple to the floor and I land on my hands and knees, inches from the roach. I look at it. This ugly, ugly thing. With its brown wings, its red face, its six spindly legs. I hear this little sound, like a wheezing chirp. It's crying out. To me maybe, or to others of its brood. I hold the hammer above the roach. Sensing it there, the roach extends its six legs, trying to make contact with the hammerhead, stretching, stretching toward the ceiling. This could be its deliverance.

I raise the hammer slowly, and bring it down fast.

THREE

The next morning I get a text from my boss. She's been feeling nervous downtown lately and just read something about packs of wolves living in old buildings and so she's going to take the rest of the week off and would I take her clients k thx. I'm already taking appointments for my colleague Brian, as well; he's on vacation. Sheila is out with flu-like symptoms, so I'm taking her appointments, too. Our other consultant is Walt, who can't be bothered to take on extra work, so although it will be only the two of us, Walt will do his work and I'll do the rest. Which is fine; I'd just as soon be busy while there and not have time to sit around and listen to him complain about TV shows. There's a certain kind of person who, even as the sane world falls apart, will still complain about TV shows.

Today the city is quiet. I wait for the Brown Line for a few minutes, and when it pulls up, it's four cars long instead of eight. The shorter trains run only on the weekends, and this causes me a momentary shudder of panic and doubt that I don't know what day it is. But I check my phone and it tells me that yes, it is indeed Wednesday, so I board the train.

At one end of the car, I see two men who look like they're brothers. Black men of almost identical build and skin tone, similar bone structure in their faces, similarly manicured hands, similar smiles, though one is missing several teeth. He wears Chicago police blues. The other is wearing an old gold-and-black par-camouflage uniform with green boots, a signature of CURE sentries. They start comparing weapons. The CURE sentry's weaponry is more state-of-the-art, and I can tell from their conversation that yes, they are brothers, and that the police officer is the elder. The younger one is proud that he outguns his big brother. Chicago police have very impressive guns, many of which they inherited from the US military, but CURE sentries have military combat weapons as well as lots of other toys: pulsar weapons that emit a directional pitch that causes severe nausea, gas bombs, seizure bombs, tar bombs, mosquito bombs, acid spray (because pepper spray is for sissies), an utterly foul thing called the "SID," and of course standard-issue automatic weapons—and that's to say nothing of their armored vehicles, their long-range capabilities, their aircraft. That's a big sore spot for the police, I'm aware. Federal and state legislation still prohibits police officers from carrying fully automatic weapons, so all guns carried by Chicago police officers (and all public officials outside California, Alabama, Arizona, East Arizona, Florida, Homa Territory, Missouri, Okla, and Texas) are limited to semiautomatic. Police officers also have limits on the types of chemical weapons they can carry, whereas certain ranks of CURE specialists are walking laboratories. It's plain that it gets under the skin of the older brother (like so many fine, sharp slivers from CURE's proprietary "diamond dust").

The doors open at Southport, and the police officer exits. As the train pulls away, the police officer can be heard yelling; it's unclear why. The CURE sentry sits, taking up two seats, staring daggers at a young woman across from him. It's hard to interpret his gaze, what is behind it, but it is persistent and it is awful. She won't look at him, seems to be unaware of him. Her brow is sharply furrowed as she scratches her arm. She looks Chinese, her hair is unwashed, and she wears a man's flannel shirt. A very thin strand of blood can be seen coming from under her sleeve, running over her wrist and into her palm. It's collecting on the underside of her curled fingers, but not yet dripping to the floor. The sentry adjusts his crotch and looks over at me. I avert my stare in time to avoid eye contact (lucky thing, CURE sentries do not like to be looked at directly, as I have learned the hard way myself and have seen many others learn the hard way as well). His earpiece lights up, indicating that he's receiving a message. He says, loud enough for everyone to hear, "Where at?" He stands, adjusts his crotch again, eyeballs the young woman one more time as though there's an opportunity being missed, and gets off the train at Belmont. I could transfer here but decide to stay out of his way. I'll stay on and transfer at Fullerton instead.

After he gets off the train, I notice at least one reason he may have been staring at the woman. She appears to be unarmed.

She gasps, and, like a balloon popping, a red mark appears on her sleeve and a steady flow of blood rushes out from her cuff. I stand and move toward her to offer her help, but she looks up at me like I'm a crazy person and dashes off the train when the doors open at Wellington. There's a hospital right off the stop (Right? There used to be—is it still a hospital?), so that must have been where she was going in the first place. But the train waits at the stop long enough for her to get down the stairs to the street, and I see her dash off to the west, away from the hospital campus, clutching her arm. A biker collides with her as she darts across the intersection. The biker pulls his gun on her, but she gets up and just keeps on running, like she doesn't even see him. The biker puts his gun back in its holster and looks down at himself. Her blood is smeared on his white shirt.

There's an ad at Wellington for a bank: "Free at Last."

At Fullerton, I transfer to the Red Line. My car has a lot of roaches on it, a lot even for the Red Line. There's a group of youths gathered around a cell phone nearby, watching a video of a small girl being picked up off the ground by a hawk. I can recognize it by the audio; I've seen it before. A family in a park, the father videoing a hawk circling in the summer sky, then the hawk dives and snatches the girl off the ground from where she sits, mere feet from her mother. The hawk carries the girl a few yards and then drops her. The little girl falls like a bag of laundry and hits the ground sprawling. The father hollers and then runs over to the terrified little girl and her horrified mother. The father laughs in relief, his fear dissipating, and the mother gets angry at him for it. A nice touch—the marital spat adds a bit of personality, a bit of authenticity. But it's not real. That one was debunked weeks ago. I consider telling them it's a fake, but they'll figure it out in their own time. And besides, they're enjoying themselves, and that counts for something.

At the end of some train cars there's a small space separated from the rest of the car, like a little auxiliary room, with two backward-facing seats that fold up. In this car, that space is covered by blankets and looks very lived-in. There's a person lying on the blankets, an obese white woman in sweatpants. She sits up on the blankets and starts laughing, a hoarse, whining laugh. There's no one around her, no one she's sharing this laugh with, but she laughs for several minutes straight. Her face turns red. She has teeth the color of brass. I decide I don't want to look at her anymore, so I direct my attention elsewhere. My eyes meet those of an old black woman with glasses and long grey hair. She frowns at me. No—she's been frowning at me.

I exit the train at Grand, and as I walk toward my office I notice the quiet. The usual sounds of horns, shouts, and shrill tones aren't present. I stop on the southeast corner of Grand and Dearborn and just listen. All around me I hear a scraping noise, like that of a metal pipe being dragged along asphalt. The sound is incessant and low. I can't ignore it. What could be making that sound? I look around for any indication of the sound's source, but no, the sound is so faint, so ambient, that its origin must be far away, or possibly underground, and it could be coming from any direction. I look for the tallest buildings. The Trump Presidential Hotel and Tower is the only one I can see from this intersection. I can't see the Hancock. Can't see the Willis Tower (or as some older Chicagoans would call it, Sear's Tower). When I look at the Trump, the scraping noise gets louder and seems to rise in pitch.

Next to my ear, I hear the telltale metallic click of a gun being cocked.

"Your phone and your cash."

The assailant says "your," even though he doesn't see the phone and cash as "mine," but rather as "his." He says "your," because language doesn't matter. Or maybe he is alluding to the transitory nature of property. (I did get held up once by a young man who had the courtesy to ask for "his money." "Gimme my money," he said, implying that the funds I had earned at my job and converted into cash were, in fact, his and not mine. So it was more of a disagreement than a mugging, but all in all, I respected his adjective use.) This current assailant is no such wordsmith. "Your." He admits to the wrongfulness of his actions while they're in progress. At least he's honest in his way.

Another click. A heavier one with more action. A voice.

"Get gone, fucko. Go. Don't look at me. Go. Put your gun away, cross the street, get the fuck outta here or this'll take your whole fuckin' head off, trust me."

I turn and see that my assailant is running north on Dearborn. Behind me, a huge bald man in old gold-and-black par-camouflage with green boots. He puts his enormous gun in its holster.

"Thanks," I say.

He looks me up and down. As he walks away from me, I hear him mutter to himself. "Faggot."

I walk up to my office, and someone is already there, waiting for me.

"Oh, are you Charlotte?"

"No."

"Oh . . . um, all right. What's your name?"

"Jackie."

Walt's client. "You're a little early, Jackie, Walt's not here yet. I can give you something to fill out while you wait."

I give Jackie a personality survey, which asks a whole bunch of questions and gives you a profile based on the combinations of different categories. This, not that. Strongly agree. Scale of one to five. Charlotte arrives ten minutes past her appointment time, and we get started. Charlotte is a college graduate who is trying to decide if she should go to grad school. But she's no longer interested in the field she majored in (visual communication). She wants to get a master's degree in English literature, but she says that everyone has been trying to talk her out of it because she's already drowning in debt and "there are no jobs in English."

"You should do what you have a passion for. That's my opinion. Do you love literature?"

"Yes, it's all I ever want to talk about or think about."

"Then that's what you should do, seriously. Be an English teacher, or a professor, or work in digital publishing or something, literary management, something that allows you to read and analyze literature."

"But what about finding a job?"

"You can't worry about that. So many jobs have disappeared, been automated or virtualized, and you never know how fields are going to change."

"No one can find a job right now, seems like. Unless you want to work for CURE."

"You don't seem like the paramilitary type to me."

"Yeah, don't worry, I don't want to work for CURE."

"I think you're the first this month to say so."

A roach walks next to Charlotte's notepad; she picks it up and brushes the insect off the desk with a hard sweeping motion. The sound of it hitting the wall is like a dry leaf underfoot.

"Sorry. So you think I should go for it?"

"I think you shouldn't be afraid to go for it, and I don't think you should let people talk you out of something you'll love because of money. Do you think ten years ago that anyone foresaw the demand for surgeons dropping so dramatically? And now nurses are becoming more and more obsolete. We have no idea how industries . . ."

Blah blah blah. The conversation goes on like this a little while longer, we talk about different grad programs and financing options and standardized tests and inequities and dubious ideals . . .

Blah blah blah. When Charlotte and I emerge from my office, Jackie is still sitting in the waiting room, looking pissed.

"Walt never showed up?"

She shrugs in a way that suggests it's my fault.

This is odd. Walt is lazy and obnoxious, but he isn't undependable. It's not like him at all to not show up for work. No message. No note. No email. He just isn't here. I call his phone. No answer.

My appointment with Charlotte ended early, so I should have time to at least touch base with Jackie before sending her off. Might be stepping on Walt's toes a little, but we'll deal with that later—if he comes to work at all, that is, because, really, when someone just plain doesn't show up, you have to wonder if you'll ever see him again.

Because that happens. Never seeing people again happens.

I have a nice chat with Jackie (who is "interested in animals"), and am more pleased than I should be when I check the messages and find that my next client has cancelled. "An incident on the bus," is his explanation. I go to my computer and stream NPR. They're just finishing up talking about a special election in South Korea.

The next story is about hackers who are perfecting a new kind of identity theft that has to do with the stealing of gained knowledge. Something having to do with a process by which, say, you go to college, get a degree, education, knowledge, skills, and then these hackers steal all that knowledge from you. So these hackers are threatening to make years of education uploadable (Directly into a person's memory? This step is unclear.), and thus are creating a knowledge black market of sorts and destroying the higher education industry. I'm glad I didn't know about this before talking with Charlotte about grad school.

Drones in Pakistan.

Helicopter crash in Syria.

C'est la vie.

A story about a team of researchers at Johns Hopkins who believe they've discovered a cure for autism. Trials have shown that their cure has a high rate of success, especially in children under the age of six. Despite this, they've lost their government funding. The radio report is about their committee hearing. Where's the proof? says Senator So-and-so. The scientists say, "In the trials we've already done, what we've already accomplished. More than two-thirds of the children who underwent this treatment showed no signs of any autism spectrum disorder within six months." Yes, very interesting, but where is the proof? "We have results, Mr. Senator. The results are the proof. We've improved the lives of these children and their families, and could improve the lives of countless others." Sounds like a wild goose chase to me; until you can substantiate these claims with data and facts, I don't see how we're gonna get anywhere. "We have years of data. Everything we've reported is a factual account of clinical trials." You know, professors, my mother had a saying: a real banana's only yella on the outside . . .

A mall shooting.

Militants in Kenya.

Mudslides.

Israel.

FOUR

At this point in my life there hasn't been a gun in my hands. Even in childhood, running around with my brother Jack, we'd never even pretend to have guns. No cowboys and native peoples. No cops and criminals. Something deep within me has always rejected them; that's how it was for Jack, too. We'd pretend we were astronauts, archaeologists, athletes, adventurers—never anyone with a weapon. Well, not a tangible weapon, anyway. Our weapons were our words, our quick wits, our indomitable intellects, our catlike agilities. Our best versions of ourselves were always unarmed, whether we even intended it that way or not. Our dad kept guns in the house, so it's not like they were hidden from us. We just always leaned away.

I wish that the world were a better place, a less scary place. Not for me. For Jack. He deserves better. The world's darkness hurts him. That kid. All I want, really, is for him to move to Chicago. Where he is, in that small town, he feels so alone, I know he does. The city is lonely, but it's nothing compared with what he must be feeling. Where he is there's literally no one else like him. No one he can talk to. No one he can share his ideas with. Here at least he'd have me. He'd make friends in no time. Everyone who meets Jack likes Jack.

I try calling him, but it goes straight to voicemail.

***

Another workday ends, and as I leave my building, I smell smoke. An acrid smoke, like burning rubber, or fuel maybe. There's a commotion around the bend. Lots of people are standing around, but no guns are drawn. I walk over, and I see a chemical tanker on its side, on fire. The smoke coming from the tanker is brown and green. I ask someone what's going on, and he tells me he thinks it's a film set. Or . . . he was told it's a film set. He can't seem to decide which.

The daylight dims, as though a cloud has passed over the sun, but it's a clear day.

A sudden hunger takes hold, and I realize that I never ate lunch. I duck into the restaurant by the train station and walk up to the counter. The guy preparing food (who is maybe also the owner) glares at me. He's muscular, looks Italian, and is covered in green tattoos. He finishes putting together an order for an elderly white man standing by the cash register. When it's my turn, I order a hot dog. The guy at the counter slaps a frank in a poppy-seed bun and asks me what else I want on it. I say "ketchup." When I say this, he freezes, and I see his forearms flex. He points at a sign by the register that says *absolutly !!!no ketchup!!! on hot dogs recuesting ketchup will earn the offender a lifetime ban.*

"What else you want?"

"Nothing else. I just want ketchup."

"I'm not putting ketchup on this fuckin' thing, what are you, ten years old?"

"I don't want it then."

"You're a fuckin' idiot, putting ketchup on a hot dog. A fuckin' idiot. A child."

"That's not even the rule."

"Huh?"

"The rule is 'no ketchup on a Chicago-style dog.' Not 'no ketchup on a hot dog in Chicago, ever.'"

"No ketchup. What, are you fuckin' retarded?"

"You don't even understand your own arbitrary rule, is what I'm saying."

The guy, without putting down my hot dog, pulls a gun from behind his apron and points it at my chest. Goddamnit. You can't talk to anyone.

"I'm not gonna argue with you about this, tough guy. If you don't put mustard and relish on this and eat it right in front of me, I'll fucking shoot you."

"I don't like either of those things."

"Kill yourself," he says with a weird little chuckle as he slathers yellow mustard and sweet relish on the hot dog, adding, "That's $4.25."

"I'm not gonna pay for something I don't want."

"If you try to walk out of here without paying me, I'll shoot you in the back, I don't care."

He scratches an itch on the side of his head with the gun. (If it went off, I wouldn't have to eat mustard.)

Not wanting to die, I hand over five dollars. He gives me three quarters back and says, quite sincerely it seems, "Thanks very much." He stares at me as I stare at this savory snack drenched in two things I hate. I don't want to eat it. And yet I must eat it. C'est la vie. I buy a Sprite to wash it down with.

I eat the hot dog quickly. I chug the Sprite. When I finish, the guy lowers the gun and smiles, saying, "It's better that way, isn't it?" I don't answer, which worries him. He reflexively tightens his grip on the gun. I say, "Yeah, way better." He smiles and holsters his gun, comforted that we now agree.

I make one other stop to pick up a six-pack and food for Larry. I had already planned on stopping for the cat food. The beer was an impulse.

***

Across from me on the train, there's a woman with a cybernetic leg. She taps on it with one long fingernail.

Ting-ting-ting-ting-ting.

A man walks up and down the train car, either blind or pretending to be blind, with a sign around his neck that reads *veteran.* He carries a large plastic cup to collect money. His feet are wrapped in plastic bags, and he says, "*Please* help me. *Please* help me. *Please* help me. *Please* help me." The blind man approaches a young gay couple, and they each put their hands on their guns but don't take them out of their holsters. He walks past them, expertly feeling the way with his cane, saying, "*Please* help me. *Please* help me." No one gives him anything. When he gets to me, I give him my hot dog change. In my pocket I also find two packets of saltines. It isn't much, but I assume he's hungry. I put the saltines in his cup. "God bless you, sir or madam. My heart thanks you." He smells like bad milk and dirt. He puts his cane and his change cup in the crook of his elbow and pulls out the saltines, opens the packet, and eats one. He sits down and falls asleep.

On the Brown Line, a man with olive skin boards the train at Irving Park and sits near me, despite the fact that most of the car is empty. He is unarmed. He looks at me without looking at me, smiles, and says, "Hey." The way he says it, it is as though he were saying, "Get a load of this." He hands me a pristine business card that reads:

RT
Unarmed Citizens
XXIIWIIN

"Addison Red, chief."

"What?" I ask, taking the card from him.

"That's all you need to know." He has an Eastern Euroish accent that I can't place. He smiles at me and gets up, gives me a friendly whap on the arm. He looks around the car at the other people, but says nothing to anyone else. The doors open at Montrose and he's off. I look at the card in my hand. XXIIWIIN. I assume that means something, but I have no idea what. It dawns on me that this card might be dangerous to have, but I don't want to just drop it either. I pocket it and pretend to relax. I look at everyone else on the train and see that all of them are carrying. None of them are looking at me. Or at each other.

***

That night, I feed Larry and crash on the couch watching a movie. A real old one called *Casablanca*. It's strange, though. I've seen this movie before—it was years ago, but now something isn't right about it. Parts of it are in color. I don't remember Ingrid Bergman smiling this much. Instead of "You played it for her, you can play it for me," Rick just says, "Play it again, Sam." They stay together at the end. The plane on the tarmac is a 797. The last line of the film is "I'm pregnant."

At the end of the movie, I lift Larry up to my chest and we snuggle. There's some salt on my fingertip, which he licks off with his rough little tongue. I look around the apartment. Larry's apartment. I pay for it, but he spends the most time here. All his time, really. I just sleep here. He licks and licks, making sure he didn't miss anything, his eyes closed, his ears flattened, his mouth like a little lion's. Sometimes he's so cute and gentle that it's hard to breathe.

Suddenly, Larry's head shoots up. His ears stand. He's alert.

"What is it, bud?"

His eyes follow something into the corner of the wall, but there's nothing there. He relaxes, but now I can't stop looking at the corner. I pick up the phone and call my parents. It rings three times and my mother answers.

"Hello?"

"Mom, hey, it's me."

"Oh . . . hi . . ."

"Hi. What's new?"

"Nothing, just . . . well, you know your brother died."

. . . nothing to see here . . . move it along now . . . nothing to . . . see here . . . nothing to . . . nothing to . . .

"What? My . . . what? Died? He's dead?"

"Jack, yes, your brother."

"Jack, yes I know what you—but you can't be serious? He's dead?"

"Well, yes, I wouldn't joke about that."

. . . see here . . . see here . . .

"He's dead? Jack's dead? Wh-*when?* When did he die?"

"About three weeks ago."

"Three *weeks!*"

"Well, twenty days. Three weeks tomorrow."

"Why didn't anyone tell me?"

"I assumed you must have known."

"How on earth would I know unless . . . *Fuck, Mom!*"

"I guess Jack is the one who would call you, normally . . ."

"How the fuck did he die?"

"He got into an argument with a man at Walmart. Something silly."

"Something . . . silly . . ."

We're both silent for a long moment. I believe I hear my mom crying, but maybe it's just me.

I ask, "When's the . . . shit, three weeks . . . he's already been buried, hasn't he?"

"Well, yes. Of course."

"Oh, of course. Of course he was. Of course he was buried. No one thought it was strange that I wasn't at my own brother's funeral?"

"Well, sure, yes, we all thought it was strange. Everyone did. We just told them you were busy."

"I didn't know he was fucking dead, Mom. No one told me!"

"OK. OK. I'm going to put your father on."

She hands the phone over to my dad.

"Hey."

"Dad!"

"You gonna come home?"

"Come home?"

"Visit your brother's grave? Least you could do."

"Dad, no one told me he was dead!"

"Well, someone had to."

Before we get off the phone, my dad says he's going to arrange a flight for me to come home to Ohio on Monday. Be on it.

I call my boss and tell her I'll be missing a few days. No big deal, the week is very light, she tells me. Oh, and by the way, Brian quit.

"Brian quit? Just like that?"

"Yeah, he called from wherever he's on vacation, told me he's not coming back. He was kinda laughing about it; it was weird."

"Hmm . . . must be nice."
"What do you mean?"
"Oh, nothing."
"Have a nice trip home."

***

I stay in for most of the weekend. No matter how much I clean my apartment, it never feels clean.

I spend Saturday night reading all about a nuclear power plant in China that melted down. Shanghai is reportedly unlivable—there are evacuations, millions and millions of people. The radiation cloud is covering the Korean Peninsula as well. Japan. It seems like much bigger news than it's being treated as. I had to dig to find it. And even the tone of the main article I read is dismissive. The reporter peppers his writing with phrases like "could have been much worse," "will not have a lasting impact," and words like "error" and "mix-up." At one point he even writes, "It's not a big deal." I scroll down and read some of the comments. Very few of them actually respond to the content of the story, the plight of these millions of Chinese people and others in the region; most of them argue about whether or not the story is fake. "GARDIAIN is an satire paper btw, ppl, do ur fuck ing reserchhh! smhhhhhh" says one of the top comments. Another says "im soooo f*#king trred of hering abt how hard the CRY-nese have itttt!!!! there billons of em how hard can it relly be!!" And another, "Chinks deserve it, amputate them all." It devolves into insults and death threats.

On Sunday, I knock on my neighbor Simon's door and ask him to cat-sit Larry while I'm away. When I come back my beer will be gone, but that's fair. He asks me where I'm going, and I tell him Ohio.

"Ooh. Yeah, OK, figured you might."

"Why do you say that?"

"Nothing, it's . . . you haven't seen your family . . . in a while, right? Be careful, been reading some crazy shit about Ohio."

I know what he means. Cleveland's been in the news a lot recently, although I don't see why. There's nothing happening in Cleveland that isn't happening here. Well, except that their roaches are apparently more aggressive and numerous; the Cuyahoga River is just full of them, like, certain days, the river looks like a big churning column of bugs. I thank him for watching Larry, and he says, "Hey man, us barebacks gotta stick together."

I tilt my head, puzzled at the term. "Bare—huh?"

"Barebacks, man, you haven't been called that?"

"Um . . . not to my knowledge."

"Barebacks. Barebacks!"

"I um . . . yeah. What?"

"*Unarmed*, dude. Bareback. Without protection."

"I get it, yeah."

"Yeah. Get with it," he says with a smile, and gives me a high five. "I mean, all the fuckheads started using that term, 'barebacks,' and they meant it as a derogatory one, but you know, hey? Shoe fits. I'm surprised you never heard that."

"I tend to keep my head down."

"Yeah, no doubt, no doubt. Hey, don't worry about Larry, OK? Me and him are like brothers."

"That's what he said, too."

"For real? Fuck, man. I love Larry."

***

I call a cab to take me to Midway. The cab is a little late, but I asked for it to pick me up four hours before my flight, so—like a nuclear meltdown in China—it's not a big deal. Something about a driverless car pulling up in front of my place fills me with anxiety.

Traffic is pretty light, and the roads are dry, so the drive is about as pleasant as a ride in a Chicago cab can be. NPR plays as we go. Warfwarfistan. I say "we." There is no we. I am the only one here. Still, there is a driver's seat. There is negative space, an emptiness. More and more, this emptiness. This lack.

Midway Airport, however, is surprisingly crowded. Lots of travelers, and the security line takes a good long while because there are a lot of, what Simon would call, fuckheads. TSA, Chicago police, state police, CURE. FAA regulations have (somehow) held strong, and civilians are still not allowed firearms in the cabins of commercial aircraft; of course, people still try to get them on. The pilots and flight attendants are armed, and that makes a lot of people paranoid (they want to be able to protect themselves and their families in case there's a hijacking or the flight crew revolts). The FAA has some of the lowest approval ratings of any federal agency due to its restrictions on firearms. The FAA director once insisted in a press conference that "people can live without their guns for a couple hours"; afterward, he received thousands of death threats and had all his personal and financial information hacked and leaked online. The airline industry sided with the FAA, not wanting open carry on airplanes, which made it deeply unpopular, too. There were boycotts, proclamations that air travel was un-American, threats from Congress that legislation would be passed requiring airlines to allow concealed weapons on passenger planes. By some miracle, that legislation was defeated. Op-eds about government overreach and tyranny, calling for the abolishment of the FAA. Many disgruntled travelers try to bring weapons aboard in protest; the most brazen try to waltz through security with heavy weaponry, while others may try to sneak a plastic printed model through. Sometimes they're arrested; usually they aren't, they're simply forced to put their guns in their checked baggage. Armed citizens treat flight attendants like they're fascist shrews, and in turn, flight attendants act like fascist shrews. They still serve you coffee, tea, and soft drinks, though. Beer, wine, and liquor are ten dollars.

The security line at any major airport is a clusterfuck. CURE sentries will look the other way when someone has a concealed weapon (especially if said weapon was manufactured by CURE Corp.), so TSA agents have to be on their game. Chicago police officers provide a last line of defense before you get into the concourses. By the end, you've gone through two metal detectors, been wanded, had your hands swabbed, behind your ears swabbed, you've been eye scanned, tongue scanned, patted down, and had your baggage searched. But there hasn't been a midair firefight on a major airline in the United States in over three years, so the security measures have been pretty successful.

It's rare that flight attendants have to use their weapons; they're mostly symbolic. But damn if those people aren't tough. A cell phone video of an incident a few months ago showed a drunk guy trying to take a flight attendant's firearm on a Northern Airlines flight. He had been hurling insults at her, saying some pretty nasty stuff about what "she deserved" and what he'd "do to her" if she didn't watch her "bitch ass." Finally, he put his hand on her gun, and as a result, got to experience firsthand her mandated mixed-martial-arts training. In the video, you see (and hear) her snap his wrist (he howls), then watch her pull him up and out of his seat like he weighs nothing, chop him in the neck, and throw him to the ground without hitting any other passengers, then get out her flex-cuffs. Several passengers clap and cheer for the flight attendant; a couple of other passengers make like they're going to pull her off of the guy, but the other flight attendants appear, guns drawn to keep anyone from interfering. (There's a lot more yelling, mostly unintelligible . . . some people start chanting, "U-S-A! U-S-A!") Then the flight attendant gets off the guy. She's got blood on her neck and the side of her face, but how it got there isn't clear. She and another flight attendant carry the guy off camera and the video ends. According to one of the comments on the video, you can tell by the way the drunk guy's wrist breaks, and by how his clothing behaves when she pulls him out of his seat, that the video is a fake. They claim that it was distributed by the FAA, the TSA, and Northern Air, who wanted it to go viral as a deterrent to those who might assault flight-crew members. The FAA and TSA never responded to the claims, Northern Air insists the video is real and that the crewmember in the video is one of their best, a woman named Selena Santos. Ms. Santos, as well as the man who took the cell phone video, one Mark DeWare, also have claimed the video is real; although the existence of "Mark DeWare" has since been questioned as well.

They change my gate three times, but it seems like this fourth one will stick. A plane rolls in and comes to rest outside. I like the look of the plane; it doesn't look super old. I can see the runway out the window. There's something about the way the planes are lining up that makes me uneasy. Everything looks crowded, crooked. A plane goes out on the runway too early, and a landing flight comes in right over the top of it. A businessman sitting next to me senses my nerves.

"That's normal. Used to call it an incursion, but really it's just efficient. Gotta get as many of these puppies in the air as they can to stay profitable, ya know?"

There's a TV on in the gate area. There's a story on the news about an investment bank that is under investigation for engineering the deliberate poisoning of the drinking water in Wheeling, West Virginia, which led to a spike in medical expenses there. The bank then bought up the medical debt, converted it into equity somehow, because that's how finance works, and paid out huge bonuses to its top officers. Then something called a "deferred-life swap" was created and sold, and somehow somebody was making a lot of money when one of these poisoned people died. The process is all very opaque, even though the people on TV are talking as though it makes a lot of sense. No one, at present, is being charged with murder or wrongful death or reckless endangerment or even pollution. One correspondent uses the word "shenanigans."

The guy next to me points at the TV and says with a smile, "Man, those guys are really fuckin' smart."

We get on the plane, and it's full. I sit in a window seat on the wing, and wonder whether anyone on Wall Street or in Las Vegas or elsewhere can make money off whether or not a plane crashes. There are roaches on the wing, but only a few. I haven't seen any in the cabin, but they're definitely here, and if not, they'll come in on people's pant legs, their carry-on luggage. I close my eyes and listen. All around me I can hear a rumbling. In the plane and outside, a creaking, a snapping. The chimes sound and our plane pulls out onto the runway.

"That sound means we're cleared for departure. We would like to remind you that federal regulations strictly prohibit any attempt or threat to disarm uniformed crew on this or any aircraft. Threatened crew may respond with force. Also, smoking is never permitted in aircraft lavatories. Please sit back and enjoy this one-hour, five-minute flight to Columbus."

***

There is turbulence. The skies are very choppy. You never hear of a smooth flight anymore. Actually, if I were on a flight and there weren't any bumps, it might scare me. Wouldn't feel right. The bumps don't bother me; I know enough about aviation to know that a plane isn't going to fall out of the sky due to turbulence alone. The sudden drops in altitude are what get me, that feeling of free fall, the leaping of your stomach. Never get used to that. Our flight has two big drops in altitude—perfectly safe I'm safe I'm safe—and some child behind me shouts "Wheeee!" which fills me with an uncomfortable anger and I have to massage my forehead. My hands shake. The kid keeps laughing and I'm not seeing straight. I have to listen to some music before I shout at him. This isn't fun, I want to say to him. This isn't a ride. Some of us are on our way to visit our dead brother. We could all be dead brothers. Show some respect.

We hit a couple of big bumps and the captain comes on.

"Good morning folks, from the flight deck. Obviously a pretty bumpy ride, so for the safety of our flight crew and passengers, we're going to ask that our flight attendants remain seated for the duration of the flight—"

I can't hear the rest of what he says, because there is an uproar from the cabin. There will be no in-flight service. That's what he's telling us. There will be no coffee. No ginger ale. No pretzels or booze. "Bullshit!" A ruddy white man with a belly demands a refund for the flight. The loud kid screams "Nooo!" I'm pretty sure a woman is crying. A fight breaks out. I put in headphones and listen to music for the rest of the flight, grimacing when the plane shakes, reminding myself that it's still, statistically, the safest way to travel.

FIVE

You have to go through security screening on your way out of the airport, too, for reasons that have never been fully explained. People are reunited with their guns.

My parents pick me up at the airport, and we begin the drive to Plain City.

My mother asks, "Where are your bags?"

"I'm only staying one night, I just have my backpack."

"Still."

We take the beltway to Route 161, which heads over to Plain City. Traffic is a little thicker in Columbus than it is in Chicago.

"People behave themselves here," my dad says, "don't want no trouble."

He's referring to the number of traffic-related skirmishes in Chicago. That's old news and old data; highway violence has been much lower in Chicago in recent years. But you know how parents are.

"In Chicago most of the cars these days are driverless. There aren't any accidents anymore."

"This one can go driverless, but what do I want my car driving me around for? Nobody wants to do anything for themselves."

"It's a lot safer."

"I like driving."

On Route 161, there are lots of gun stands. Signs and banners demanding that I *protect [my] freedom, be on [my] guard,* and *defend [my] kids.* My mother asks me if I want a gun, because she always does. I say no. She asks me to think about it. I tell her I will. We drive past a car set aflame. My father looks at it as we pass and grunts. All along the road are people sitting with coolers of beer and guns, doing no visible harm. My father waves at most of them as we pass, and they wave back. My mother asks me about my job.

"Business OK?"

"It's slow. We've started offering a steep discount."

"Still don't get what you do." My father.

"It's not that complicated. We help people make decisions. I think they just like to forget about what's happening in the world and talk about themselves for a bit. Their future. A little individual attention."

"And people pay for that?"

"They want to believe there are opportunities still. Most of our clients are pretty hopeful, which is kind of amazing, all things considered."

My mother smiles and nods. I go on.

"So . . . Jack is dead and no one called to tell me."

"You're always so busy."

"I am not."

"Well, you could call us more."

"Can we talk about it, please? Tell me what happened?"

"He was being stupid," my dad chimes in. "He was at Walmart and this fella is walking around with one of these new

ARs, which are designed with safety in mind, by the way, and Jack goes up to the guy and says it's an 'awful lot of firepower just to go shopping' or something like that—"

"Good point," I say.

He shakes his head, ever so slightly. From this angle I can see the very edge of his frown. "Stupid thing to say. This guy's not hurting anyone, exercising his God-given rights, and Jack—"

"Not hurting anyone, you mean, until he killed your son."

"Jack confronted him."

"So the unarmed kid was posing an imminent threat to the guy with the combat weapon?"

"You're being childish. You can't get in someone's face like that."

"So you're saying he was asking for it, right?"

My mom interjects with a scolding. "Boys."

"We're upsetting your mother."

"Right. One of her two sons was murdered by a guy who couldn't take criticism, but this conversation is what's upsetting her. Did you press charges against the guy?"

My mom turns around in her seat. "Sweetie, the law is not on our side."

"But, it doesn't—"

"Sweetie. The law is not on our side."

The roaches are bigger outside the cities. I see two on the roadside, twelve legs skyward. Size of rats. Maybe that's why I don't live out here.

My parents' house seems to have been fortified more since my last visit. There's a new layer of razor wire around the perimeter, and my dad must have put upgraded bars on the windows (they look thicker). We pull into the driveway and I can hear their dogs barking inside. Boxers. They won't recognize me;

we go through this every time. They'll smell Larry, and it'll be intense for a couple of minutes.

Once the dogs have their freakout and settle down, it's nice inside their house. Smells like pine trees and bread.

"Did you hear," my mother asks, "about the firefighters in Pennsylvania?"

"The ones who saved all of those babies from that hospital fire?"

"Yes!"

"I read about it. It was a fake."

"What do you mean it was a fake?"

"It didn't happen, there was an updated story on it."

"So all those babies died?"

"No, Mom, the hospital fire never happened."

"Oh. It . . . oh."

I take my bag up to my room. Atlas, one of the older boxers, follows me. As soon as I open the bedroom door, he jumps up onto the bed and gets comfortable. I open the closet and inside are a couple of things I hate to see: (a) two huge dead (or playing dead) roaches and (b) an assault rifle and a shotgun. I'm tempted to pick them up and throw them out the window, but that would require touching them.

My dad peeks his head in.

"Everything all right?"

"Yep, everything's fine. Got a couple big suckers in here." I let him decide which I'm referring to.

"Yeah, they're everywhere. You know that, bein' in the city. Can never get rid of 'em." He lets me decide which he's referring to.

We eat a quiet dinner, during which we avoid all conversation that doesn't have to do with sports. I always check up on sports a little when I'm going to see my dad—it's one of the only things we don't find cause to fight about. We avoid politics, guns, whether or not I'll ever move back to Ohio, public health, the environment. We know better. We don't talk about Jack. The Buckeyes are number one.

"I haven't seen a whole lot of roaches out here."

"It's the dogs."

"It's bad for them to eat them, you know."

"That's a wives' tale. Nothing wrong with eating a roach."

"Oh really? You eaten many yourself?"

"Funny."

My parents' back porch looks out onto a wooded area. Between the woods and the house there's a man-made pond, two fences, and a big open field. My mom comes out with a couple of the dogs, who go running off to chase each other around in the field. My mom smiles at me, then puts her arm around my waist. She's shorter than me, but I always feel small next to her. We stand and watch the dogs wrestle, listen to them bark.

***

Jack is buried in Forest Grove Cemetery. My parents ask if I want them to come with me, and I say no. I tell my parents I don't want to know where his grave is. I want to find it. I bring a flashlight in case it takes me until dark (Forest Grove isn't a huge cemetery, but it isn't tiny either). My mother puts a handgun on the passenger seat. Just in case.

It's the middle of the afternoon when I drive over, and the car continually reminds me that it can go driverless if I want, like it's bragging.

I leave the gun in the car and walk around, looking at the headstones as I go. I'm trying not to pay attention to the earth, whether or not it's disturbed. Trying to not give anything away for myself.

I want to find his name.

I remember when we were kids, going out to the cemetery near our house in Worthington. Telling each other scary stories, making each other jump. Jack and I were a lot alike, as kids and adults. He stayed behind in Columbus when my parents moved out to Plain City. He moved downtown. Lived right near the Ohio State campus, which I always thought was crazy. All those armed college kids. (Something like eighty-five or ninety percent of college students nationwide have carried weapons ever since the Incident at Rice. A bad day.) He'd hit a rough patch these last two or three years, couldn't find any steady work, and so he had moved in with my parents in Plain City. Had been here only about six months.

Jack always used to say I was smarter than he was, but I don't know if that's true. I never felt that it was true. I wouldn't have confronted a guy with an AR at a Walmart, but that's beside the point. It isn't Jack's fault he's dead. I can think of a few people who are more to blame for his death than Jack is. A few hundred. A few hundred million.

The grass is dried out. It rustles as I walk up and down the rows of graves. There's a wind that blows through, gentle, constant, hissing. The sky is clear. No planes. I close my eyes and listen. I hear a faint bubbling, a rasping, but that's it. I consider lying down but then decide against it; I've been so tired lately that I might fall asleep. And as peaceful as I find cemeteries, as peaceful as I find this cemetery, I don't want to sleep here. There was a story about a man who passed out drunk in a cemetery in Kansas. A bunch of teenagers came across him where he slept, and got it in their head that it would be hilarious to bury him alive. So they did. Some reports claimed that the man died down there; others claimed someone heard the man crying out from his shallow grave and dug him up. One story claimed that the teenagers stole three hundred dollars from him, while another suggested he paid the kids fifty dollars each to bury him. The news cycle moved on before there was anything definitive, so that man is both alive and dead. C'est la vie.

This cemetery is more full than I remember. The sun begins to set. The twilight glints off the gravestones. There is beauty.

Jack was better than I am. I used to think that he and I would both leave Ohio and open a business together. Something big, something creative, something that could make a difference. Cut through all the darkness and meanness and vitriol and hate, and provide something of substance, something bright. That would have been easy for Jack. He always wanted everything to be better. That's what made him drink, made him sad, made him angry and bitter—that the world wasn't better, wasn't as good as he was, didn't reflect his light. I live in the world, I observe it, I tolerate it. I've even accepted it. I still don't carry a gun, which would make my big brother proud. Don't give in. But Jack, he was big on complaining, big on raising his voice, big on challenging those around him. That's what ultimately killed him, or ultimately served as the justification for what killed him. Being himself. I wonder if it's a flaw in my character that I don't get as mad as he got. That it says something about me that I live where I live and I don't go crazy. That I'm not constantly shouting in outrage. That I'm not seizing everyone by the collar and yelling, "*What* the *fuck* is *wrong* with *you!*" I wonder if he'd be disappointed in me, come to think of it.

Dusk settles in, and I click on the flashlight. This is when life gets interesting. Nighttime. A flashlight. A graveyard. A search. The shaft of light darts between the ground and the stones. Here lies. Eleanor Bates. Charles Bates. Step, step. Francis Franklin. Step, step, step. Harold Brown. Here lies. Margaret Brown. Here lies. Ashley Brown. Step. Here lies. Step. David and Sarah Corcoran. Step. Violet Driscoll.

Step.

Step.
Step.
Here lies.
Here lies.
Here lies.
John "Jack" Palazzo.
Found you.

***

I stay with Jack for a while. We share one more drink. I brought with me two tiny bottles of scotch. I drink one and pour the other on Jack's earth. I'm careful not to splash any on the headstone, because that'd be tacky and a waste. I talk to him. The sounds around me change: a high-pitched whirring noise hangs in the air; underneath it, a sound like digging. It's soft, though . . . both sounds are soft. Back toward the parking lot, I see lights. Flashlights. At first it's just one, so I assume maybe it's my parents. But then I see a second light. Then a third, a fourth, a seventh. I hear laughter. I hear aluminum cans hitting asphalt. Some of the lights are still, others erratic. I don't know if these people mean me well or mean me harm or mean me nothing at all, but they're here. And whoever they are, they know I'm here. I can tell that they're by the car. The sound carries:

"Gunonna seat. Passner side, lookit."

"Ey! Oo'souddere? Leff yergun, dummass!"

"Woop! Woop!"

I see most of the flashlights start from the parking lot into the cemetery. One stays behind. They aren't on a line toward me at first. I say good-bye to Jack and counter them, figuring if I take the long way around I might be able to get back to the parking lot without them seeing me. They start spreading out with their lights, hollering. I duck in and around some of the larger headstones and monuments. One of the encroachers is near. I can't cross to the grave on either side without being seen. I pick up a small rock and wait. One of the encroachers shouts from the other end of the cemetery. The one approaching me turns that way, his beam no longer facing toward me. I wind up and throw the rock as hard and as far as I can back in the direction I came. Back toward Jack. These are very, very long seconds, not being able to watch the path of the rock, not knowing if it already came down without striking a headstone, not knowing if adrenaline had somehow given me the strength to throw the rock all the way across and clear over the entire cemetery. Then the quiet is broken by the *clack* of rock hitting stone, echoing across the night. The encroachers all hear it, and start to move toward it, whooping and calling.

"Woop! Woop!"

When I get near to the parking lot, I see there are, indeed, others waiting for me. I'm dressed like a city boy. Hair on the long side, button-down shirt, nice jeans, nice-ish shoes. This won't do.

I take off the button-down, leaving my white crew-neck undershirt. I rub some dirt in the underarms. I take off my jeans and use the knife attached to my parents' car starter to cut them into shorts. I put dirt on them. I take off my shoes and socks and leave them. Luckily, I haven't shaved since Thursday and haven't cut my toenails in weeks. Hair. Not sure what to do with my hair. No good way to cut it. I find a discarded beer can. It still has an ounce or two of beer in it, and I empty this into my hand and put it in my hair; this'll make me look a little greasy at the very least. As I get closer to the car, I hear two voices. One flashlight, but two young men, white with sunburns, drinking and sitting on the car. They listen to country music on a phone. Which I'm glad for, the sound will give me cover. I crawl over to the car and crouch by the passenger door. I get on my belly and wriggle under the car. I know if I think about it too long, I'll decide it's a bad idea and talk myself into something else, so I grit my teeth and press the unlock button on the starter. The car unlocks and the lights flash. Both men exclaim and jump off the car, looking around. As I had hoped, they assume I'm hiding somewhere nearby and start looking around for me. I roll out from under the car and open the driver's side door as quietly as I can, and I slip inside. Both men have their guns drawn, and they call across the cemetery to the others. I duck down so I'm out of sight, feet on the pedals, stomach under the steering wheel, hands on the wheel and the shifter. I put the starter in the ignition, engage it, and the engine turns right over, which I couldn't possibly be more thankful for. The car reminds me that I left it in manual drive mode and do I want to go driverless? And I think at first, yes, now is a perfect time to go driverless—I need to start moving *now* and I can't see— but then I remember that in driverless mode the car will drive safely and in no particular rush, and I'm not interested in either of those things.

Someone yells, "*Tha fuck?*" but I don't stay to hear what they say next. I put the car in reverse and back up blindly, cutting the wheel. I pop the car into drive, lift my head up so I can just see above the dash, and I floor it.

I hear some shouting behind me, but no shots fired. I guess their hearts weren't in it tonight.

When I get back to the house, my mother is sitting up, waiting for me. She gives me a mild scolding for staying out so long, asks me what happened to my clothes, and then what happened to me, but then casts off that line of questioning and makes me macaroni and cheese instead.

PART II

*After my visit to Forest Grove
Cemetery, Plain City, Ohio*

*Prior to fleeing my apartment,
following a murder*

SIX

The country is quiet; when I awaken in the middle of the night, it is the quiet that wakes me. But if you listen closely enough, you can hear a grinding noise, like stone being pulverized, or a cinder block dragging on brick. Two of my parents' dogs are sleeping in the room with me. I tiptoe past them. I walk down to the kitchen and grab a beer out of the fridge. I take a sip, and it goes down as though I haven't had a drop of water to drink in days. I feel the liquid coat my throat, hit my stomach, chill it. I feel it being absorbed. I hear something then, a sound from underneath me. Objects being moved. Heavy objects. I open the door to the basement and walk down the stairs.

The first thing I see are a couple of boxes of ammo piled at the foot of the steps. Then I see the grenades. Hand grenades. Flash grenades. Then guns. Dozens of rifles, shotguns, some in racks and some laid out neatly on couches, or leaned up in rows against the wall. Handguns, so many handguns. Boxes of ammo piled chest high, loose magazines scattered in piles. I spot two heavy-duty crossbows and quivers of bolts. Knives, knives, knives. More grenades. Three sawed-off shotguns. Assault rifles, at least half a dozen assault rifles. The Ping-Pong table is set up. It is covered in guns. I don't know all their names. Body armor. At one end of the table I see my dad.

I want to say something to him, but my voice refuses. I'm afraid of him.

"Can't sleep?" he asks me. He's reading some kind of instruction manual.

I nod, look around.

"I've uh . . . grown my inventory. You might say. Your mother thinks I have enough, but I keep adding to the collection."

"The arsenal, you mean?"

"Well . . . yeah. I guess it is."

"This . . . *shit* . . . this is . . ."

"Lower your voice. Your mother's sleepin."

"What the fuck is this?"

"Listen. I wouldn't expect you to understand. I don't expect you to. I know how you feel. And I don't care. You have your priorities and I—"

"This is insane."

"Be insane not to have 'em."

"This is hell down here. What the fuck is going on with you?"

"I promise you, son, you walk into any basement in the county and my collection will be small compared to most."

"Jack lived in this hou—"

"Don't talk to me about Jack. Jack's not around anymore, and neither are you. It's just me and your mom, not any business of yours. I'll be prepared no matter what."

"You're armed for World War IV and the zombie apocalypse combined down here."

"Aliens, too. Don't forget aliens."

"Right. You mean from space . . . or foreigners?"

"Either. Both. Like I said, I don't expect you to understand."

We are both quiet for a long time. The central air clicks on with a deep, sinister *whoooosh*. That's when I notice it behind him, something that looks like a cross between a medical scanner and a vending machine, with a large open window and intricate mechanical parts that look like the inside of a huge printer . . . because that's exactly what it is. I've never seen one in person.

"Got yourself a 3-D printer, I see."

"Yep . . . damned thing isn't as easy to use as you'd think."

"I suppose there's no mistaking what you plan to use it for."

"Arts and crafts, mostly." My dad smirks, and it chills my blood.

"Yeah. You know, I've seen a lot of those in Chicago. Printed guns, I mean. Seen one explode in someone's hand, take the whole thing off. Left a gory stump, nothing left of his hand anywhere, or the gun either, just all blown apart. Which I only mention in passing, not that you're planning to mass-produce plastic guns for yourself and everyone in town, because of course you know that's extremely illegal."

"Sure it is." He puts the instructions aside and adds, "For now."

"You can't just do whatever you want because you don't agree with the law."

He stares at me—the way he stares at me has not changed since I was a child—and in this moment, I feel a sharp pain in my chest that is hard to describe accurately, so I'll call it heartbreak.

"Your mother worries herself to sleep about you every single night. Living in that place, one of the worst places in the whole goddamned country, and you're defenseless."

"I'm careful."

"How careful can you be? Murder capital of the country. Might as well live in Nigeria, with all those crazies—what do they call themselves?"

"It's bad everywhere."

"You're vulnerable, don't you realize that? What if someone puts a gun in your face?"

"It's happened."

"Has it?"

I nod. The information seems to affect him, which isn't nothing.

"What if," he continues, "you're walking down the street and some nut starts pointing his gun at a playground?"

"I'll call the police."

"You'll call the police."

"The police presence in Chicago is amazing; they're on every corner, and you've heard of CURE. I fuckin' hate them but they're everywhere—it's like they're in the bushes."

"There's no one around, you and this nut and his finger's on the trigger."

"Kids don't play outside anymore, everyone's too—"

"A family on the street, just walking."

"I wish he didn't have a gun."

"He does. Of course he does."

"I tackle him."

"He's stronger than you."

"Oh well."

"He puts a bullet through your skull."

"So be it."

My father shakes his head and looks genuinely sad. Not frustrated. Wounded. By me. My father has hurt feelings and combat weapons, including one of the new ARs, lying ominous and gigantic there on the Ping-Pong table. I point to it.

"Just like the one that killed Jack."

I go back upstairs. In the kitchen, there's a large cockroach on the cutting board. I grab the meat cleaver, aim, and swing it down. The roach dodges at the last second, and the cleaver lodges itself in the wood. I watch the roach skitter-scuttle down the counter and disappear behind the stove.

"Tricky, tricky."

I try to take the cleaver out of the cutting board, but it's stuck.

***

That night, I dream of a sickly sky, but a sky that is not unfamiliar. Tornado sky. I'm standing on top of a tall, tall building. The city doesn't look like Chicago, but I know it's supposed to be Chicago from the civil defense sirens. Fighter jets buzz the city, weaving in between buildings. Maybe it's Air and Water Show weekend. I feel energy in my hands, as though they are electric, but no, that description is inadequate; it is beyond electric—it is volcanic, it is oceanic. These fail, too. I can't describe it, but I don't need to describe it, because language doesn't matter. I'm King Kong, high atop this skyscraper, and the jets are coming for me. I'm filled with hatred for these jets and whoever's piloting them, and I want them to crash. I want them to crash. I'm thinking about how to make them crash, wondering if I can do it with my mind, with my hands. I feel that it is within my control, but yet out of my control. A power I can tap but cannot yet harness. I'm fearful and I hold back, but the jets get closer, their pilots like giant grinning cockroaches. One of the jets fires a cloud of bullets. They strike all around me. Maybe they hit me, but I feel no pain. Another jet fires a missile, and I feel the building shake under my feet as the missile connects. Steel crumples and shrieks. My whole body feels on fire when, suddenly, the yellow sky darkens, and the air is filled by the sound of a woman screaming. Screaming at the top of her lungs. A strong wind picks up. The scream is wild. It blinds me and I fall.

***

The next morning I find my mother in the kitchen, searching for deals online. The cleaver is still stuck in the cutting board. She smiles at me.

"Sleep OK?"

"Yeah, fine."

"I'll make you some breakfast."

She makes me bacon and eggs, toast. I can't remember the last time I had bacon. She watches me eat, and it seems to bring her enormous pleasure to do so. I consider asking again why no one told me about Jack's death, but then I don't. I know why.

The newspaper lies open next to her. I see a headline that reads "NOW FEAR THE WORST." I look again and it actually reads "New Fire Chief Welcomed."

Being in this house fills me with a dull sort of panic. One of the boxers comes over and rests his head on my lap. It dawns on me that I don't know all these dogs' names, or if they're even the same dogs that my parents had the last time I was here. I hope Simon is taking good care of Larry, and being careful not to overfeed him. Larry will eat himself to death if you let him.

I eat my bacon and eggs so fast that my mother figures I want more. I tell her I don't want more, but she makes me more and sets another helping down in front of me. This second plate I just stare at, and it fills me with a melancholy more vast and deep than any breakfast deserves. My mother tells me I "look so thin." But then, so does she.

I felt compelled to come here when I learned my brother died, but now that I've come, I don't know if anything was gained or improved or changed by my coming. Jack is still dead. My mother is still lonely. My father is still isolated. Plain City is still a small town like any other small town. My well-being—and maybe my life—was threatened last night at the cemetery, but this morning it's like it never happened.

I'm still here. People are violent. The world turns.

My mother drives me to the airport in the afternoon. I don't see my father again after our conversation in the basement. When we're getting ready to leave, I ask my mother where he is, and she says he's probably "at one of his meetings." And I really, really, really don't want to know.

We get on 161 and head back over to Columbus.

"I'm worried about Dad."

"Don't be."

"He's obsessed with guns."

"A lot of people collect guns, sweetie."

"What's he going to do with all of that?"

"I think . . . your father . . . just wants to be able to protect us if anything happens."

"Anything happ—Like what? Like if what happens?"

"We don't know. Could be criminals, could be the government tries to seize the land or there's a coup."

"If the army showed up at his house and wanted to take his land, what's he gonna do? Fire on them? What does he think would happen?"

She doesn't answer this.

"Mom? What would he do? Lob grenades at the police? What's he going to do with—"

"He just wants to be prepared."

"He bought a 3-D printer. He's going to start making guns. His own guns. This isn't right."

"Nothing is right, sweetie."

"Well, it's also not legal."

"Don't worry about your father."

"OK, fine, I won't. I'm worried about you."

"Me? That's funny, coming from someone who lives where you live. Why on earth would anyone want to live there? It's so unpredictable, so dangerous."

"It's no more dangerous in Chicago than it is anywhere else, there's just more people."

"More crazy people, more criminals."

I could tell her about what happened last night. I don't. What good would it do?

"In Plain City I'd stick out—look what happened to Jack. Someone who thinks the way we do can't be in a place like this. We get singled out. At least in Chicago I can find my people."

"Your people . . ."

There's a pause; we enter the remains of a commercial district, but everything is boarded up.

"Mom, you sleep fifty feet from a military armory. It's a fuckin' terrorist stockpile is what it is."

"You watch your mouth." Whether she's objecting to the f-word or the t-word is hard to say.

"Doesn't he scare you? At all, I mean? Do you feel safe with him?"

"Of course, what kind of thing is that—"

"Mom . . . I think . . . I believe that Dad thinks Jack deserved to die. For provoking that man. That Jack was to blame."

"We all miss Jack."

"Does he blame Jack? Mom?"

She's silent. Watches the road. She sighs.

"Mom? Do you blame Jack?"

"It's . . . it's . . . very complic—"

She slams on the brakes. The roaches on the hood don't fall off—*look at that grip!* Out in the road, I see a man, normal looking enough, standing in front of the car as though bracing himself.

"Oh no . . . they always do this."

The man launches himself hard onto the hood of my mom's car. It's surreal, a carefully perfected self-throw, smacking his knees and face on the front of the car and hitting the ground hard. My mom looks peeved. No, she looks furious.

"And . . . yep, there's the other one."

Another man appears, across the intersection, pointing at us.

"*Hey! Hey!* You just hit that guy! *Hey!*"

My mom closes her eyes and frowns. Shakes her head, exhales. She unholsters her handgun and gets out of the car, faster than I've ever seen my mom move. She fires two shots into the air, then lowers her gun and fires again, striking a yield sign feet away from the man across the intersection. He ducks.

"*Not today! You hear me?*" she yells, louder than I've ever heard her yell. It doesn't even sound like her. She walks to the front of the car and aims her weapon at the man on the ground. "Not me. Not today. Enough of this. Get up. Go." The man on the ground gets up. He got hurt throwing himself onto her car. (I guess you have to for this scam to work. He has a limp now and a pretty nasty laceration on his face.)

"You . . . hit me . . . you . . . you goddamned . . ."

"I said go. I don't have the patience for this today."

"With your car . . . fuckin' bitch."

My mom cocks her gun and points it right between his eyes.

"You don't get to call me that. No. No."

The man snivels, sputters. He misjudged her. (Serves him right.) He walks away, checking his shoulder to see if she pursues. She doesn't. She holsters her gun and gets back in the car, takes a deep breath, and grips the steering wheel. After a moment she smiles and opens her pleasant eyes.

She looks at me and says, "C'est la vie."

***

After a long, long hug, my mother leaves me at the airport, and I move through security like a sleepwalker. When I travel, even though TSA agents and CURE sentries treat me like I'm more dangerous than anyone else for not having a weapon and for not trying to sneak something through, and even though I draw extra screening and get hands and fingers and instruments run through my hair, and even though I get multiple pat downs and am blasted through with so many X-rays and gamma rays and sensors of all kinds that I may no longer technically be human, I usually try to be polite and friendly with these people. I try to remind them that kindness is real and it is possible. I try to remind them that not everyone is a threat.

But not today. Today I wordlessly, smilelessly shamble through the gauntlet and emerge on the other end, with plenty of time before my flight to get a beer. I find a bar near my gate, sit, and order a Guinness. I watch the stout cascade in the plastic cup. I take a sip and marvel at the fact that Guinness is now solely brewed in Missouri, but somehow the flavor, color, and body remain. Some things stay good.

My flight back to Chicago is only half full, which always makes me a little nervous; something about the empty seats feels not right. Like when a classmate's seat goes empty one day and she never returns.

This time, the flight is smooth to begin with, and so we get service. I eat my pretzels. I drink a scotch, neat. One of the flight attendants betrays herself and smiles at me when I thank her. I look out the window and over the clouds, and they look like snow. I find them comforting because they're so close. If the plane were to fall out of the sky right this moment, I feel as though we'd bounce on those clouds rather than plummet through them. The clouds look solid, strong, like you could build a city on them. Like you could build all cities on them. When the clouds rear up into vast towers, when they heighten and flatten like giant doors, there's nothing to say that there isn't a castle on the other side. Or within. A skyscraper. A subway system. The clouds go on forever and ever, broken up only by the flashing lights of other passenger jets careering toward their destinations.

Flashes of lightning, from above, look like underwater light. The clouds are a magic floor that glows when you set your foot on it. I forget whether I am up or down, whether I am meant to be where I am. I walk on the clouds and find that it is easy. You don't need to be an architect to know solid ground when it's right under your feet. There are no cockroaches on the clouds.

I am disturbed by a noise.

Eeeeeeeeeeeeeeeeeeeeeeeeeeeeeeeee.

A whining in the machine. The people all around me have their air nozzles open to full blast. They screech and growl. There are tones, the captain speaks:

"Ladies and gentlemen, this is your captain speaking. We're coming into Chicago airspace but, uh . . . something's happening on the ground that's preventing anyone from landing right this minute, so looks like, uh . . . we're going to be put into a holding pattern, not sure for how long, but we'll keep you updated." Then he gets much louder. "*Clear skies!* In Chicago." (That is plainly untrue.) "Winds coming out of the southeast, gusting at fifty-five miles per hour, and warfwarf visibility. Uh . . . try to get you on the ground as quickly as possible." I hope he doesn't mean that literally.

I lean my head against the window and look out, and it takes me a moment to realize just how strange what I'm seeing is. We're not just being placed into a holding pattern. We're entering one already long in progress. Dozens of jets, like vultures circling prey at different altitudes, a tall cylinder of hulking metal birds. I can see in the distance another jet, which is at the highest level of the holding pattern. And it's impossible to trust your depth perception when you're twenty-nine thousand feet up, but I'm fairly certain we're entering the pattern at the same altitude as that plane. In fact, there seem to be multiple aircraft at each level of the holding pattern. I can't tell how many levels there are, but there seem to be planes in every direction. The flight attendants appear calm, as though this is normal, as though it's routine for procedure to court catastrophe. The captain comes on. "No word as to what's causing this delay, folks; they aren't telling me anything, ha-*ha!*" Ten minutes later, we descend one level. Twenty minutes, we descend again. With each passing minute there are more and more raised voices, more necessity for flight attendants to strong-arm people back into their seats. One passenger tells a flight attendant, "If I had my weapon, I'd blow that smirk off your face." Other threats to shoot the flight attendants in the eyes, the ass, the breasts, the womb, with the guns every passenger had to place in checked baggage. The more people say they want to shoot the flight attendants, the more people feel at liberty to say they want to shoot the flight attendants. A well-groomed white man in a suit (who doesn't even seem to be angry) insists to the youngest-looking flight attendant that he'll take his weapon and "find the right spot." He adds, "Little bitch." There's a note in his voice that suggests this is not a threat, but a fantasy.

The sensation I get looking out the window is even stranger as I see planes above and below. The row across from me is empty. I take off my seat belt and cross over. A flight attendant demands I return to my seat. When I look out the window, I see a jet a few hundred feet below us. It looks as though I could jump off our wing onto its roof. I look up and see another jet above us, maybe a minute or two behind us. I can see another jet not far behind that one. The flight attendant grabs me by the arm and returns me to my seat. When she does, I catch a glimpse of the inside of her wrist and see a tattoo of a block letter *C* inscribing a rifle bullet, which I recognize as an insignia of CURE. I stay seated, but I don't put my seat belt back on. The captain comes on and says, "Just a little traffic congestion in Chicago. A little weather. Police activity. Understaffed. We should be landing soon, just keep to your seats. Flight attendants stay seated as well." We are in a sea of aircraft, flying fish, a rebel air force invading the capital of the American Midwest. People keep asking the flight attendants what the fuck on earth is going on, and all they say is, "There's nothing to worry about." Also, "Be quiet." The *eeeeee* noise goes away, which makes me more anxious; I feel it more deeply in its absence.

The captain checks in, but all he does is lie.

In what feels like an age, we descend again. Then again. Then again. The plane banks hard to the right, and I look out the window, up, up, up into the atmosphere. My vision is obscured by clouds, but what I see is like standing on a pier and looking up through a flurry of twisting gulls. The planes seem to be ignoring the racetrack oval of the holding pattern. Now they're flying free-form. Looking up through the center of this chaos, I see the sky darken and I hear a scream. From outside. From the clouds. From space.

I plug my ears. It's like being underwater.

Rumbles, as though surface-to-air missiles are detonating around us. I feel the plane shudder as the landing gear deploys, a sound like an ancient beast inhaling deeply. The aircraft seems to be working much harder than it's supposed to. The wings shift mechanically, transform, look like they're coming apart. They are computers inside, valves, wires, horrible angel wings.

Houses come into view. Train tracks. It's raining in Chicago. The runway will be slick, but who gives a shit? We all just want to be out of the air, put 'er down on her belly for all we care. The plane speeds up as we approach Midway, pressing us all back into our seats. I can see through the wings. The landing gear hits the runway with a violent bang, and the sound of a dragon's roar silences everything else as the jet tries to slow itself on the wet ground. We brake enough to swerve off the runway so another jet can come screeching in behind us. Our wing almost clips a smaller plane taxiing just off the runway. It isn't until we're parked at the gate that I'm confident another plane won't just land on us (and even then . . .). We sit at the gate for twenty minutes waiting for someone to connect us to the jet bridge. Many passengers get unruly, and one of them rushes a flight attendant in the rear of the craft. She subdues him with stunning ease and violence; something snaps, we all hear it. He moans and moans. I don't know if anyone catches it on camera. If anyone here is Mark DeWare.

In the end, the doors open. On my way off the plane, I see a flight attendant sitting in a window seat in the front row, gun in her lap, hands shaking, drinking a can of beer with a thousand-yard stare. I raise my eyes, and they're met by the captain's. A svelte black man with white hair and a face like a poorly baked pie. He'll be back in the air soon. Glancing past him into the cockpit, I see the Automat copilot with its long obsidian face, forever gazing out the windshield, its flat chrome fingers on the yoke, flexing, pointing, flexing, pointing, flexing, pointing . . .

SEVEN

My mother gave me cash so I could take a cab when I got back to Chicago, but like a good son I spent that money on drinks. I grit my teeth and board the Orange Line. It's a long crawl from Midway to downtown on a very dirty train. The rain pelts the roof of the train, surrounding me in a loud wash of metal static. A woman at the other end of the car is screaming. I don't see an earpiece, so I can't be sure if she's on the phone or not. She says, "*Time's up no time's up no no no no fuck you what I'm sayin' what I'm sayin' is I want chu be real with me know I'm sayin' I want chu be real no no and knock out this fake shit know I'm sayin' fake-ass fake-ass and I ain't even givin' you mine know I'm sayin' time's up you know time's up know I'm sayin' hell no hell no hell no!*" and so on and so on and so on. More than once she looks at me as she speaks, gesturing emphatically. Nearer to me, there's a wet sound. A man is spitting blood. I can't help but stare at him; he doesn't seem to be in pain, rather confused, or a little embarrassed. He looks young, in his twenties, Latino, precise facial hair, a chiseled jaw. He puckers his lips and rolls his tongue around in his mouth, collecting fluid, before spitting another wad of blood and saliva on the floor in front of him. The red mark is like a shadow.

The lights on the train flicker, which makes the blood seem to dance.

***

Back at my apartment, Larry is at my feet the second I walk in. He mews hungrily, but Larry can't fool me. I go to his dish and there are pellets of food scattered where there previously were none. Simon was here and Larry's been fed.

Larry rubs his head against my leg, and for some reason this contact makes me finally understand that I will never see my brother again. I sit on the floor, hold Larry to me, and sob loudly. The look on Larry's face expresses that he finds the sounds I'm making to be utterly strange but not disconcerting enough to flee. He makes himself comfortable, and the very tips of his claws poke the skin of my arm. He purrs, and for a few precious seconds it is the only sound in the world I can hear. Then, outside, in the alley, I hear yelling and a loud arrhythmic metallic clanking, like a hammer or an aluminum bat being slammed into a lamppost. My refrigerator emits a low hum. Something startles Larry, and he sprints into the other room. I stand. It's then I notice it. On the counter. A small white rectangle. A card.

SB
Unarmed Citizens
VIIIELXXXIXN

Another of these. Just like the others, this card has an arrange-ment of letters and numbers, only this time, they're struck through. A scrawled arrow points to the edge of the card. I flip it over, and on the back Simon's handwriting reads:

VIIISIIIE
Where you stand this second.
All you need to know, bud.

Where I stand this second. This second. VIIISIIIE. This second. My memory begins to fire away. I couldn't stop it if I wanted to. IXS, Kedzie Brown. XXIIWIIN, Addison Red. VIIISIIIE, my kitchen. That's all I need to know. A map appears in my mind. Nine south from Kedzie Brown Line; Twenty-two west, two north from Addison Red Line; eight south, three east from me at this moment. Blocks on the grid. The directions from these three points all lead to the same intersection: Kedzie and Grace. Without even knowing why, I run out my front door so fast that I forget to lock it.

EIGHT

Albany Park at night is a contradiction, as many American neighborhoods are. There is nothing to indicate that it is dangerous except that it is an American neighborhood. It looks peaceful. But every corner has seen a skirmish. I do not take my time. People are much less likely to mess with you if you look like you need to get somewhere, because nothing sparks a firefight quite like slowing someone down. People will protect their appointments.

I walk down Saint Louis Avenue. Most houses are dark; it's hard to tell what's abandoned and what isn't. I feel eyes on me. Wilson sits at 4600 N on the grid, Grace at 3800 N. Eight south. Saint Louis at 3500 W, Kedzie at 3200 W. Three east. When I get to Elston, I could take it to Grace, but I decide to honor the instructions instead. Eight south. Three east. No shortcuts.

I walk across the six-point at Grace, Bernard, and Elston. The asphalt of the intersection and several storefronts facing it are scorched black, as though there was a massive fire that engulfed the entire area. A couple of cars are still gently aflame. There was nothing in the news about such a fire, and yet I see it. Nothing here. Except cockroaches. They slither, skitter-scuttle, and crisscross in haphazard formations through the urban soot. Their brown-and-yellow bodies are coated in the black stuff, making them invisible. Countless and invisible. But I hear them. I pick up my pace, but I do not run. If I run, it will only attract them.

Then among all the tiny movements is a singular large movement. Out of the shadows lopes what looks like a large dog, maybe a wolf. It is pitch-black, but its eyes glow cruelly in the darkness. The clicking sounds of the cockroaches seem to slow, and I can hear the breathing of this hound. Low and throaty. Beyond throaty, that fails. An industrial, hellish sound. That fails, too. The rumble of this hound's snarling evokes plate tectonics. Redwoods snapping.

I freeze as it passes, even as cockroaches crawl up my legs—well practiced, me, at stillness and silence. Despite my loathing of the roaches, I know to fear this hound far more. I am somehow certain that this hound has a name, and that I am primevally aware of that name, and that she is a she, and that I have seen her before and will see her again. It occurs to me that the cockroaches are swarming to me for protection.

I reach my destination without encountering a single other person. There are no random civilian patrols, no police, no CURE, no codgers on their front porches, no youth militias. I arrive at the corner of Grace and Kedzie. There is very little here except a few residences that appear empty, an old post office that is now a pharmacy, and a dive bar. The bar, called simply C's Pub, has the lights on, but there doesn't appear to be much activity inside. No music. No laughter. The occasional solemn *clack* of billiard balls. The windows are all covered up, and the door is a forbidding slab of faded dead tree, opaque and unbroken by so much as a list of specials. I pull on the handle, expecting the entrance to be locked, and am surprised to find that it swings right open. Inside, the place is just as dumpy as the exterior suggests. It seems patched together; everything looks added on, washed out, stapled together; the bar looks hastily constructed, repeatedly repaired, jerry-rigged, and uneven. There's a large Blackhawks season schedule (last year's) tacked up and curling at the edges, surrounded by beer-branded mirrors and memorabilia, and ironic street signs. The bartender is a young white girl in a tank top and zip-front sweatshirt, her hair falling around a thick headband. She eats a small bag of chips (many other bags of which are hanging on hooks behind the bar and can be had for a dollar). When I open the door, she is watching a child standing by the pool table. He rolls the three ball along the beat-up rails of the beat-up table. He sings a nonsensical song to himself. The look on the bartender's face is neither a smile nor a frown.

It isn't until the door closes that the bartender looks up at me (as if anything said, any interaction here, had to happen behind closed doors).

"Hi. From the neighborhood?"

"Wilson and Saint Louis."

"Right by the high school. Well, former high school."

"That's it."

"Lotta action over there."

"Same as anywhere."

"Anyone in the school these days?"

"Just roaches."

"Which kind?" She smiles. There's a loud *clack*. The boy has found the nine ball and is banging the three and the nine together. "Somethin' to drink?"

Figuring there's no point in delaying it, I pull out Simon's card and lay it on the bar. "Actually, know anything about this?"

Upon seeing the card, she immediately drops all artifice and strides out from behind the bar. She thrusts her hands under my hair and feels around my scalp. She says to me, "Arms up," but has already forcefully raised them and starts to pat me down.

She runs a hand over my back, massages my forearms through my shirt. She unceremoniously reaches down my pants and gets her hand under my testicles. I am momentarily self-conscious—wondering when it was I last showered—as her small hand lifts my balls and touches the inside of my thighs (but only momentarily, as, of course, there is nothing even remotely sexual about this). She pulls her hand out and continues the pat down, outside of the hips, legs, grabs my butt, checks my ankles. She says, "Take your shoes off." The boy is watching all of this. Maybe ready to sound an alarm. She checks the weight of my shoes, takes one last quick look behind my ears. "Open your mouth." I do. She puts two fingers in my mouth and feels around the inside of my cheeks. I try to ignore that her hand has been on my scrotum and in my shoes.

She takes out a small flashlight and shines it into my eyes. Off. On. Off. On. She asks, "Any cybers?"

"No."

"It's OK if so, I just need to know."

"None, no."

"Give me your phone."

I do. She takes out a small device and holds it up in front of me. "This won't hurt." I notice the child covers his ears. The device glows yellow and hums, then flashes green and lets out an irritating, pulsing sound. Seconds later, two cockroaches fall from somewhere on my body. They land on their backs and twelve legs kick. She nods and goes back behind the bar, pours me a beer from the tap and one for herself, hands Simon's card back to me, lifts her glass, and says, "Cheers."

Clink.

"Mind crushing those?" she says as she picks up a phone and dials. I put my heel on one of the roaches and press down. It sounds like plastic snapping. Then again.

A moment later the bartender says into the phone, "Yeah, hey. Got an interested party. Uh, I already did. Fuck off." That last part she says with a smile and a stifled laugh.

I stoop down and inspect the crushed bodies of the two roaches. They're not sooty, so these weren't roaches that came with me from the street. These came from somewhere else. The nine ball hits the floor right in front of me with a *boom-boom-boom*. I jump and look over toward the pool table. The little boy stares at me, expressionless.

Behind the bar on a small TV, a news story plays. Thousands of flights grounded. Railways delayed. Travel is being choked up, but I can't make out why.

The screen changes, and the bartender and I watch in silence. A virus rapidly spreading in India. The virus causes the levels of hydrochloric acid in the stomach to spike, and victims turn into human acid geysers, spewing the stuff from their mouths and noses all over everything in sight, corroding all surfaces around them. If so much as a drop of the acid touches another person's skin, it burns down into the bloodstream and infects that person as well. Symptoms start in under twenty minutes and most victims are dead within hours. Thousands of people have been infected, especially in urban centers, and it seems to be out of control.

Oh, wait—no. It's a trailer for a movie.

Oh, wait—no. It's real.

I hear a door open and close somewhere within, and Simon appears behind the bar. He leans on the bar and takes one of the bartender's chips. He gives her a fraternal pat on the back and says, "Thanks, Maggie."

"Dude. He had one of your cards from last week."

"Yeah, I know, whatever."

Maggie shrugs and goes back to watching the boy at the pool table.

Simon says to me, "You're in the right place."

Simon leads me into the back of the bar, to what looks like a very normal storage/office space, cluttered and taped together as you'd expect the back room at a dive to be. The floor creaks at an alarming volume, and dust coats everything. An outdated computer displays a spreadsheet. There are boxes of promotional giveaways, pint glasses, coozies, bottle openers. In one corner there are two glass-front refrigerators full of bottled beer. Simon goes to one of the fridges and opens it.

"I'm OK, Maggie already got me a beer."

"I know. Watch this," Simon says as he reaches inside the fridge and flips some sort of lever or switch so well hidden that I can't even track what he did. There's a loud click, like the latch of a window has just been popped open, and, using both hands, Simon pushes the interior compartment of the fridge out of the way, revealing a ladder. A funny look must run across my face, because Simon giggles at me and says, "I know, right? Mind blown."

"This is like a secret hideout? For unarmed citizens?"

"Not a hideout, it's a meeting place."

"What is it, a political group?"

"You'll see."

The false refrigerator is ingenious, as it isn't false at all. It's a real fridge with real, actual cold beer inside, and in turn the chute and ladder underneath are quite chilly. As we descend, he tells me a little more.

"Like the name implies, we're a group of unarmed citizens who reject a fully armed society. We meet here once a week, sometimes a little more, and discuss action and strategy for combating that vision of the world."

We walk down a short hallway toward a large sliding door.

"Combating? You don't mean like, actual combat?"

"Well, not in a conventional sense. But we're working for a safer city."

"So what do you do?"

"All sorts of things. We impede or intercept arms deliveries. We disable and destroy 3-D printers engineered to make weapons. We steal guns. Anything we can."

"That sounds . . . really dangerous."

"It is, although the stuff you'd think is the most dangerous is actually pretty tame. The most dangerous thing we do is organize, stage protests. That always gets ugly in a hurry."

We come to the door. Simon turns to me and lowers his voice like he's about to say something very important.

"You know, man, I'm really disappointed you didn't bring Larry. Bring him next time."

***

Simon slides the heavy door open, and inside are far more people than I expected to see. I don't know what I was expecting, maybe eight or twelve, but there are more like sixty or seventy (or maybe more; I'm bad at estimating) men and women, some very young, some very old, crammed into pretty tight quarters. As soon as the door opens, all eyes are on us.

He takes me around and introduces me to a few key players. The room is more like a conference than a meeting; rather than everyone convening around a single agenda, there are breakout groups each talking about different projects. This group wants to infiltrate a CURE storehouse. This group wants to tamper with ammunition stockpiles. This group wants to hack into the systems of large weapons-advocacy organizations and lobbying groups and screw with their finances, their registries. Some of the plans seem so grand that I doubt whether they're being discussed in earnest.

Simon brings me to a young Chinese American woman in a scarf, whom he introduces as Lacey. "She's gonna ask you a few questions, if that's cool. You in a hurry?"

"No, not really."

"Awesome. Lacey'll take good care of you."

Lacey and I go off to another room lit by several standing lamps. She offers me a beer, which she calls "the truth serum." I laugh, and she gives me a knowing smile.

She proceeds to ask me a number of questions, some more prying than others, some very open-ended. Everything from my name and occupation to my political leanings to my attitudes on foreign wars or any kind of wars; my opinion on the various uses of unmanned drones; have I ever owned or operated a deadly weapon; have I ever owned or operated an unmanned drone; do I have any cybers or other bio-modifications; does anyone in my family belong to any radical or reactionary groups (I answer no, for the record); have I ever used force to defend myself or another, and if so, do I have any formal martial arts or other combat training; do I have any special degrees, certificates, or licenses; do I have any experience in the law; do I have any experience in life-saving medicine; do I speak any languages other than English; has anyone in my family been killed by a gun (I answer yes, and that leads to many, many more questions, all pertaining to that, then an entirely separate questionnaire about grief and vengeance); how do I personally interpret the First Amendment of the United States Constitution; how do I personally interpret the Second, Thirty-Third, and Thirty-Fifth Amendments of the United States Constitution; do I believe it's moral to kill someone who threatens me; do I believe it's moral to kill someone who threatens another person; do I believe it's moral to kill someone who disagrees with me?

She has questions about my recent trip to Ohio. I omit the part about my father's arsenal. I do briefly describe the encounter with the mob at Forest Grove Cemetery.

"Fuckers. I hope their guns backfire on them." Then her cheeks flush. "Sorry, that was intense. What I mean is . . . I'm glad you got away."

The last question is a doozy. "I can recommend you for membership. Do you want to talk to someone about how you can support the mission of Unarmed Citizens?"

I hesitate.

"Is it a one-time offer?"

"How do you mean?"

"Like, I need to accept now or . . ."

"Oh . . . well . . . no. You could go, like, sleep on it or whatever, come with Simon next week, and let us know."

"OK. I think I'll do that. It's just a lot to . . ."

"Process, yeah, I know. But as a person who has had a sibling murdered, I think we have a lot to offer you, and vice versa. Many in UC have lost family. It can be helpful just to talk to people who have had similar experiences."

"Were any of them my brother's brother?"

"Hmm?"

"Was my brother any of their brothers?"

"I don't follow."

"I'm just . . . the experience isn't similar, none of them suffered the same loss as I did." I pause; she stares. "Sorry, I'm being—"

"It's all death."

"Right."

"Think about it."

Two Unarmed Citizens named Dave and Jeff walk me back to my apartment. On the way, I ask them what Simon meant when he alluded to protests being the most dangerous thing they do. Dave responds at length.

"Well, we stopped doing that for the most part, because there were so fuckin' many open-carry and militia-building and no-restriction groups, it was impossible to keep track of all of their activity, first of all, and secondly, open-carry became so common that it was hard to distinguish what was an open-carry rally from just, like, a group of friends hanging out in a park."

Jeff chimes in, "Confront either, you're gettin' the same treatment."

Dave snorts.

Off to our right we all catch a glimpse of a bright-orange glow. A man sits on his porch, smoking a cigarette. An assault rifle leans next to him. We quiet as we pass him. I look up at his house. A dark figure stands still, silhouetted in a second-floor window, staring down at us. The imagination runs wild.

When they drop me off, they each shake my hand. I'm home for about twenty minutes when there's a knock on my door. My heart drops into my gut, wondering who it could be. The police? CURE? The cigarette-smoking man? My father? There's another knock, and I hear a familiar voice.

"Hey man, you in there?" It's Simon. I go to the door and open it a crack to greet him.

"Hey Simon, what's up?"

"Just wanted to say thanks for coming by the meeting. And uh . . . I don't think I need to tell you this, but . . ."

"I won't tell anyone anything."

"Yeah, good. Cool. That's . . . yeah, it's important. You never know who you can trust. But I've had a good feeling about you for a while."

"About me?" This strikes me as ridiculous, but he seems to mean it.

"Yeah, you're a good neighbor, seem like a solid guy, and I knew you'd lost a brother to violence, so . . ."

"You knew?"

"What? Oh. Yeah."

"How?"

"Sorry, right, yeah, that's . . . we keep apprised of weapon deaths all over the country—Jack's murder didn't make national news, but Ohio stations covered it and a few in Indiana. You'd mentioned you had a brother Jack and I figured, how many Jack Palazzos are there? You wouldn't believe how the press and the local officials blamed him, just really baldly—"

"You knew about Jack's death and didn't say anything to me about it?"

"Well . . . sorry, man, wasn't sure if you'd want me to bring it up."

"It's just . . . no one told me about it. You knew about my brother's death before I did."

"Seriously? Wow. Um . . . OK. That's fucked-up. Never would have guessed you didn't know."

"Yeah."

"Well, hey man, I'm really sorry about it and really, there's a lot of people in the group who—"

"Lacey already told me, many losses, similar feelings, yadda yadda."

"OK, you're upset, I'm gonna leave you alone. Think about it, though, man. There's a place for you. Good people."

Simon walks into his apartment, and I shut the door.

***

Larry joins me on the couch. I pull out my tablet and start looking up videos. Tonight it's strange creatures. Cryptozoology. The videos have titles like:

ALIEN IN THE CROWD?

and

*^^GINAT TRANNATULA SITING IN NALT PARK!!!!!!!!^^*

and

STRANG BODDY WAS A SHORE IN VAUNCOUVAR (CANNADIA)

and

RIVER BEAST?? ~ ~ WAT IS IT U DESIDE?!?!

These types of videos are easy to fake, so the message boards go nuts. Claiming all the creatures are puppets, they're people in costumes, they're animals in normal states of decomposition, they're animals in costumes. The comments suggest that not only are they fakes but they're *bad* fakes, and people are really mad that someone even went to the trouble of making them. They shouldn't have made them. They shouldn't have done anything. It's such a fake. They're all such fakes. You're retarded if you think otherwise. Prove me wrong. You can't. Kill yourself. I STADN BYE MY SATEMENT U CAN HTE ME IF U WANT!!! I'm a man of FACTS. Another parasite. I'll kill you. I'll kill you.

Again, there's one video that troubles me. It's a cell phone video taken on a subway. There's a group of young friends on a train at night, and they are very excited about a concert they just saw. The car is a typical one, very dirty, a flickering light. Somewhere off camera someone is ranting and raving incoherently. In the background, a homeless man sits slumped over, his face cannot be seen, his hands and feet are wrapped in garbage bags and duct tape. The kids carry on for a minute or so about the concert, offering reactions to the show, when suddenly the person raving off camera just starts laughing. A dark, hysterical laughter. A laugh of cosmic madness. The camera swings to the right to capture the laughing person, and it does, briefly, centering and focusing on a raincoat-clad old white man with a partially cybernetic jaw, his head thrown back, mouth wide open, laughing in a way that may cause him injury. When the camera comes back to the original angle, the friends look creeped out by the laugher but are unaware of the development behind them, which is that the homeless man is quaking. The one with the camera says, "Whoa, hey . . . hey look . . ." The friends all slowly turn to look at the homeless man. One of them calls out, "Sir? Sir, you need a hospital?" And that's when it happens. The train lurches, and the homeless man is cast out of his seat. When he hits the floor, thousands of cockroaches scatter from every opening in his clothing, pouring out into the car. The friends shout and swear—I do as well—and get up on their seats to avoid the roaches. The bugs stream out of the homeless man's clothes until there's nothing left. No body, no skeleton, no nothing. Just clothes. The video is titled:

*ROACH MAN ****WTF**** NSFW*

The consensus is that it's a fake. That seems like the logical conclusion. But it also seems like the easy conclusion. Don't think about it. It's a fake. I'll kill you.

Nothing to see . . .

People create fake videos to deceive, manipulate, and scare you. You can't trust anything you didn't see with your own eyes. And even then.

Move it along now . . .

I look into some of the less-sensationalized forums. Inspired by my conversation with Dave and Jeff, I decide to look up some videos of protests. I find one of students at a small liberal arts college staging a peaceful protest regarding the school's indifference toward sexual assault on campus. The group of mostly female students is gathered on the quad with signs, and a CURE sentry in a gas mask and riot gear (stepping forth from a line of CURE sentries in gas masks and riot gear) walks up to them and, without warning, uses some kind of chemical weapon on them. There's a lot of screaming and shouting, and the camera work becomes shaky. The sounds coming from the attacked students are revolting. Before the video cuts out, there is the sound of a helicopter above.

The commenters claim this video is a fake for many different reasons. Some say it's a fake put out by activists to make CURE look bad. Others say CURE and the government put out the video as a warning to student demonstrations of any kind nationwide. It looks pretty damn real to me, but everyone claims that since the video could have some political benefit for someone, it is probably a fake. Not that it *might be*, but that it *is*. If someone stands to gain from it, then there is no way it happened by accident.

I click on another video. And then another. And then another. I finally come across a video titled:

CC FOOTAGE OHIO WALMART SHOOTING
[GRAPHIC] #death #kill

It's Jack's death. It's been viewed a lot. There are a lot of comments posted. I can't bring myself to click on it, not only because I don't wish to see my brother's murder, but because I cannot stomach the thought of what people have to say about it. That the shooter didn't do anything wrong. That he's the real victim. That he deserved to kill Jack. That the gun used is a sweet gun. Dude went down hard LOL.

I don't need to read any of it, because I don't need to know why so many have chosen to watch the moment of my brother's death. To deconstruct it. To criticize it. Besides, I already know what they say.

The video might not be real. The story might not be real. There never was a Jack Palazzo.

In the sidebar there are other recommended videos. One has no title; I notice this because that's odd, most videos have titles that shout at you in all caps. The preview shot appears to be an empty street corner. It has over twenty million views. I assume that because it has so many views, it must be something really profane, and so I decide not to watch it.

I shut down the tablet and realize Larry is no longer on the couch with me. I decide to go find him, and when I do, I'll feed him. Not because he'll need it, but because we'll both enjoy it, and that's enough of a reason.

***

I'm shaken in the middle of the night by an explosion. It sounds like it was right down at the end of the block. There are immediate shouts and cries, I get up and go to the window, open it a crack, and see a few men running toward the explosion, guns out. Two of them appear to be already injured, bloody and hobbling. As they run, I hear the sound of cockroaches being crushed underfoot.

Larry's eyes are wide and searching, looking to me for a sign.

Is this it? Is this the end?

After a tense moment in which I believe Larry might actually say something to me, and I might actually understand it, he blinks and his little pink tongue flicks his nose.

I grab a beer from my fridge, and before opening it I hold the cold can to my cheek and forehead. I crack it open and stand in my kitchen, listening to the sounds outside. Something is happening. I recall a story out of San Jose last year—some people had a nuclear weapon in a storage unit of an apartment building. There was never any (confirmed) information about what the device's purpose was, if it had an intended target, if it was being delivered to another party, or if its owners were just going to set it off one day. The reports were that the neighborhood watch had investigated and neutralized the threat, but that never sat well with me. The media spread the narrative that a group of concerned citizens took action and rooted out the radicalized terrorists in their midst, that they heroically took up arms, devised a strategy, stormed the apartment building, and took 'em out. San Jose is saved. Honor is restored.

But there were whispers of another story. Sophisticated surveillance. CURE sentries rolling into the apartment building overarmed and underinformed. CURE sentries dressed for full-scale combat, peppering the building with tear gas and filling it with diamond dust. CURE sentries killing everyone in the building. There were descriptions of the group's movements, their formations, their grenade launcher, their armored van, their gleeful mocking chants. It all sounded like CURE. But the media told us that CURE had nothing to do with it. Nor did the police. They told us that it was regular people like us who had had the bomb, and regular people like us who had thwarted them. They want us to suspect our neighbors, they want us to invade each other's privacy, they want us to presume, and mistrust, and inform.

They, they. They they they. I wish there were a better word.

The noise from outside dies down. No more explosions. Tonight. Only distant gunshots. Could be raindrops on an air conditioner.

Larry stretches, yawns. I do the same. I go back to the tablet and find that the thumbnail of the video I ignored earlier is still present on-screen, the one with no title that appears to be only a street corner. It now has nearly forty million views. I click on it. A street corner. A silent, still street corner somewhere in a city that is not surrounded by mountains. It's hard to tell whether it's shot on a dashboard camera, a phone, a face computer, or what, but the picture is pretty clear. None of the usual tells of inauthenticity like grainy footage, low light, or extreme angles. There are no loud noises, or even strange noises. The only movement at first is wind in the flora and, of course, a few visible cockroaches. Then, out of the right side of the frame, there is a sudden color. A vibrant blue. A girl has walked into the frame. She wears a knee-length lightweight blue coat. Her hair is curly, a shade of chestnut. She walks slowly, with a downward gaze, but she doesn't seem forlorn. She appears to be deep in thought. Her hands rest in her pockets as she strolls just past the center of the frame. She stands there a moment, still looking down at the ground. I am met with a moment of panic, expecting that someone is going to abruptly emerge and assault her (rape videos tend to get a lot of views), or perhaps she's going to pull out a gun and shoot herself (suicide videos tend to get a lot of views). But that panic leaves me. She is safe, and somehow I know that in this video at least, no harm will come to her. She stands on the sidewalk in whatever place this is, and she pauses. She contemplates. I make the video full screen, and I see her face in greater detail. The color of her coat seems bolder. Somehow hopeful yet cautious. She stands like this for eleven seconds, then she looks to the sky. Her hair falls back from her face. (Her hair is so gorgeous it's unreal.) After only four seconds of looking at the sky, she lowers her head again and walks on, leaving the frame much as it started.

And that's the whole thing. Fifty-eight seconds. Nothing. Girl. Nothing.

Blue coat. Chestnut hair.

There's no commentary, no notes, no explanation. And again, no title. I might expect "GRRL ON STREET!!" or "WAT COAT IS THIS???" I reload the page. Sixty-one million views.

I keep rewatching it. The stillness, her entrance, her coat, her hair. Her downward gaze. Her upward glance. Exit. Over and over. The first dozen times I watch it, I keep looking in the background for what might be a point of curiosity. The sky is mostly out of frame, so whatever she might be looking at, or might be hearing, isn't visible. I consider the color of her coat, melancholic in its way, and I wonder what that color is called. It resembles a cornflower . . . or a sapphire. I get another beer. I watch it over and over again for an hour before I stop looking for what's wrong with it, what's strange in it, what I might be missing, and I just accept it for what it is. The video is her. She is the video.

Sixty-eight million views.

Seventy-three million views.

Eighty-one million views.

Still no comments, and then I get it. The video is going viral because it's real, and everyone knows it. There's no narrative in it. No motive. No politics. No advertisement. No violence.

A girl, with thoughts, in a coat. It's breathtaking. She's breathtaking.

The sun comes up. I have to go to work.

NINE

I have one client today, name of Joe; he's typically laid-back and is about my age, so I feel no need to dress up. I don't shave, only kind of wash my face. Joe won't care. I consider not brushing my teeth, but then a belch forces its way up that is pure beer, so as a courtesy to both of us, I brush. Mouthwash and gum for good measure.

On the train, we keep stopping between every station. The train slams to a halt and there's a *boop-boop-boop* over the speakers. A recorded voice:

Your attention please. We are being delayed because of an equipment problem on a train. Warfwarfwarf to correct the problem. We regret this inconvenience.

We crawl into Belmont, and I switch over to the Red Line. The Red Line is no better. We stop just north of Fullerton.

Boop-boop-boop.

Your attention please . . .

Sometimes when this happens, the operators get off the trains. We could be abandoned here. I got in the habit, a long time ago, of starting my commute much earlier than I should need to, because you never know when this is going to happen.

The trains, the tracks, the whole system has been slowly falling apart. I've always assumed I'll die on the train. C'est la vie.

There's only one other man on my car. He leans forward in his seat, appearing to be mulling something over, but then I realize he's staring. He looks a lot like me actually, probably about my age. Armed, though. He stares at the seat across from him, as though inspecting an object left behind, or a stain. Then I see it, what he's staring at. It's a single cockroach. The roach is doing something I've never seen before. It looks almost as if it is standing. Standing up. Between them there seems to be a staredown happening. A confrontation. The man does not seem to be afraid or intimidated. I see blood on the man's ankle, soaking through his sock and into his shoe. His hands stay in his lap, not moving for the gun. The cockroach's antennae wave, taunting. Somewhere, outside, a shrill tone sounds.

Warfwarf! Warfwarfwarfwarf! Someone is being arrested. There's a lot of crime around the old university in this neighborhood. Shots are fired. The man takes his eyes off the cockroach for a fraction of a second, his gaze darting ever so slightly in the direction of the shots. The cockroach spreads its hideous, papery wings and flies right at the man's face, landing on his cheek. The man hollers and tries to pull the offending insect off his cheek, but much to our shared horror, the cockroach will not come off. The man takes out a large knife and attempts to pry the roach from his face but to no avail. He shrieks, and blood runs down his cheek. I'm not sure whether he's cutting into his own face with the knife or whether the cockroach is making him bleed. The man pulls out his gun and holds it up to his cheek, to blow off the roach (and half his face along with it). I rush over to him and knock the gun from his hands, at which he fulminates, calls me names, throws elbows. I wrestle him to the floor of the train and take his knife.

"Don't move, I'm gonna get it," I say. Even as I say it, I don't know how I'm going to accomplish it. He keeps alternating between begging me for help and verbally abusing me. He's in a full panic. I put the point of the knife under the roach's body, and it flits its wings. I realize it's hooked into his flesh, and the realization causes my knees to buckle.

Then the train jerks forward. My hand slips and the knife slices the man's cheek. He howls in pain and blood immediately begins flowing down the side of his face and neck, collecting grimly in the grooves of the train floor. I apologize, but I don't get off him. I press my hand down on his chest, and, not knowing where exactly the words come from, I yell, *"Fucking stop!"*

He stops thrashing, and as the train creeps into Fullerton station, I grasp the cockroach's wings between my thumb and forefinger. I lift, and the folded sections of its little brown body begin to part like an uncoiling spring. The wings part from the abdomen, the legs extend but stay latched into the man's cheek. I have an image in my mind of how Larry looks when I grab him by the scruff of his neck, his lean body elongating and going stiff. I give a firm yank, and I expect the wings to rip away from the body, but they don't. They hold true. With the serrated part of the knife, I saw at the roach's legs. It's much more difficult than I expect.

I say to the man, "Just a second."

I manage to cut through the roach's legs and hold up the body in front of my eyes. My hands and fingers don't want me to be holding it, autonomically try to flick it away, but my eyes and brain want to see it. The roach's body dangles from the wings. It lives because of course it does, because these fuckin' things . . . I throw it to the other side of the train.

I look back at the man, and the segments of the roach's legs still stick out of his face like hairy fishhooks. He yells, "G' off me!" and pushes me away as the train comes to a stop at

Fullerton. He doesn't wait for the operator to open the doors. He pulls the emergency lever and forces the door open, charging out onto the platform, stumbling into people and then running down the stairs. The other doors open. About ten or twelve people get on the train and take their seats. I walk over to where the cockroach landed. I find it on a seat, on its back. It's curled up, its leg stumps pulled close as though dead or sleeping, but I know better. At the North/Clybourn stop, two women get on and come toward me, like they want the seats I'm standing over. I gesture toward the injured roach. They frown and sit elsewhere.

I look back at the roach and laugh. The laugh sounds wrong in my head, as though it comes through a fog. I pick up a discarded iced tea bottle. Without knowing why, I unscrew the bottle cap, grab the roach, and drop it into the bottle. It kicks its legs and rights itself within. I don't know what I intend to do with it, but I feel that I need to look at this roach more closely, understand why it was so . . . resistant. I put the bottled roach in my bag.

When the train reaches Grand, there's an old man struggling to get up from his bench to board the train. I ask him if he needs help, and he looks at me with wide eyes and a slack jaw. "God, yes" is the expression. He leans his weight on a cane and offers his other hand to me. The hand is fully cybernetic. I take his hand in one of mine and grasp his arm with my other hand. His entire forearm, I feel, is cybernetic. A tangle of machine, fiber, and computer. His arm could withstand a blow from a sledgehammer, these cybernetic limbs are so sophisticated and durable, but somehow, in my hands, in this moment, it feels fragile, delicate. I get the man safely onto the train and into a seat, but the doors close before I can get off again. Lake station is shut down, so I'll have to walk to work from Monroe.

***

As I walk up State, the wind whips violently. It comes in bursts, as though there is a giant winged creature hovering over the lake, its wingbeats sending gale-force gusts through the urban corridors. It's accompanied by a loud flapping noise in the air, like a giant flag catching the breeze (also, wings). I get to the river and find that the State Street Bridge is closed. I turn to look east toward the lake and west to where the river curves southward. Many other bridges appear to be closed. There are no boats in the river at this moment, though that's not out of place. The cockroach bodies and thick, mephitic slurry of pollutants in the water are deadly to boat motors. Can't get far in that particular waterway unless you're in a Marine ClearWay, which only the police, CURE, and the US military possess. I've heard older Chicagoans talk about these guided boat tours that used to be popular; they would take folks up and down the river and then out onto the lake, sharing anecdotes about the history of the neighborhoods and the architecture. The greatness of the city. Cocktails were served. Those boats have all been decommissioned. The very idea of such a thing now is unimaginably quaint.

The one bridge that's open in the vicinity is the Wells Street Bridge, so that's where I make my passage. With each step, I feel in my feet, in my whole body, the emptiness below. The flutter and bounce. Above me, the tracks carry the Brown Line across the river and into the Loop. As I walk north, halfway across the bridge I find a very old homeless woman. Her skin is a deep, deep brown, but she has large patches of vitiligo all over her face, neck, and hands. She has a sign next to her that reads *wating 4 colaps*. I pause and look at the sign and her skin, and when I stop and listen, I can hear the rusting, the buckling. I hear a deep, mournful groaning in the bridge, like a gigantic old dog stretching its limbs, unable to get comfortable. A gust comes west from the lake, and she snatches the sign, holding it in place. The steel shudders, and then I hear a rumbling from the north. A Brown Line train roars overhead, and dozens of cockroaches are shaken from the beams and tracks above, landing all around and on top of us; one skips off my shoulder like a stone and falls into the river. There are wings and legs everywhere, the color of filth. I pull my jacket over my head so they won't get in my hair. The old woman closes her eyes, and when the rush of the train fades, I hear that she is humming a tune. She hums loudly, but as soon as I take a few steps to the north, I can no longer hear her.

Once I get across the river, I decide to head east toward the lake rather than continue north. The closer you get to Michigan Avenue and State Street, the more people there are, which to me is always a toss-up; the more people you have around, the less likely you are to get mugged, but with crowds come more arbitrary altercations, people bumping into each other, flare-ups, more police and more CURE. From somewhere a block or two away, I hear the shrill police tone cry out, warping as it echoes. Seconds later, from the south, another shrill tone. (No wonder no one lives downtown anymore—that sound must get unbearable.) Two CURE armored trucks go past, heading south, with sentries hanging off the sides like it's spring break.

From the east I hear a rumbling coming from the sky. I look and see a plane, westbound toward O'Hare. It flies low over the city. I swear it's low enough to hit the Hancock. It doesn't.

I get to my office and find Joe outside, waiting. He grimaces. I pull out my phone and check the time. It's almost an hour before our appointment.

"Hey Joe. You're early."

"Got nowhere else to be, so . . ."

"OK. Well, let's head up."

There's no one in the building yet. No other businesses are open. Just me and Joe.

"Had a good weekend?"

"Meh. You?"

"It was OK. Went to visit my folks, that's always a little strange."

"Sure."

When Joe was in last week, he seemed up. Now he seems edgy. Maybe something happened on his commute.

"You want some coffee or anything?"

"Nah, let's just get to it."

"Have a seat for a minute. I'll be right back, and we'll start."

I gesture to the whole lobby, which is full of empty seats. Still, Joe looks around as if there's nowhere to sit. He remains standing.

I go into the office and check the messages. No messages. I check the email. All spam. I send a text to Walt: *Coming in today?*

I sit at the computer, morning light streaming in, making everything feel strangely out of time, like I wasn't supposed to see it yet. I pull up the video of the girl. Her blue coat. Her curls. I watch the video two or three times. Then I take the bottled roach out of my bag and set it on the desk in front of me. The incident on the train rushes back, and I am newly disturbed. I hear the man's screams, see the roach hooked into the flesh of his cheek. I have blood on my cuffs; I hadn't noticed it until now. My shoes, too. I watch the roach move easily around the bottle, despite the fact that I mutilated two of its legs. It's grotesque and yet extremely impressive. I can see how it effortlessly compensates for the missing appendages. Having it behind glass allows me to observe it much more closely than I normally would.

I go back out to the lobby and find Joe still standing, staring at the wall.

"Hey Joe, you can come on back if you're ready."

"If I'm ready? Why wouldn't I be ready?"

"Oh, not . . . I was just saying."

"I was ready when I showed up. Now you're ready."

"Yes. Great, we're both ready."

Still no one in the building. Still no other businesses open. Still just me and Joe.

We go back into my office. Joe stands by the chair that would be his, I stand behind my desk at my chair. Joe's eyes dart around. He may be looking for surveillance or checking the exits, but then I notice that there are quite a few cockroaches on my walls. More than we usually get in here.

"Can we . . ." Joe begins, and then seems to struggle to form words. He looks ill suddenly, holds his stomach. "Can we go somewhere with . . . fewer of . . . them?"

I wish there were such a place, but anyone who lives in the world knows that cockroaches are ubiquitous. There is nowhere you can go to get away from them entirely. No room secure enough, no lock tight enough, no warehouse remote enough, no tundra cold enough. I have heard that cockroaches have found their way onto the International Space Station. They are cunning and tenacious and fast. They are fast, fuck damn are they fast. I see their speed in my dreams, feel their speed in my nightmares. They seem to appear, like ghosts, from nowhere. There is no escape from them, not even in death. Especially not in death. They are the dominant species.

"We could switch offices, but every room is going to have them."

"Could we go to the roof?"

"There will be cockroaches on the roof, Joe. And we'll be watched."

"I don't know, then."

"I never knew you were so averse."

"Oh, what? You aren't? You love cockroaches?"

"No, but I deal with them."

"These old buildings have more."

"Can we talk about your job search?"

He looks at me crooked.

I add, "Please?"

"Yeah. I guess. Why I'm here, right?"

"You tell me, Joe."

"You keep saying my name."

"How's the job search going?"

"You know how it's going. Every interview I've had in the past two weeks was for an internship that I didn't get."

"That's frustrating."

"You have no idea. I applied for a job as a waiter, OK? I went in and talked to the manager, and he said he liked my energy but they were looking for someone with more on their résumé."

"Don't you have six years of serving experience?"

"They wanted someone with a master's degree."

"Oof."

"Everyone's telling me I need a master's at least, but I'll be paying back the loans I already have until I'm fifty, and that's if I get a job today. My savings are gone."

"Have you considered leaving Chicago?"

"There are no jobs anywhere, man. Leaving isn't gonna fuckin' help. Where am I gonna go? Some small town? There's even less nothing out there."

"Joe, I'm just here to help you. All I can do is give you advice, ideas—that's what I'm here for."

"How much you get paid for this job?"

"Very little."

"Do you have a master's degree?"

"No."

"How did you get this job?"

"Luck, I guess. I don't want to talk about me."

"A *master's degree*. That's what they . . . yeah, I'll get a master's in anthropology, so then I'm qualified to wait tables? Good. Or I get an MBA and that qualifies me to tear fucking Hawks tickets? Maybe I'll go to law school, then *who knows?* With a law degree maybe I could dream big and work in retail! Oh wait, no, that's all automated now."

"I know it's hard; I was unemployed for years before I got this job. It seems impossible, and everyone looks at you like you're the one with a problem, or that you are the problem or—"

"Yeah, my parents keep asking me why no one will hire me, keep asking me if I'm a drunk, if I don't dress well for interviews, if I've gained too much weight do I think?"

"Don't listen to that, they don't get the situation."

"The situation? I'd give my left fuckin' arm for a situation, man, there isn't even a situation, there's just randomness and goddamned chaos. I got harassed twice on my way here by two different CURE sentries. *Two.* Just starting some shit with me because they can. The second one seemed like a wackjob; I thought he might draw his weapon on me. Isn't it funny we fuckin' sit here and complain about the job market, meanwhile we could get killed for no reason today? Like hey, the dying can't be helped, but maybe the economy will improve. That sentry could have blasted me today and would probably face no repercussions whatsoever. I don't even know why I say 'probably.' No one would even know I was dead."

"I'd know."

Joe winces and grasps at his stomach. I feel more comfortable with him the more upset he gets. Somehow he feels less threatening when he's releasing it.

"You OK? Your stomach, I mean?"

"I'm all right, recovering from something."

"Virus?"

"Something like that." A cockroach flits from the wall and lands in between us. Joe slams his fist down on it, trapping the back half of its body underneath, crushing it. The front half reaches and squirms, struggles, its antennae stiffening. I hear it . . . gasp?

"I had an interviewer, some HR dipshit the other day, look at me and say, apropos of nothing, 'Your generation expects to be handed everything.' When your interview starts that way, it doesn't bode well, you know?"

"No. Definitely not." I pause, and I remember what it was like to be in Joe's position. "Before I landed this job, I tried to volunteer at a couple different places, just to . . . have an excuse to use my skills, I guess. And I kept getting rejected. From volunteering." As I say that, I pick up a notepad and brush a roach off my desk; we both watch it hit the wall and stick. It hangs on, doesn't fall. We share an uncomfortable moment, marveling at it. Joe winces, and his hand goes to his stomach. He struggles to say these words:

"Everything I hear is about how our generation are leeches, that we don't want to work. We don't want to do anything or be anything. Everyone talks about 'why don't we get jobs?' like there are jobs to get. Even if I get a job, by some miracle, it won't pay me enough to actually own anything or keep me out of debt, and I'll be made to feel like I'm lucky for it. I want everything that everyone says I'm supposed to have, but it doesn't exist. It's a sick fantasy. There are people in the world who get rich off murder and fraud and theft and just fucking *lies*, and I'm told I'm entitled because I'm honest and expect more than a slow death."

The cockroaches seem to respond to the sound of his pain. They start to skitter-scuttle down the walls toward the floor. He chokes back his emotion and steadies himself, and they start to crawl back up. He stares into my eyes, and after a long moment, he starts to lift his shirt, wincing.

Underneath, I see that he has what appears to be a large piece of machinery embedded into his abdomen. He also shows me—perhaps unwittingly, perhaps not—that he is armed. The machinery whirs and hums, and he adjusts something on it, some valve, which seems to give him very momentary relief. I try to not alarm him, call attention to his abdomen, his weapon, I try to continue the conversation as normal.

"I'm on your side, I want you to know that."

"All I have to show for my work is debt and loss. I'm half expecting to start being charged fees to apply for a job, just wait till that gets going. It's coming. Thanks for your interest, that'll be one hundred dollars, and good luck to you. Just take and take and take. I'm thirty years old and I have nothing."

"No one does, Joe. There's less and less out there all the time, everything's a scam, nothing is real. Right? So why even try? Is that what you want to hear?" As soon as I say it, I wish I could take it back.

Joe looks like he may say something else, like he may confess something to me, but instead he gets up from the desk and storms out. In the empty building, I can hear him descend from floor to floor and out onto the street. The sounds travel through the structure, vibrating the walls and floor. I look out my window and see Joe emerge onto the sidewalk. He's no longer wearing a shirt; sunlight glints off his abdominal device. A CURE sentry walks past and says something to him. I can't make it out, but sentries almost never say anything kind.

(Joe is doomed. Maybe he always was.)

As soon as the CURE sentry makes his remark, Joe turns back. Then a dark spot appears on the sentry's forehead, which I can recognize, even from this distance, as a cockroach. Joe's weapon comes up from his waistband. He shoots the cockroach, and beyond it, the CURE sentry's brain. The sentry is dead before hitting the ground. Joe stands over the old gold and black with green boots and lets out a scream that reaches my ears even through my window's bulletproof glass. The scream is ghastly, triumphant. There is a yawning void in this scream that invites the darkness. I swear I hear another scream mix with Joe's, a scream from the sky.

A shrill tone cries out, "PUT YOUR FIREARM IN ITS HOLSTER AND STAND DOWN."

Joe drops his gun and stands still.

"STAND DOWN—STEP AWAY FROM THE BODY."

Joe makes like he might comply, but then he falls on the body of the sentry.

"STEP AWAY FROM THE BODY."

I'm surprised that he hasn't already been taken down by the police. From somewhere on the sentry's person, Joe removes a metallic-gold canister. I recognize it, and I shiver. I've only seen them in videos online, and they're so vile that I had wondered if they were even real. They are real. Joe is holding one.

A SID.

"DROP THE WEAPON AND STAND DOWN."

The CURE-issued spherical immolation device, a.k.a. the SID, is typically used to disperse violent crowds as a last resort; they've seen a lot of use at large-scale demonstrations. It acts like a self-contained, multidirectional flamethrower, spraying a thick chemical fluid in all directions that ignites when oxidized. Joe activates the device and holds it against his body. I can't look away.

The police call out one more time in vain.

"DROP THE WEAPON AND STA—"

The fluid ejects from the canister with a high-pitched whine, and within seconds Joe is engulfed in robes of black and orange. The fire looks as fire does in outer space: heavy liquid ribbons, crawling up, over, and around his body, following each curve of his shape. The CURE sentry's body catches as well, and the two of them become a roaring pyre. The burning figure of Joe leans back and holds the canister aloft, and the dread liquid jets from it like a fountain, coating and incinerating everything within a fifty-foot radius.

Watching this all, I feel my heart race, my skin itch, and a clawing weight grow on the back of my neck that is hard to describe accurately, so I'll call it guilt.

More and more police officers show up on the scene, some in cruisers, others on Segways. They all hang back at a safe distance, ineffectual, watching the bodies burn. They make no moves to put the fire out. Maybe they just don't want to. At least four appear to be laughing. The way friends do.

There are a few bystanders farther down the block, and I wonder if any of them are catching this on video.

I pry myself away from the window. There isn't any reason I need to continue to watch. Joe and I weren't friends, but I talked with him enough about his dreams to recognize the perversity in watching them literally go up in flames. There was a time when such a rash gesture may have sparked protests, may have started a movement, but Joe's spectacular death will not even make the news.

I wander dull-headed back into our business office, and I have trouble picturing my coworkers in the space. I vaguely remember someone sitting over there, and someone slapping the printer, and someone leaning up against that table, and maybe someone talking on the phone, but it's been so long since I've shared a workday with my colleagues—at least, it feels so long. I lose track of relative time when I spend too long alone, it starts to become difficult to distinguish hours from minutes, days from months. I wonder if maybe I have an undiagnosed condition of some sort. Or maybe it all just blends together and that's how things are. Maybe everyone has this problem. Maybe it isn't a problem. This is an old building, and the sounds it makes are hypnotic. Humming. Creaking. Machinery on the ground floor, the boiler, the air condition-ing, the wiring, the virtual systems—it's almost like I can feel energy swelling in the walls, spiking, singing. I can feel the sounds in my feet, in my hands, and in my throat. I close my eyes and breathe deeply.

The phone rings, and it fucking scares me, OK? It's fine to be scared by a phone ringing. Many things are scary, and it's fine and normal for a phone's ringing to be one of those things, even when the other things are things like hurricanes and disorder and space. A ringing phone is a weapon, like a knife or shrapnel; the sound is so alien, so loud and angry. I wonder how on earth it still works, or why our service hasn't been turned off, as I'm fairly sure no one has taken responsi-bility for paying it in months. I certainly haven't. Maybe it's all autopay. Or does someone else come in when I'm gone? I get the unshakable feeling that there is someone in the room with me. Someone who is both inside and outside. The radiating of breath. A faint pulse. Moisture. In the right light you have no shadow. The phone stops ringing.

Was everything as I had left it?

Am I the only one here?

If there is not an entity already present, I feel certain that sudden movements will create one, so I'm very careful. My motions are fluid, as easy as I can manage. I glance around the office. The cockroaches behave and stay away from me. The floor creaks underfoot. I get to the desk with the computer and phone and lay my fingers on the surface. Over here, I feel the presence even more. A nameless, growing angst. I sit at the desk, and the pressure lifts enough to say hello.

The phone rings again. I reach out and pick it up. It's the call box from downstairs. Someone's . . .

Someone's . . . trying to . . . hmm . . .

. . . trying to buzz up . . .

There's . . .

There's no one else on the calendar. I worry that perhaps it's one of the police officers. Maybe I was spotted in the window. On the matter of Joe, I don't know what my statement would be. We talked about his future and then he died. I want to cry, but I haven't yet.

I answer the phone. I'm supposed to say the name of my organization when answering a call, but I'm struck with doubt as to whether my organization still has a name, if it really exists anymore at all, and instead I say, "Yes . . . ?"

On the other end I hear a strange whining. Like a small dog. Then, a tiny, unsteady voice.

". . . what . . .

". . . have you done . . .

". . . with my . . ."

(The voice gathers, crashes through the receiver like a great glass breaking.)

". . . *daughter?*"

I have to pull the phone away from my ear. I hang up on her. Is it a her? I think it's a her. It could be a man. Whoever it is sounds very small.

The phone rings again. I answer. I again hear the whining, and noises behind as well; perhaps it's the police activity. Before the small person can say anything, I say, "There's no one up here."

". . . what . . .

". . . have you done . . .

". . . with her . . . ?"

"Your daughter was never here. There are no . . . girls at all here at the moment. At all."

". . . where is she . . . ?"

"I don't know. I'm sorry. She's not here."

". . . my daughter . . ."

"Nobody's daughter is here." I hang up. I stare at the phone, expecting it to ring again, but it does not.

I pick up the phone and call our head office. No answer. I can't remember the last time I spoke to someone at our head office. The last email exchange. The last newsletter.

I did, however, get paid last week. (But that's definitely all automated.)

I look in the fridge, and I'm thrilled to find half a bottle of white wine that my boss left behind. Pinot grigio. I start sipping on it, staring off into space, listening to the sounds from outside. The sounds. I need to block them all out, so I go online. I pull up a video of a dancing bear first. Lots of negative comments, though. Bears dont dance like that. ANMAL OBUSE!! ———>that barre shuld ate his tranor lol jus sayin. 4yr zoolgy degree cum loud so wats up betchez. My cuz a bear expert, so. Do you eat meat its THE SAME THING! How you figure????? Show proof before I'll believe you! Shut up. I'll kill you.

I click around and find footage of a chemical plant in North Texas exploding. The video of the blast, caught by a dashboard camera, is shocking, and the story that accompanies it is one of negligence and poor safety records, of hazard and risk and a brazen defiance of already thin regulations. Over two hundred killed in the blast, many more expected to suffer debilitating effects resulting from the chemical fire. There are calls for the owners and management of the plant to be held accountable, fined, imprisoned, and worse. But then I reload the page, and it loads differently than just a moment ago. Now it's just a "plant" in "the south." Now "possibly as many as eleven" were killed. The commentary all becomes speculation about what really happened and what are the facts and who's reporting what? The forum devolves into an argument over whether or not the plant's owners bear any responsibility whatsoever for those deaths, regardless of the number. Someone named warrrmdonuts says the owners are real heroes for operating a business in this economy; that he's sick of the anti-American lefty bullshit and fuck all y'all; those people are dead but at least they had jobs to die at, says warrrmdonuts.

I pull up the video of the girl in the blue coat. I finish the pinot grigio.

I look up, and it's just after noon. There's no reason for me to be here. No one is going to call. No one else is going to call.

I gather my things and head for the door. I set the alarm and very carefully start to descend the stairs. It somehow feels safer than taking the elevator. That small person who called up with the missing daughter could still be lurking about.

I creep down, stair by stair, and I can smell the remnants of the SID. I'd try to describe the smell, but it doesn't smell like anything else. (Like wet, dirty ammonia? That fails.) When I get to the first floor, I hear a lot of action and raised voices coming from outside. I don't see a woman or small person who might have been the caller. I wonder where she went, and now I find myself wishing I knew what she looked like. I hope her daughter is real and that she finds her.

The police mill about, and now there are a lot of CURE sentries. It somehow escaped me that the place would be crawling with CURE, and I know better than to walk right out of the building and into CURE activity; I'll end up detained for hours, overnight, maybe longer in some warehouse on the West Side (I picture shackled bones). They'll want to know what I saw, what I'm doing here, who the fuck I am; they'll want to pick through every corner of my phone's memory. No one sees me, and so I sneak, undetected, back up the stairs, and go out the fire escape.

I come around to the front of the building from the side. There's a brown, smoldering circle, roughly a hundred feet in diameter; there are spots around its circumference with small flames still burning in earnest. The bodies have been removed. There are armored vehicles and barricades blocking traffic from the west, east, and south; to the north, traffic is being blocked by a tank. The CURE sentries and police officers are all discussing what happened with Joe. (No, I realize, they aren't discussing; rather, the CURE sentries are, in fact, questioning the police officers. The police are being interrogated, and this makes me very, very uncomfortable.) A lot of conflict is created by the murkiness around the respective jurisdictions of the police and CURE, and where those jurisdictions begin and end. The police are publicly funded and are empowered to uphold the law, to protect citizens, and to minimize disturbances. CURE, on the other hand, is a privately held, corporate-owned WRM (that's a "well-regulated militia") that is empowered to "improve communities by responding to criminal acts or the threat of criminal acts in which the primary victim is the United States Constitution." The police are limited by public policy; CURE is limited only by the whims of its board and its definitions of "freedom," "enemy," "liberty," and "threat." *The Coalition of United Response Engineers v. City of Philadelphia* was a landmark Supreme Court decision in which CURE sued Philadelphia on grounds of antitrust and won, breaking what the complainants and their legal team referred to as the ineffective and failing "monopoly on action" and paving the way for the private sector (but really just CURE, as it devoured all competitors) to roll out its own brand of civic law enforcement in most major cities, universities, and corporate campuses in the country. CURE's funding dwarfs that of the police, and therefore it has more sophisticated technology and much more terrible weaponry and artillery. Make no mistake: CURE is an army.

CURE has a tenuous partnership with local and federal authorities alike, but in a business sense, they are rivals. I wonder what would happen if CURE decided to turn its entire force on the cops nationwide. I'd wager CURE's rank and file have wondered the same thing.

I stare too long at one cop giving a statement, and she narrows her eyes at me. She looks lost and mean but also scared. A sentry comes up beside me and grabs me by the arm.

"Fuck're you?"

"I'm just walking."

"See what happened here?"

"No, what happened?"

The sentry, a squat, reddish-white man with a lip scar, gives me an up and down. He doesn't like me but also doesn't need anything from me. That is to say, he doesn't immediately see what use I may be. (Which means I'm succeeding. I wonder if the dead sentry was a friend of his.) He holds his assault rifle up, on display, his arm flexing across his body. He never takes his eyes off my eyes. He says something about "per second" and something else about "throats."

I nod and start to peek over his shoulder. He shoves me.

"Go around. Yeah, look, turn around dickface, you can't come through this way, you gotta go around. That way." He points over my shoulder. He shoves me with the gun, even though I'm making no effort whatsoever to get past him. Although something does catch my eye. In the middle of the burning circle, a large object sits. It appears to be metal, but its shape is so irregular I can't even begin to guess at what it is.

"What is that?" I ask, almost to myself, not expecting an answer. He looks toward the circle. Sees what I'm eyeing. He laughs.

"That was the guy's large intestine—well, what was in place of his large intestine. The rest is—"

"What'll happen to it now?"

The laugh dissolves. He shoves me hard and tells me to "get the fuck outta here. You wanna piss me off?"

As I walk away from the scene, I look back. A pale-skinned white woman with a lab mask and heavy gloves places Joe's cybernetic intestine into a yellow bag. Her clothing is neither the two-tone blue of the Chicago police nor the old gold and black of CURE. I can't tell whom she's working for, whom she's with. I keep my eyes on her and walk backward. I stumble off the curb and land in the street, knocking my head on the pavement pretty good. A car—fortunately one with an Automat driver—comes through the intersection but stops short of hitting me.

I look back toward the scene in front of my building. Or, I should say, where the scene had been. Looking back now, there is no sign of the police. No sign of CURE. No sign of anything. As though there had been no death. No bodies. No story. Just a street in Chicago. Taped off with the orange hazard tape favored by CURE. But while the sentries have all gone away, the area is definitely not unoccupied. You hear of snipers staking out and firing on anyone who crosses the orange tape. It's best, in general, to never give CURE an excuse to shoot you. Because they would love to, and they will. The cost of security is paid in gallons.

The foot traffic is starting to pick up all around. It's lunchtime. People walk past the tape without even looking at it. I get a text from my boss: *busy?* I consider for a moment that she's monitoring the office and knows I've left, but then I remember she barely cares about such things.

I write back: *so busy.* I wait a moment, then write: *You coming in ever again?*

She writes back: *haha.*

I text her again: *Hey, have you heard anything about Sheila? Did she ever kick that flu?*

No reply.

TEN

On the train ride home, I catch myself looking at a young black woman sitting across from me. She's noticed me but is acting like she hasn't. She reads a book, her hair falling along the sides of her face. I don't want to make her uncomfortable, but the reason I'm looking at her is that I recognize her as someone from Unarmed Citizens. I wait a couple of stops, considering how to start talking to her, feeling awkward, not wanting to be rude. I slowly lean forward, thinking maybe she'll look up, like maybe she'll think I'm fainting or something and she'll look up. I keep leaning. A little more. A little more. A man walks past with an assault rifle strapped to his back, and I sit back in my seat. He stops and stares at her. She masterfully keeps her focus on her book, like she's not even aware of him. (I'm good at that, too!) He stands there for an uncomfortable few seconds, like he may sit next to one of us, or start talking to one of us. But then he moves on and sits farther down the car. I start to lean forward again, just a tad faster this time. I keep leaning and eventually I'm doubled over, my chest on my knees, my head craned up awkwardly toward her. She doesn't look up at me.

A cockroach runs in between our feet and stops. I keep my eye on it, watch its antennae sway, alert for any sudden movements, any opening of its wings. I watch its legs. Then a foot slams down on the roach, crushing it with a crack that seems to echo through the car. It's her foot. I look up and she's now staring at me. She doesn't seem like she's gonna speak first, so I do.

"I saw you," I say vaguely. I'm shocked to find that this is enough to make her talk. Maybe she was waiting for it.

"You saw me."

"Yeah, at the um . . . the place."

"The place?"

"The meeting."

"I don't know what you're talking about."

"The meeting. The Unar—"

Like lightning, she hits me on the head with her book. I shoot back in my seat. I ask, "What'd you do that for?"

"Don't be an idiot."

Ah, yes. We're in public. Rookie mistake. I smile at her through the pain pulsing on the top of my head. She smiles back, but in her smile there's a certain "just how dumb are you?" being asked.

We don't talk the rest of the ride, but she happens to get off at my stop. We walk shoulder to shoulder. She tells me her name is Emerald.

She says, "So . . . do you live up here or are you following me?"

"Wh— Oh no, I live here, right down the street."

"That's right. You live with Simon, don't you?"

"Not with him, but in the same building."

"Well, yeah. That's what I meant."

"How long have you . . . I mean when did you join . . ."

"Ten months ago. After my dad was killed."

"With a gun, I assume?"

"Uh, yeah."

"Sorry. My brother was killed just recently. In line at a freakin' Walmart. Got into an argument with some asshole."

"No, not some asshole."

"Huh?"

"The mayor is some asshole. My landlord is some asshole. The guy who killed your brother is a murderer. And a coward." She pauses, I don't respond, because she doesn't need me to. To my silence, she adds, "Most people in the group have suffered some kind of senseless loss."

"What happened . . . can I ask what happened to your dad?"

"He was in the security line at the airport, Dallas–Fort Worth, and a fight broke out. Shots were exchanged between a TSA agent and a couple angry travelers. Two people were killed, my dad and an old nun who was also in line. None of the people involved in the fight had so much as a scratch. The police arrested the guys who opened fire, but they weren't charged, not even with manslaughter. Something about . . . how they weren't liable because they were shooting toward what they considered a threat, the TSA agent, and it was my father's responsibility to get out of the way. For some reason, it held up that the TSA agent qualified as a threat. Also, my dad wasn't armed, so the judge was very unsympathetic, said if my father was armed, he could have protected himself from his attacker. Except, of course, that he wasn't attacked, he was just there, but apparently that was besides the point."

I have a thought that waiting in line might be the most dangerous thing in America. Take impatience and entitlement and toss in boredom and weapons. Violence waiting to happen.

"So, have you done many missions with UC?"

"Yep." That's all she says about that. She asks, "Will you be at the next meeting?"

"I don't know. Yeah, think so. I assume Simon will tell me."

"Cool, I'll see you there. Or . . . hey, what are you doing tomorrow night?"

"Tomorrow? Nothing."

"A few of us are raiding a house. Wanna come?"

"Raiding a house why?"

"We found out about this guy who has been developing an app that would override the smart functions on a lot of single-user weapons, which means anyone who has the app could use any gun, all of those weapons could enter the black market, et cetera, et cetera. We're going to steal his computer and anything else of interest."

"Oh . . . all right."

"So you'll come? It's in Lincoln Park."

"Yeah . . . I think I will."

"Great."

She tells me when and where to meet them, then walks away, and I stand on the sidewalk, watching her go. I look down and there's a dead rat covered in roaches. Nearby, there's a young man sitting on the stoop of his building, wearing a face computer and loudly talking about tsunamis as though they're a sporting event. I hear a low sound—coming from a distance but feeling very close—like that of a massive furnace clicking on.

***

Inside my apartment, the lightbulb in my kitchen flickers. This keeps happening. Every time I mention it, my landlord says, "Your wiring is fine. Change the bulb. We know you have many choices when renting; thank you for choosing to lease from us." I'm not even sure if I have another lightbulb. Larry must be hiding somewhere, I imagine the flickering drives him a little crazy. Before dealing with that, I really have to go, so I duck into the bathroom and sit on the toilet. I start doing what I came in here to do, but just as I begin, I look down and see what appear to be two long, quivering, dark hairs sprouting from under the seat. I usually do a quick check of the toilet before sitting on it, for this very reason, but today I didn't. (It's always this time, when you didn't.) A single cockroach comes darting out from underneath and stops on top of the seat, between my knees. In response, I try to do too many things at once. I try to stand, jump, swat it away, and run. What happens instead is that I trip on my pants, fall, and hit my head on the doorknob.

It's maybe the best nap I've gotten in years. Sure, I'm lying on the floor of my bathroom in full light with my pants around my ankles and a cut on my head, and I'm sure any number of bugs crawl on me while I'm out, so it's not the most dignified position I've ever found myself in. *But!* The sleep is glorious. I'm pretty sure I dreamed about eating a pizza.

When I wake up, three hours have passed. By now, Larry is past being polite. When I open the bathroom door he's sitting right outside in the hallway, vocalizing his hunger and discontent. The kitchen light is still flickering (which I'm glad for . . . it would be creepier if it weren't). I brave it, I go in there and pour food into Larry's dish. He won't come into the kitchen due to the sinister light, so I bring his dish out to him.

There are more cockroaches in my apartment than usual, and Larry seems very bothered by them. Me too, Larry. Me too.

But OK, let's talk about cockroaches for a minute. Cockroaches used to be guileful, they used to stay in dark places, out of sight . . . they used to be those things that you'd catch out of the corner of your eye, this flash of dark when you turned on the light. They'd scurry under the fridge, under the stove, to a crack in the wall, as though they were trapping the dark in their bodies and taking it away. These motherfuckers. They have unimaginable malleability and can fit into impossible places. The saying always was that if you see one, you're already infested; they stay hidden until the time is right. This is why oppressed peoples have always been likened to cockroaches: because cockroaches proliferate in secret, you don't always see them, but you know they are there, spreading, building, that one betrays the presence of hundreds, thousands. They're already here. Also, cockroaches are associated with decay and filth, a sign that a structure is crumbling or weak, that rot and mold have crept in, and that things are taking a turn for the worse. So yes, cockroaches (a) are furtive and spread in darkness and (b) suggest a creeping filth and rot. Death, too. Makes sense why cockroaches are often used by the majority to characterize minority groups, or dissidents, or rebels. Filthy and secretive. Scurrying beneath the homeland. And obviously, (c) cockroaches are disgusting. And ugly. The perfect familiar object for reactionary propaganda: the only truly effective way to destroy them is to never let them in.

Then, the irony: calling a person, or a group of persons, "cockroaches" may be an unwitting article of praise. Cockroaches are dirty, yes, but so are humans. Cockroaches are ugly, yes, but so is the world. Cockroaches, however, are like nothing else so much as ideas. Quick to move. Quick to spread. Hard, sometimes impossible, to crush. Or no, I got that backward. Cockroaches are not like ideas. Ideas are like cockroaches. Cockroaches have been around longer than ideas. They've been around forever, have survived everything from ice ages and urbanization to global warming and chemical warfare. They don't just survive, they strengthen, adapt, and multiply. Ideas have learned from cockroaches how to infiltrate, infest, and rule from within. Calling a group of people "cockroaches," while a clear attempt to show them as insignificant filth, may, in truth, describe them as something essential, ancient, and much, much greater than. Something connected to history. Something universal. Something that was always here, waiting and superior.

Because honestly, they are superior. Cockroaches. They're a superior life-form. Human beings can invent languages and build cities, but modern cockroaches can survive for up to a year without food. They don't sleep. They're expert colonizers. Their brains are spread throughout their bodies. I'll repeat that: their brains are spread throughout their bodies. So a cockroach can lose its head and still think and function, because it's lost only a part of its brain. The only thing a headless roach can't do is eat; a human without his or her head dies in seconds, but since roaches can live up to a year without food, that means a headless roach can theoretically live for up to a year in the right conditions, which for a cockroach are pretty much any conditions. They are so much less fragile than we are. They're fast. Touching everything. Tasting everything. Going everywhere and living everywhere. They're fast. They're fast. They can dramatically alter the size and shape of their bodies. They can fly. They are perfectly constructed and nearly invulnerable; one of the only things that used to kill them reliably—cypermethrin—no longer has any effect. A substitute poison was never created or found, and R&D dried up in the United States a long time ago, so supercockroaches are here to stay. They die when it's time to die. When they want to. They rule the ecosystem. They've outlasted. They've won.

I started collecting them, I should have mentioned that. Ever since that day on the train when I bottled the injured roach and took it with me. That was the first. I have more now. I feel it's important that I observe them. I modified an aquarium so that I can deposit cockroaches into it, both alive and dead, and they can't get out. Of course, they're cockroaches, so

I can only assume that they'll find a way. But in the meantime, I can watch them, study them. In swarms they seem abstract, almost imaginary. Individually, they're very real. Something I can touch—not that I want to touch them, because as much as I see to admire in them, they're still cockroaches with six foul legs, and I realize now that I have so many confined in close proximity that they give off a strange odor, too. I'd never noticed this odor before; I suppose it's something you just get used to when you live in it. But I can smell it now. It's an inky, chemical smell.

They smell like money.

One thing that amazes me is that they share the space; they crawl all over each other, and yet I can see no conflict. And these are cockroaches from all different places. Some from the street, some from my office, some from my house. But they don't seem ever to fight; they seem to be at general ease with each other. Of course, the absence of conflict does not imply peace. I know very little about how they might resolve disputes, how they communicate displeasure, how they enact justice.

I really don't know much of anything about them at all. It would be foolish of me to assume otherwise.

***

The following night, I take the Brown Line to Fullerton and walk a few blocks to our meeting place near the old university campus, a little sandwich shop getting ready to close down for the evening. I find Emerald; she and I are the only ones there from the group (Am I part of the group? Does this make it official?). She tells me that we'll start toward our target on foot, and others will meet us as we go.

The walk is quiet. I can tell Emerald is hyperaware of our surroundings, and I don't want to be a distraction. She tells me

that this developer is supposed to be attending a play downtown tonight, so we should have a few hours to get in and out
with the assets.

I say, "Simon was telling me a little about the woman who
founded UC, Bonnie?"

Emerald pauses. "Yeah, what about her?"

"Ever met her?"

"Of course. She trained me."

"Trained you? In what?"

"How to defend myself."

"Oh. What sort of things did she train you to do?"

"Well . . . she's military. When she was younger, anyway,"
she says, kind of answering my question and kind of not. "And
after that she was a mixed martial artist. She competed inter-
nationally for a while."

"Yikes. I had no idea."

"You never heard of Bonnie Shale? I feel like she was actually kind of a big deal when we were kids."

"I guess I didn't pay attention to stuff like that."

Emerald doesn't say anything else about her training, or
Bonnie. Up ahead we see a young man sitting on a bus bench.
As we pass him, he stands up and starts to follow us.

"Don't look," Emerald says. "That's Fletcher. He's with us."

We walk a little farther, and we pass a young woman whom
I recognize as Maggie from behind the bar. She joins up with
Fletcher. The four of us arrive at our destination, a three-story
town house, new looking. Fletcher uses a device attached to
his phone to disable the various locks on the mark's side door.
I'm impressed by these three right away. The operation, while
lean, is organized and well researched. Maggie wears a device
around her wrist that looks like a simple white bracelet; she
gives out three more to the rest of us.

"What are these?" I ask.

Maggie replies, "We call them Dog-Collars. They give off a sound and scent that will mask us from the owner's dog. Or, if he does detect us, he won't care."

We go inside. The place is impeccably decorated, lots of windows. Fletcher holds us up so he can scan for and disable security devices and cameras.

"So you're the resident hacker, I guess?" I ask. Fletcher doesn't respond. Emerald smiles at me and then gives Fletcher a smack on the back. Fletcher makes a noise like he doesn't like something he's seeing, and Emerald asks him what it is.

"The place is crawling with nanobots. They're everywhere. There's even a few airborne ones around us right now." At that, all three of them pull out Maw-Gards. Emerald hands one to me, and I put it on.

Maggie pipes up, "Are any of them gonna hurt us?"

"They're surveillance, I think. But that means we've already been recorded."

"And the owner might be alerted."

"Maybe, so let's be fast."

The team divides like this: Fletcher is on extraction. He knows what we're looking for and how to disable any security hurdles we encounter that are technological. Emerald is on protection. She is trained to disable any security hurdles that are alive. Maggie is on alert. She watches the approach to the property to make sure we'll all know if anyone gets close. And I'm the shadow. Just here to observe and learn.

The owner's dog lies at the top of the stairs, watching us. He looks like he'd be pretty tough under normal circumstances, so I'm glad for the jewelry. Emerald goes up the stairs first, followed closely by Fletcher and then me. We step right over the dog, who just makes a little moan as I pass him. Maybe he smells Larry.

Emerald cautiously but confidently works her way down the hallway. She stops outside a door near the end, and listens. Nothing. She opens it with a gloved hand. Inside, it looks like what I see in my head when I imagine a room at the Pentagon. Supercomputers. Wall-to-wall workstations and consoles. So many machines. So many lights. Fletcher scans the room and one by one cripples the security measures.

Emerald said we were coming here to steal the guy's computer, but he looks to own about fifty of them. Regardless, Fletcher sees what he's looking for and starts toward it. Emerald can't stop him in time.

"Fletcher, wait!" she says, right at the moment Fletcher's hand touches the targeted machine.

In an instant, there is a flash of light and Fletcher's body seems to levitate. Then he starts to fall. But the ground doesn't move. Fletcher's body flips around, as though he were falling, perpetually, into a hole whose cylinder I can't see. He looks as though he is in a skydiving simulator without a chute, wind whipping at his hair and clothes like he's falling at terminal velocity, even though where I stand some fifteen feet away, the air is still. He is held, trapped in a suspended plummet, eerily hovering a few feet off the ground, falling endlessly toward a floor he will never reach. The look on Emerald's face is one of horror. I take a curious step toward Fletcher, and Emerald's hand is on me, pulling me back.

"*Don't touch him*," she says. She phones down to Maggie.

"It's Fletcher. He stepped into a FallSpot. I need you up here."

Emerald takes off her Maw-Gard and covers her mouth with her hand, as though she might be sick. She asks me, quite upset, "Ever seen one of these?" I shake my head. She continues, "They're called FallSpot traps, or Remote Fall Simulators. They were developed by CURE to protect their own facilities;

you don't usually see them in homes. We had no idea there'd be something like this—"

"What's happening to him?"

"He's falling. To us it looks like he's floating there, but what he's experiencing right now is a bottomless pit. We have to get him out fast—people go crazy if they're stuck in a FallSpot for too long."

She's not kidding. The look on Fletcher's face is a blank sort of panic that is deeply disturbing—as though being in this thing for only a minute has already deadened him with fear. Emerald tells me that we can't just pull him out, because we'll get dragged in. Nor can we simply use some sort of implement to push him out, explaining, "It would be like pushing him off a building. He'd fall those couple of feet and splatter in front of us. To his body and mind right now, he is in free fall."

Maggie comes in and gasps. I have a feeling they've seen this before, and that it didn't end well. Emerald asks Maggie a question about the FallSpot that I don't quite hear, because I'm focused instead on Fletcher's eyes. His cheeks. His hands.

"I saw Bonnie do it one time, but I don't know where his control panel is, and we shouldn't just pick around in here, because there could be others."

"We can't just let him fall."

"Right, right. I might be able to find it, but I need something from Fletcher's bag."

"Where's Fletcher's bag?"

"I saw it in the kitchen."

Emerald grabs me by the shoulder and says, "Follow me." We head out into the hallway. The dog is no longer there. We go downstairs. There on the kitchen floor sits Fletcher's heavy black tech bag. I dash over and grab it. As soon as I do, the lights come on. Standing by the door with a dog at his feet and a heat weapon in his hand is a man whom I presume to be the master of the house. He's a handsome guy, well dressed for a night at the theatre. I've heard the pain from a heat weapon turned up to ten is maddeningly unbearable. Boils your brain.

I stand frozen. The guy doesn't say anything. No "Freeze." No "Gotcha." No "Hold it right there" or "Who the fuck are you?" I want him to say something; instead, he just starts to smile. It's terrifying. I glance toward the stairs. Emerald is gone.

Just then, Maggie rushes halfway down the stairs and says, "What's taking so long?" Startled by her entrance, the developer turns the heat weapon on Maggie and fires. The end of the weapon glows blue, and Maggie crumples and falls down on the stairs, holding her head and screaming in pain. The developer turns the weapon on me, but before he can fire, Emerald appears, seemingly from out of the floor, and charges him. He tries to blast her but misses. Emerald disarms him and the weapon falls with a heavy clunk. She punches the developer in the throat, incapacitating him. The dog attacks her. She jams one of her arms (which I now see bears a protective sleeve) into the dog's mouth and picks it up with the other arm as though it weighs five pounds. It thrashes in her arms, growling, but she keeps her arm pressed hard into its jaws so it can't bite her anywhere else. The developer, struggling to catch his breath, reaches into his coat. Emerald takes the dog to an open door leading down to the lower level. She chucks the dog down the stairs and closes the door. The developer pulls a gun out of his coat. Without thinking, I run straight at him. He points and fires twice. His aim is bad. I bodycheck him into the wall. He points the gun at me again, but it's too late; I've distracted him just enough. Emerald is on him, and I have never witnessed anything quite like the beating she gives him. Within seconds, she has broken his nose, broken his wrist, broken his foot, slammed his head into the kitchen island and thrown him to the floor. Emerald jumps into the air and stomps her feet down hard on the developer's abdomen, then drops her full weight, knees first, onto his chest. She strikes him twice more in the face for good measure. She snatches him by his now-no-longer-perfect hair and shouts into his face, "*Get my friend out of your FallSpot!*" She gets the developer off the floor and up the stairs, half dragging him, half shoving him. I check our supplies and find a cold pill to counteract the blast from the heat weapon. I take it to Maggie—still groaning in agony, her entire head and face a molten red—and I pry her jaw open. I shove the pill back between her molars and press her jaw shut. Within a few moments, she starts to regain her composure. Her breathing slows down. The redness in her skin softens. I grab a carton of milk from the fridge and hold it to her head to cool her down. She takes it from me, opens it, and dumps the contents all over her face and neck. Maggie sighs, in immense relief.

Emerald appears at the top of the stairs with Fletcher flung over her shoulders.

"Did you give her a cold pill?"

"Yeah."

"We need to get out of here. Maggie, can you walk on your own?"

"I think so."

"Let's go. Get Fletcher's bag."

Fletcher looks like a zombie, ashen and slack, staring. I try to remember why we came.

I ask, "What about the guy?"

"Don't worry about him."

Emerald rushes out with Fletcher. Maggie staggers behind her. I pick up Fletcher's heavy bag and loop the strap over my shoulder, heading for the exit. Behind me I hear the dog barking in a frenzy, frantically scratching and ramming the door.

***

Once outside, an Automat car awaits just down the block. We run to it, and inside are two other members of UC. We get Maggie and Fletcher inside, and Emerald says, "Get them home." The car pulls away, leaving Emerald and me standing on the street corner. We're silent for a while. I see a cockroach with another cockroach on its back, seemingly carrying it. The one being carried looks dead.

"That was . . ." I stammer. "I've never really . . . um . . ."

Emerald grabs me and kisses me. I'm pretty sure we're the same height, but in this moment, she seems to dwarf me. Her hands are quite strong. She tells me I'm going home with her.

***

I had forgotten what warmth was like. Real warmth. Lying in Emerald's bed, a cocktail of endorphins, I listen to the sound of her breathing. We keep the discussion of the evening's events to a minimum, but we're both thinking of little else. (At least I think so. I have no idea what she's thinking.)

It starts to rain outside. There is shouting. Emerald gets out of bed and goes to the window. She pulls the blinds aside, her lovely, imposing figure silhouetted by the streetlight. She looks. I look.

"Did you kill him?" I ask. There is a pause. Rain. "The developer," I add, as though she wouldn't know who I was asking about.

"Had to," she says, with no hint of inner conflict. "Does that bother you?"

"I don't know."

That's the end of that conversation. I can tell she isn't interested.

The shouting outside ceases, and she goes into her kitchen. She comes back with two bottles of beer. She hands me one and gets under the covers. She holds the neck of her bottle out toward me. I clink mine against hers, and she smiles.

"Will you be at the next meeting?" she asks me.

"I hadn't thought that far ahead." This is a lie.

"I hope you come. You should. You were really great tonight; Bonnie will want to meet you. Besides—" She pauses for a long time, hesitates, as though considering whether or not to say what she plans to say. Then she leans over and whispers in my ear, "I think they're planning something big."

ELEVEN

The next time Unarmed Citizens meets, I don't need to decipher any codes. Simon just knocks on my door, and away we go. I tuck Larry into my coat when Simon insists that I bring him. Frankly, I'm shocked that I can bring my cat to a clandestine meeting of a resistance group, so maybe I agree to bring him out of the sheer novelty. I've never tucked Larry into my coat before, but when I do, he takes to it immediately and purrs like crazy, like it's what he's always wanted and finally has.

We walk, but we take a few shortcuts and avoid the scorched landscape I wandered through last time. The place where I saw that . . . hound. I ask Simon if he's ever seen any strange animals in the neighborhood. Like a wolf, or a fox; I avoid the word "hound" because that sounds very "something." He affirms that he hasn't seen anything like that, but that others have.

"Coyotes, man. I've heard about coyotes. There are thousands of 'em in the city. Downtown, man, they're everywhere. In the subway? If you're in the subway and your train stops and they won't tell you why, there are probably coyotes on the track."

"Thousands, huh? That's alarming."

"Coyotes are all right. I don't think they'd, like, attack you or anything."

"You don't think that?"

"That they'd attack? No."

"Based on what?"

"I don't know. Why would a coyote attack a person?"

"It's starving? Or feels, I don't know, threatened?"

"I think you stay out of a coyote's way and he'll be cool."

We walk a little farther. When we're just a block or so away from the spot, Simon says, "So I heard you went out with Emerald and them?"

"Oh . . . yeah, I did."

"It's not always crazy like that; I heard what happened."

"Yeah. It was . . . unexpected. But I went to Emerald's place after and she . . ."

"You went home with her? You sly bones. She's a cutie."

"Yeah, no. Not . . . I mean, yes, but what I mean to say is, she said something . . . interesting."

"Interesting? How interesting."

"She said . . . that the group . . ."

"What about it?"

"That something might be . . . in the works."

"In the works."

"Yeah."

"Like what?"

"I don't know. I thought maybe you'd know."

"Something . . ."

"I don't know . . . big, maybe?"

"Don't know what Emerald knows about any of that. And shit, man, I'm glad you aren't some mole, 'cause you've only been to one meeting, and she could get into some serious shit talking like that."

"Oh, damn, really?"

"Yeah, when this gets around, she's gonna be in some bad trouble, like, I don't know what'll happen to her."

"What? I didn't mean to get her in trouble."

"No, I'm fucking with you." Simon laughs a laugh that makes him feel very far away or makes me feel very small, I'm not sure which, and continues, "You must like her, though, you looked really concerned. She's cool, and you're cool, and yeah, you'll hear all about it. There are plans. You're in on the ground floor, brother. And so is stone-cold Larry." Simon pats Larry through my coat. "Hey Larry, you beautiful fuckin' animal. You're gonna be a major player, you in?" He then imitates Larry: "*I'm in, Simon, I'm so in, I can't wait to do the big thing, hehehe.*" Simon then meows, then laughs, then his tone changes. "Oh, hey, crazy about the airports, right?"

"Airports?"

"You didn't hear? Midway and O'Hare, both closed until further notice."

"Closed? That's . . . scary. Why?"

"There were three major disasters involving airliners yesterday, so a lot of airports are closed today."

"Terrorists?"

"That's what they'll say, but who fuckin' knows?"

Even though there are such things as buses and trains, receiving the information that flights are grounded makes me feel trapped in the city.

Just inside C's, we run into Ethan, a nice guy a little older than us with a great red beard and heavy-rimmed glasses. Ethan shakes my hand from behind the bar and says, "Welcome back, friend. Hey, Maggie wanted me to say hi. She's feeling a lot better, said you had a lot to do with that."

Ethan hands me a short stack of business cards. They read:

KP
Unarmed Citizens
XXVINXVIW

He taps the top of the stack with his index finger and says, "This week the marker is Division Blue."

Right then Larry pokes his head out of the top of my coat, and Ethan bellows excitedly, clapping his hands, which scares the shit out of Larry, causing him to scratch me and jump out of my arms onto the bar. You'd think these people never saw a cat before.

*****

We go down into the meeting place, and there's an air of excitement, lots of murmurs and general electricity. Smiles and expectant faces. Simon grabs a spot on the wall to lean on and calls me over. I lean next to him, with Larry at my feet, eyes huge and cowering. I stoop and give him a little scritch-scritch on the top of the head. He pushes his head into my hand in gratitude.

When I look up from Larry, I see Emerald. She smiles at me, but not enough for me to really read too much into. (Which, by acknowledging, I realize means I already read into it.)

The room quiets down as a woman enters, who looks to be in her forties, fair-skinned, wearing black and blue.

"That's Bonnie. Ol' mastermind."

Even though I'm technically on her side, there's something about Bonnie Shale that instantly makes me nervous, like she has a bomb strapped to her torso. She smiles and then begins to speak.

"Neighbors. Hi. I've come upon some disturbing information, information that is going to require immediate action from all of us, but before I get into that, there's something else I want to talk about if you'll bear with me."

The entire room gives a sort of welcoming grunt of support, as though Bonnie is their mother and asking for their attention so she might sing a song (I picture a campfire). One woman in the corner bounces a baby and listens intently. Bonnie has a pleasant voice. Her tone suggests a Thanksgiving dinner speech about all the things she's thankful for. But there's something in her eyes.

"I want to talk about empathy. I don't question whether anyone in this room is unclear as to what empathy is, but it's good to remind ourselves, say it out loud, I guess. Empathy is the ability—the basic and essential human ability—to feel what another person feels. To put yourself in their place. Whether it's the exhilaration of a triumph, or the anguish of deep pain . . . maybe a loss. Empathy is that thing, that crucial thing that allows us to make each joy, each sorrow, each truth our own. It is a gift we have as humans, an innate ability that so many of us—through trial, hurt, cynicism—eventually lose or cast aside. Empathy dies in a world like this.

"People have been encouraged by their country, their media, and their own darker corners to judge rather than understand. Not to feel, but to attack. People have learned that nothing and no one can be trusted, not their neighbors, not their government, not even their families. The enemy is everywhere. We no longer recognize what's harmless. A story just made the news in Des Moines. An eighty-five-year-old man with Alzheimer's, living with his sixty-year-old son, slipped out of the house late at night and wandered about the neighborhood. Before moving in with his son a few years prior, he had lived just a few streets away in the same neighborhood. The old man ended up on the doorstep of his former home, believing it was still his home. The current resident, without warning, without calling the police, burst from the house and shot the old man six times in the chest. By now, the old man's son was out looking for him—he heard the shots and came running. When he came upon the scene, he saw his father lying there, on the front porch of his old home, and he rushed toward him. The homeowner, again without warning, opened fire on the son, hitting him twice in the chest and once in the neck. He died where he fell, in his father's old driveway. The homeowner didn't call the police for twenty minutes, by which point, of course, there was absolutely no chance that either man had any hope of survival. The homeowner, a heavily armed thirty-six-year-old man, said he felt imminently endangered. Endangered by the frail, doddering octogenarian in a bathrobe and by the distraught, unarmed sixty-year-old who was rushing to his father's side. The homeowner will face no charges under Iowa's Fight Back laws. That's the level of empathy we now have in society. Rather than recognizing pain, or confusion, or people in need, we see only threats. Threats which can be leveraged into righteous homicide. The old man could have easily been helped, or even ignored, but the homeowner decided that his conscience would be best served by removing the old man from existence. Killing is now easier than empathizing. Maybe it always has been."

She pauses a moment. Something flits across her face. I know it. I've felt it, too. It's rage.

"The media, of course, is broadly in support of the home-owner. Many say the unarmed men had it coming, that a man that age shouldn't be living at home, that he should be in a senior center. A neighbor was interviewed and said that she had often seen the old man and his son out for walks in the middle of the day and was tired, tired of them trying to strike up conversation with her. She said that she expects the neighborhood will be more peaceful now."

At this, Bonnie looks as though she may cry, from sadness, from frustration, from anger, from a volatile mix of the three. She pauses, brushes her cheek with a knuckle.

"There are countless stories just like this every week in this country. But empathy has been on my mind lately, and this story, and the response to it, suggests that empathy is a generation away from extinction. These two men who were killed—it was reported that neither one of them owned, or had ever even used, a deadly weapon. Some have blamed the men for their own deaths, arguing that if they had been armed, the homeowner might have thought twice. You heard that right. The fact that they were merely an annoyance, or a mystery, somehow that makes the homeowner's actions easier to understand and not only easier to forgive, but to support. This is why I share this, because of who we are. Who you all are. Unarmed citizens, in a society that views the lack of a weapon as the greatest threat of all. By not owning weapons, you are enemies of the state. You are a blight. A creeping filth"—she punctuates the word "filth" by stepping hard on a lone cockroach near her foot—"you are not to be trusted. You are defenseless and therefore not worth defending. These United States of America are looking for a reason to put you in the ground, and if you don't arm yourself, any violence done to you is your fault. Not just your fault, but exactly what you deserve."

She seems calm now, and there is always a warmth in her voice. Her surety, though, is alluring. No one in this room would contradict her—that is very clear. They all look upon her like a sage.

"Remember that," she says, "always," with a hint of a smirk, like it was a pep talk.

The room responds, "Always." The call-and-response gives me goosebumps. She reveals a map.

"Here's what we know. A network of Logan Square condo associations has procured a number of 3-D printers, a type we are aware can be modified to produce combat arms. When I say 'a number,' that's as specific as I can be. It could be four, it could be forty. We aren't sure. But what is clear is that they have far more than they could possibly need to arm their own residents, which would be alarming and illegal in itself, so what is it? Could be the beginnings of a printed-gun market in Logan Square or the origins of a new militia, and not a WRM but something much more insidious. I should note, the president of the condo network is a man by the name of Darien Trells. He is a suit, financial sector, but his older brother is Peter Trells, a high-ranking official for CURE.

"As you know, CURE is barred by the Detectable Weapons Act from mass-producing their own plastic or chemical weapons. They develop much of their own conventional weaponry, but the more high-tech stuff is still being purchased from a number of defense contractors. We believe, however, that the condo associations may be a cover for such a production outfit here in Chicago. If we are correct, CURE sentries would have access to limitless weapons that could not be traced back to the corporation, which I'm sure you'll all agree is extremely problematic. We need to act tonight, and since the printers are already on-site, disruption is not an option for us here. We'll need to locate and destroy these devices."

I look down. Larry is on his hind legs, his paws stretching up to my belt. He stares at me in his way, not in need of anything other than to be looked at. I look over at Emerald. She makes like she intends to walk over toward me, but then her eyes move and she stops, takes a step back. I turn again and find Bonnie Shale standing right near me with her hand out-stretched. She's got an incredible handshake.

"Let me introduce you," Simon says, a hand on my shoulder, "Bonnie, this is—"

"Your neighbor, yes, the one you were telling me about. Thank you so much for coming. I've heard a lot about you. And who's this handsome guy?"

I reach down and pick up Larry, holding him to my chest. Bonnie runs a hand gently over Larry's head. He closes his eyes and purrs.

Bonnie says, "Emerald said you saved her life."

"I did what anyone would do."

"You know that's not true in the slightest. Anyway, thank you."

"How are Maggie and Fletcher?"

"Maggie is going to be fine, again, thanks to your quick thinking, getting her that cold pill before she got too over-heated. And Fletcher is . . . well, it's going to be a long road back for Fletcher. Spending over a minute in a FallSpot tends to give you an existential crisis. I'll tell him you asked about him."

"I noticed there are no roaches down here. Other than the one you crushed—"

"We try to keep them out. I don't trust them."

Bonnie chirps slightly and looks down. Larry has lightly clamped his teeth over Bonnie's finger. He does this to me, but it's usually only when he's stressed-out; light pressure with his teeth, a little squeeze. Larry looks up at her as though expecting her to strike. She stares back at him, a steely look on her face. It's an odd standoff, and I just keep holding Larry there like a plate of hors d'oeuvres. Larry finally releases her finger from his teeth, still looking at her. He then licks her finger a few times.

"Cute," she says.

***

Where they once seemed like a haphazard collection of con-cerned citizens, or a neighborhood watch, UC now falls into a regimented sort of efficiency and fervor. Supplies are gathered, routes mapped, teams formed, strategies laid out. It all hap-pens in a matter of minutes. Bonnie gives a few people who would seem to be group leaders their directives, but then she backs off and lets them work. She's a stillness amid the flurry. The operation is out the door in less than an hour.

Bonnie invites me to have a seat with her at a small table in the corner of the room. Simon comes over to us with cups of coffee and sits next to me. For some reason I find it odd that he doesn't sit next to Bonnie, like he's more here with me than with her. (Or are they pinning me in? I wonder if he's known Bonnie longer than he's known me.) We all sip our coffees.

"So," she begins, "according to your questionnaire, you've never even held a gun. Is that true?"

I answer the wrong question. "Questionnaire?" I even answer her question with a question. She makes me uncom-fortable, and I have trouble placing why.

"You took a questionnaire, an interview, the last time you were here."

"Oh, yeah . . ."

"And you said you've never held a gun."

"Right."

"Actually, Lacey said your words were that you 'never touched a gun.'"

"OK."

"Is it the truth?"

"It is."

"Never touched a gun?"

"Yeah, no."

"Why do you suppose that is?"

"Never wanted to."

"I understand not liking them, but you say you've never touched one."

"Is that so . . . unlikely?"

"It is, actually."

"Not sure what else to say about it."

"Do you hate them?" This seems like an odd line of inquiry from a woman who runs an antiweapon activist group.

"Hate them?" I ask.

"Guns make people feel powerful. They get drunk on the weight of them, the feel of them in their hands."

"Addicted, some say," says Simon.

I almost make a crack about my father the gun addict, but then I remember my audience; my responses in the interview start flooding back to me as well, and it now seems very important that I remember them exactly.

"It's borderline illegal in today's world to be unarmed," Bonnie goes on. "No statutes commanding all unarmed peoples be locked up or anything, no, but if you aren't carrying, you have almost zero protection under the law. You're a rabbit, and it's open season."

"Hate crimes against barebacks are on the rise."

"Simon, really, that term—"

"Sorry, Bonnie, hate crimes, yeah, on the rise against unarmed peoples. Politicians almost encourage it, that senator from California, what'd he say? 'If you can't be the one to put down a threat, then you are the threat' or some shit? The Internet is full of CURE sentries caught on video picking fights with unarmed people and being cheered by onlookers."

"That's happened to me," I offer.

"It's happened to all of us," Bonnie says, "in one way or another."

"So what can be done about it? Things can't go back. I'm sorry, Ms. Shale"—I can tell she doesn't like being called Ms. Shale—"I believe in the ideal behind your group; I just don't see how society can ever go back. Unless we could somehow collect all of the guns and weapons, and chemicals and everything in one place and melt it all down or shoot it into space, but it's impossible to even know where all of the guns are, and the printers are just making it worse."

"Hence the operation tonight. We need to get these machines out of private circulation—"

"I read a story the other day about the first 3-D printer to be successfully printed by a 3-D printer."

Bonnie takes a second to really hear this, and laughs. It's a rueful laugh, like I just said something that was absurd and obvious at the same time. "I'd think that was a joke if—"

"If it wasn't precisely the kind of thing that happens in the world?"

"The world," she says, shaking her head. She sips her coffee.

"How often are your operations targeted at CURE?" I ask.

"Most," she says, matter-of-factly, "most of our activities involve CURE in some way. It's just probability, not some vendetta. Their ethical record is horrifying. There's no accountability when they injure or kill a civilian, which is a daily occurrence. Their oversight is weak—"

"And they're armed to the teeth," Simon adds.

Bonnie continues, "They're society's great antagonist."

"They'd say they're its protectors."

"I know what they'd say. You don't believe it, and you don't need me to point out the hypocrisy, so why even bring it up?"

"Guess I . . . I'm interested in what motivates you. Motivates all this." I can tell I'm making Simon uncomfortable. He never imagined that he'd bring me here and I'd question Bonnie

Shale. I suppose I never imagined it either. I never thought about it until it happened. It's happening now.

"You question my motivations?" she replies.

"I don't know what they are."

"Of course you do."

"Really, no. I don't. Ending gun deaths? Disarming the populace? No one in their right mind could expect to achieve that, and you seem like a rational person. So I don't know what your agenda is, because this isn't an activist group, or a support group. It's an insurgency."

"You think we're terrorists?" Simon bleats, incredulous.

"Insurgent doesn't mean terrorist," I say.

"We're not terrorists," Bonnie states, staring at me unblinking. No one bothered to pick up the roach Bonnie crushed.

"So what are you?"

"We're an endangered species."

"But what motivates you?"

Bonnie and I look at each other. She stalls, trying to determine if I deserve the real answer. "Did you hear that story out of Minnesota last week?"

"Which one?"

"Exactly."

"That doesn't answer my question."

"Oh, I think it does," she says.

A Latino man with a greying beard starts gesturing at Simon. Simon goes to the gesturing man, they exchange words hurriedly, and Simon returns. He whispers something in Bonnie's ear, and her face rolls to blank. White. (I picture an avalanche.)

She looks up at Simon and asks, "How many?"

***

One of UC's teams was ambushed before they reached their target. It would seem somehow that someone—some enemy force—had anticipated UC's action and set up an attack. It's possible other teams have been intercepted as well. Details are very sketchy, but before I know what's happening, we're all out the door and heading south. When I demand some sort of explanation from Simon and Bonnie, or anyone else in earshot, no one will speak to me. Before charging out the door, I pick Larry up and hold him in my arms. When we get to the 90-94 overpass at Belmont, the party stops and gathers around a large man with a huge duffel bag. He opens the duffel, and inside are myriad weapons classified as "nondeadly." Knives, clubs, brass knuckles, blackjacks, and an assortment of flash grenades, gas canisters, and the like. I puzzle over this. The "unarmed" in Unarmed Citizens would seem to take a very limited definition of what constitutes "arms" and what it means to not have them. I am offered a hunting knife, which I turn down.

Bonnie hollers at everyone to get something in their hands. She looks up and sees me standing there. She gestures with a knife to some various bludgeoning instruments.

"Get something to fight with."

"I don't like this. I knew there was something—"

"Listen." She shuts me right up. "I don't know who the fuck you are or who you think you are or what you feel like we owe you, but I don't have time for what you like and don't like. You're Simon's friend, he wanted to bring you along. None of us are here to impress you."

"I won't fight like this."

Someone signals Bonnie; she whistles, and the group starts to move.

"We're moving. Are you joining us or aren't you?"

In this moment, I can think of nothing to say. Not yes. Or no. Not "fuck this." I'm completely without words. Bonnie's face twists in frustration.

"Damn it. You could have been helpful."

I see Bonnie take something out of a bag and attach it to her waist. Seeing it makes me feel sick. An acid bomb. She turns her back on me and walks down the street. From across the mob I make eye contact with Simon. Unaware that Bonnie and I just had something of a falling out, he smiles and holds up his fist, adorned with a combination brass knuckles/serrated knife fixture.

"*Warfwarfy?*" he shouts.

"*Huh?*"

"*Where's Larry?*"

I put my hand over my belly, where Larry curls around my midsection, digging his claws into my abdomen. Simon gives a sign of the devil and sticks out his tongue (as though bringing your cat to a violent skirmish is what it really takes to be hardcore). As the ranks of Unarmed Citizens make their way south and east—into what I assume is certain death or detainment—I hang back. Bonnie said I "could have been helpful." I don't know that I could have been. When the mob is gone, it's just me and a homeless woman across the street, staring at each other. She holds a large bottle of ketchup like it's a rifle.

I start back north, with a quickening pace, feeling that I need to get as far away from UC as possible. In the evening air, I hear distant war sounds. Rattling, rumbling, screeching.

Pop-pop-pop-pop.

I walk past a small house with a sign in the window: *fuck the police. we call CURE!* A man and a woman are in the window, too, having sex in a manner that I can only describe as nihilistic. I stop just past them; I look under my collar at Larry, and he looks back up at me, wonder in his eyes. "I'm sorry, buddy," I say to him.

Just then, an explosion erupts to the south—Logan Square. The direction UC was headed. (I hope Simon is all right.) But it isn't just one explosion. There's another. Then another. The gunfire picks up. I can hear loud voices and screams. The shrill tone of the Chicago police from multiple directions. One street down I see two CURE armored trucks speeding east. The couple in the window doesn't stop, and now they're looking at me.

I need to get home. Now.

I'm about a mile and a half from my apartment, but from where I stand home feels about as close as the moon. It's a crapshoot whether a casual walk or a full-out sprint will attract deadlier attention, so I split the difference and jog.

Up ahead I see two tall figures running in my direction on the sidewalk. They move into the glow of a streetlamp, and I catch a glimpse of old gold and black, so I get off the main road. I turn down a couple of side streets and end up by an elementary school, where I stop and catch my breath.

I look up and see a low wall with statues of little kids lining its full length. The statues are life-size and eerie, backlit by a strip of floodlights above the school's exits. I assume they're meant to represent the school's student population. I start to walk past them, parallel to the wall, keeping an eye out ahead for a sudden sign of CURE. I walk slowly, silently, listening. I hear a cough. Not ahead, or behind. To my side.

They aren't statues.

I freeze.

I peek over my shoulder and see that what I thought was a statue is actually a young boy who looks to be Chinese American and the right age to attend school here. He wears black head to toe. He holds a handgun. Somehow, in his hands it doesn't look like a weapon, but like a tool. He doesn't look at me.

I look down the row of kids. Enough to fill a classroom. They all wear black, each hold a gun, almost loosely, as though they're on break. At ease. They're all probably between six and ten years old, mostly Latino, with a handful of white and Asian kids. Boys and girls. None of them look at me as I pass, they just stare at the ground. They seem to want nothing to do with me, which I'm thankful for; still, I try my best to maintain a constant speed, to not alter my gait.

I'm about halfway down the line of them when I hear something behind me. A lush, metallic clacking. Impossible to mistake, that sound. Then another clack, a bit closer. Then another, closer. They're cocking their guns. All of them, in succession. Like a reaction, a ripple, moving through them, through their hands. That sound. That sound. Like metal bones snapping. No, that fails. Like giant mechanical insects, clicking their mandibles. That fails, too. The sound swells, travels from behind me, to beside me, to the front of the line. Their movements seem autonomic, like breathing. I keep walking, and when I'm nearly past them, one says:

"Hey you."

I stop, almost not hearing it over the distant gunfire, the approaching helicopters. I look over at the boy. Can't be more than six years old. I don't know what he or any of them are doing out here. He appears to have gotten my attention prematurely, unsure what he wanted to say once I engaged, and thus he stares. I ask, "Do you know what time it is?" not really knowing why I ask it except yes I do know it's because it's really fucking late and these are kids that's why I ask it but I still don't know why I ask this kid at this moment when I could have asked him a million other things like "What's your name?" or "Are your parents alive?"

He shakes his head, not knowing what time it is. He asks, in that curious, slightly suspicious way a six-year-old would, "What are you doing here?"

"I'm just passing by. I'm walking home."

"There's fighting."

"Yeah, I'm trying to get away from it." Right after I say this, Larry meows. For him, it's a very loud, very sure meow. All the kids suddenly turn their heads and look at me.

"You got a cat?" asks the kid.

"I do. I have a cat."

And then something happens that sends the most genuine chill through my body that I've ever experienced. When I affirm, "I do. I have a cat," all the kids along the wall, all of them, say, "Can we see?"

Roaches skitter-scuttle behind the kids' dangling legs.

I have a terrible fear that if I show Larry to these kids, I'll never get him back. I'm also well aware that if I run for it, I'll catch anywhere from twenty to sixty bullets in the back. Maybe. It's not certain, but I'm also not the gambling kind. If I stand here and hold out on them, I might just get one or two bullets in the stomach. So I reach into my shirt. This, of course, provokes hands to tighten on weapons. (What these kids have seen . . . how these kids have lived . . .) I slow down my movements. I easily, gently pull Larry out of my shirt and hold him close to me. The kids just stare. None of them tries to come near or pet Larry, they just stare, awestruck. A few of them smile, and that seems incredible enough. But Larry has this effect on people.

I say, "OK, well, we have to get home." None of them seems bothered by this. "Good night."

The kid who first talked to me says, "Good night."

When I get back out to the street, I see an ad for an online retailer. The picture is of a smiling family. The ad reads "The Freedom You Want. The Freedom You've Earned."

***

I get inside my apartment and leave all the lights off. I put Larry on the floor, but he doesn't leave my side. I sit near a window and peek out through the blinds, as though there were something I could do about the situation outside. The conflict is to the south, but neighborhood battles have a way of traveling quickly.

Out of the darkness, Larry hisses. I turn and get the general impression of a person, but I can't see who it is. I lunge at the intruder and push him up against the wall, smacking his head.

Except a female voice cries *"Ow!"* and I end up with my arm behind my back, bending the wrong way. I get a peek at the intruder's face. Emerald.

"You," I say. Without even thinking about it, I put my hands on her shoulders and kiss her. For a second or two, she kisses me back. Then she knocks the wind out of me and pushes me away.

"You deserted."

"So did you."

Larry hides. Emerald is the first person to be in this apartment in . . . I don't even know how long. I really do isolate myself in here. Maybe I should get out more or—

A blast from outside. (Actually, no, I'm good.)

"Oh God," Emerald cries in response to the explosion, nearer than the others, "I wonder what's happening."

"I think it's a good thing you followed me."

"What do you mean?"

"I mean I wouldn't want to be in any of those UC groups right now."

What sounds like a fighter jet, flying very, very low, zooms overhead. Seconds later, there's a bright flash from the south and a rattling boom. It's war. I don't know if it's the military or CURE or who, but regardless, the neighborhoods to the south of us are being bombed.

"Oh . . ." Emerald says.

"What?"

"Just . . . I was just thinking what I was going to say to Bonnie when I see her . . . but then I thought . . . I may not see her. I mean, depending—"

"Yeah."

"That's . . . it's crazy."

I decide not to show her the cockroach terrarium.

"I'm gonna see if anyone's talking about what's going on."

I check news sites. Social media. I stream the local NPR. They're talking about some new research university that opened in Singapore. Or wait, actually it's some research university that was attacked by . . . I'm not sure who . . . then flooding in the Florida Keys . . . a new caliphate . . . no one is talking about any bombing in Chicago, who's involved, any damage or deaths. Like it's not happening. But it is happening. It's all we can hear.

I close all the browser windows but one, the one cued up to the video of the girl in the blue coat. I had been watching it again earlier that night, marveling at her subtle movements, wondering what her name is, where she went after the clip was shot. Wondering what's in her pockets.

Emerald makes a sound. I look at her.

"That's my friend's video."

"You know this girl?"

"No, I know the guy who made the video. His name is Pedro; he did it for a film class."

"What, uh . . . what? A film class? So it's staged?"

"Oh no, it's animated. He created that girl."

"Created her?"

"She's animated and superimposed on the shot. He used this cutting-edge technique, took him forever. Her hair especially, he spent weeks animating her hair to make it look like that."

"This video is a fake? This video of a girl standing on a street corner in a blue coat is a fake?"

"Yeah, well, I wouldn't say fake, it was produced. He produced it. Did you see it went viral?"

Even though Emerald is sitting right next to me, even though I am looking into her green eyes, I feel alone. I look back at the screen, the video paused on the girl in the blue coat with the chestnut hair looking up at the sky. There is one comment, from a user named drcomputerjr. The comment is "amzng btw." My throat tightens, my eyes well up a little, and I'm overwhelmed by a confusion that is hard to describe accurately, so I'll call it grief.

I toss the tablet away from myself and walk into the next room. Emerald doesn't follow me. I should have known better. I should have known it wasn't real. But it was just her, there were no ads, no messages, no agenda. It was just her. And yet it wasn't her. What on earth can you find that's genuine? What on earth can you find that's real? Everything is a creation. A fabrication. A hoax. I'm so fucking tired of it.

The gunfire outside intensifies and someone screams, snapping me back to reality. It occurs to me that this may only get worse.

I take out my phone and call my mother. She answers on the fourth ring. She sounds upset.

"Hello?"

"Mom, it's me."

"Oh . . . hi."

"Mom, is everything OK?"

"Oh . . . yeah. Yeah, what's happening there? I hear a lot of noise . . ."

"Mom, there's a battle happening in my neighborhood. If anything happens to me, I just want you to know that I love you."

"I love you, too."

"Is Dad there?"

"Oh . . . he isn't."

"Where is he?"

"He's, um . . ."

There's gunfire right outside my window. "Mom, if something happens, tell Dad I love him, too."

"I'm sure you'll be fine, sweetie."

"Mom . . ." An explosion a few blocks away. Everything shakes. I drop my phone, and when I pick it up, it won't turn back on.

Emerald sits with her back to the wall, a streak of blood extending up behind her like a red vine.

"What happened!"

"A stray, or . . . agh! Stupid . . . standing at the window . . ."

"Where are you hit?" She points to her shoulder. I cut the clothing away. Blood comes forth as though the wound is coughing. I run to the bathroom and wet a towel.

"Here, pressure." I hand her the towel, and she holds it against her shoulder with her other hand, wincing and moaning. I peek over her shoulder and see that the bullet went all the way through, and the exit wound is gruesome, like the bullet had claws and teeth. (It's possible that CURE has bullets with claws and teeth.)

I start looking for something to bandage her with. I don't have any gauze or anything. My phone is broken. I ask Emerald for her phone, but she says it's dead. I need to get her to a hospital. I remember that Simon has a car that he rarely drives. I bet he didn't even have his starter with him tonight. I grab his spare key-card and cross the hall to his apartment.

Simon's place smells like marijuana and garlic. I start to look around for his car starter, which is, of course, a long, thin, flat black object, and in the dark, cockroaches are long, thin, flat black objects as well. It's not by the door. I go from room to room, bumping into everything. On a small table next to Simon's bed, I find what I'm looking for. A roach sits on the starter patiently. In the shadows, it almost seems to disappear; it has the impression of an inkblot. A specter. It could be anything.

From somewhere in the building, gunshots ring out. I hear voices, commands. I duck behind the bed for a minute until the noise dies down. I look out through the peephole and see two men and a woman in black attire, tactical gear, face shields, race out of my apartment. When they're out of the building, I go back into my place, the floor creaking under each step. The fighting outside rages on. Larry runs down the hall toward me, and I scoop him up into my arms, thrilled he's all right. But then I find Emerald. She's been shot multiple times. She's had her hands cut off. She is unrecognizable through the gore.

I call her name, as though doing so will somehow help her.

Emerald's head lulls softly to the side, and she gasps, a wet, stuttering hiss. She opens one eye.

"Who did this? Those people, were they CURE?"

"Th-they were . . . huuuuuugh . . . l-l-looking for . . . huh huh huh . . . S-S-S-S-Sim-Simon . . ."

"They had the wrong address?"

"Th-th-they . . ."—she coughs and gasps several times in painful succession—"Th-th-they're going to . . . c-c-c-c-come back . . ."

"Emerald. I'm so sorry. I don't know what to do."

"J-j-j-just . . . could you . . . h-h-hold my h-h-h-hand?"

Either she doesn't know they cut off her hands or she's so out of her mind that she's already forgotten. Or she can still feel them there. It seems perverse to hold her wrist where her hand used to be, so I just lean in close to her. I put my hand where her hand would be, where it should be, the space that's rightfully her hand's space. She looks into my eyes.

"I'm squeezing your hand," I say to her, meaning every word. "Feel it?"

She nods. And then she dies.

And then I remember: this is grief.

Real. Actual. Genuine.

But I can't hang around. She said they're coming back. They're looking for Simon, but for all I know they're looking for me, too. They may have figured out that I have ties to Unarmed Citizens. I run into my kitchen and grab a few energy bars and four bottles of water. I throw them in a backpack along with a bag of cat treats and a small bowl.

I grab some socks, a few shirts, some deodorant, some toothpaste. I snatch up Larry and put him in my shirt again. I open my door and stop, looking back into my apartment, where I've lived for years but never really felt at home. I'm surprised by how easily I can leave it, knowing that I almost certainly won't return.

Outside, the air seems thicker, and everywhere is a stench of . . . chemicals? Burning plastic? I can't place it, but something has been let loose upon Albany Park. A pall or miasma. Within seconds, my eyes sting and I can barely see. My first instinct is to run back inside, but that's not an option. They'll return. They'll find me. (Maybe I should just let them find me. What kind of world is this to go on in?)

(No.)

I head east. Gunfire approaching from the west. Shouting. I cross Kedzie and look north toward a screeching roar. The Brown Line rumbles past, one car engulfed in flames. Helicopters above. To the south, the shrill police cry, over and over.

I pick up my pace but am sure to stay completely out of the light. I have about half a mile to the river. I have to get there. I don't even know why, it just seems like the only place I can get to. An artery. A lifeline.

Each block feels longer than the last.

At the corner of Wilson and Mozart, something strikes me across the shins and I go down hard. I land in a way that protects Larry, but in doing so my elbows and head hit the ground savagely. I turn onto my back and a man with scars on his face is on top of me. I don't know what he wants.

"*Fuck you doin' out here?*" or something. He's yelling. At me, or to me, but his words become less clear the louder he gets. The sounds of skirmish dull and fade as well. All I can hear is the sound of my heels scraping the pavement. Larry meows once; I hear him, too. I can always hear him.

"*Who you with, man, goddamnit, who you with who you wi—*"

My face is sprayed with the blood of the man with the scars on his face, as something forceful hits him from the side and knocks him off me. A mass. A wave of energy. I scramble to my feet and see what looks like a giant black hound on top of the man with the scars on his face, mauling him. One more block. I can see the bridge. I hop a fence and hurry through an immense yard, down a wooden staircase to a small river dock. There's a canoe. It looks filthy, flimsy, like it hasn't been used in years. Years and years. Time passes. I unfasten the canoe from the dock.

Behind me, shouting. Howling.

The shrill police tone.

Larry's claws dig into me.

From the sky, a woman screaming. I look up. I see . . . I see . . .

A detonation from behind us. Larry and I are thrown forward. I feel an impact and a cold splash of water. Maybe it was my head hitting the floor of the canoe, or the force of the blast, but the world spins, and I know I can't stay awake. The last thing I see is a nightmarish sky, lit up by ballistics and fireballs. I see a face in the sky. Eyes. A mouth. Expression.

No. No. I see nothing but clouds.

I succumb.

***

In the dreams that follow, I am trapped in an elevator for days. It has already been days. I have no food. I have no water. Larry is nowhere to be seen. I hope that I haven't eaten Larry, I can't imagine that I would have eaten Larry, but I've never been desperately hungry and I can't imagine why else he wouldn't be here except maybe that he just isn't, and that's sad, but not as sad as having eaten him.

An alarm blares. It's been blaring for quite a long time. It drove me insane long before the dream began.

PART III

After fleeing my apartment, following a murder

Prior to losing my job

*Note: Before beginning this section, the author rec-
ommends that the reader find and listen to a sample
of the Chicago civil defense/tornado sirens. Knowing
that sound will give this section its full effect.*

TWELVE

I open my eyes, slowly regaining consciousness, the maddening dream alarm still mixing with the sounds of the world. I'm in a small space, and I can hear water. I lie here exhausted, bewildered. I get a twinge in my calf. The muscle tightens up like it's been electrocuted. I try to point and flex my foot, but the pain is too great. I sit up and rub the cramp in my leg, and only then am I fully reminded of where I am. In a canoe. Floating down the Chicago River. Larry is curled up next to me. I'm amazed by his ability to be comfortable anywhere I am. All those years I've gone to work, run errands, visited friends—I seem to remember doing that at some point; I must have had friends—I always left Larry behind, in the apartment. It was his, he spent the most time there, his was the predominant scent on the furniture.

I'll need to find more food for him, I realize. This feels very daunting and urgent at the moment, even though I should be able to find cat food anywhere. Should. The way things are, though, I won't be surprised to discover that there's no more cat food one day, maybe today, an entire category of consumer goods vanished.

That happens, though. Things vanish. Just recently, yogurt is gone from shelves. Pork products. Olive oil. Strawberries. A reminder to myself to feel lucky anytime I can find something I need when I need it. With luck, I'll be able to get my hands on a can of tuna. We can share it.

Larry stands on his hind legs at the side of the boat and gazes into the water. The river is atrocious, choked with roach carcasses and sludge. There are birds perched all along the river on buildings, wires, bridges, but none of them are interested in eating these dead roaches. Seems unnatural and even a bit sad. (I picture myself buried in a cardboard box, and not even the worms want me for food.) I've seen it written, seen pictures, heard older Chicagoans talk about the river once being beautiful, but that seems impossible to believe or even envision in its current state. The flow is slow; if I'm doing the math right, I've drifted only a couple of miles overnight, and up ahead I see what I believe to be Goose Island. It's a quiet morning. An occasional shrill police tone comes from the west. A bird lands on the side of the canoe, and Larry immediately takes an interest, his body tensing, eyes locked on the winged thing.

Out to the east, a rumbling in the air, like boulders rolling through clouds. I look and see a passenger jet coming in over Lake Michigan. At least I think it's a passenger jet. I'm not sure now. It's very low, as though the sky itself is heavy on the roof, preventing it from climbing. The sound coming from the jet swells, incongruous, it seems impossible that one machine could make that noise. And then I realize it isn't one plane. Behind that plane there's another, and another. Not in a flight path, but scattered, approaching the skyline. More and more. I count eleven in all, way, way too close together.

As I watch them approach, the bird flies in front of my face and a loud, panicked scratching comes from below. I look down and see Larry hanging off the edge of the canoe. I think

I say, "What the—?" and before I can even process what the hell's happening, he falls in. For a second or two, his body is buoyed on top of the water by the dead roaches and the heavy pollutants, but it's only a second or two. I can barely reach for him and yell his name before he slips under the surface. At first, I assure myself (based on nothing) that Larry knows how to swim. I just assume, he's a creature, he has instincts—that's how he ended up in the water in the first place: instincts. But no, Larry cannot swim. I have never seen him swim, and he has never tried. I'm going to have to jump in there.

Nothing in my life has prepared me for this. I jump into the Chicago River, and immediately I feel the slight, sharp impacts of tiny bodies all around me, the vibration of kicking legs in the water—mine, Larry's, and the roaches clinging to life. I open my eyes underwater and I try to look around, but the water is so cloudy that I can't see Larry anywhere. I look up at the silhouettes of the countless dead and dying arthropods forming a dark membrane on top of the river, and I wonder if they're going to somehow keep me down here. That they'll link themselves together into a shield I can't break through, and that will be it.

No, I need to breathe.

I come back up for air, and doing this is a mistake. Drowning might have been better than resurfacing with them all over my shoulders and face. I gasp and flail, but flailing just means I touch more of them. No one is around. The planes are closing in.

I go back under and swim beneath the canoe, and swing my arms in wide circles. My hand finds soft wisps of fur floating in the murk, and my fingers close around Larry's tail.

I toss Larry up and over, back into the canoe. There's no way for me to get back in, so I hang on to the side. The planes are now right over top, even lower now; they divide into two streams, seven of them continue on, presumably toward O'Hare, and four break off to the south, presumably toward Midway. Their shapes seem to morph as they go, like I'm looking at them through some prism. I can't tell what kind of planes they are at all. Commercial? Military? Surveillance? I really have no idea. I have no idea what happened last night. I have no idea where I'm going.

I'm going to have to burn these clothes.

***

I run the canoe ashore near Wolf Point, and I stand up beside it. Larry rests inside, looking tired, soaking wet. I hope he didn't swallow too much river water. I hope I didn't either, for that matter.

An unmounted minigun bearing the CURE insignia lies abandoned on the water's edge.

I look at one of the towers that stands here, and one of them bears the CURE insignia as well; a symbol on a building where there was previously no such symbol. And that's me all over: I notice the part but miss the machine. I'm disturbed by the minigun; the building, however, seems perfectly normal. Just a part of the city. This is a mistake. And I know it's a mistake. But I still spend much more time gazing mournfully at the minigun, chewing the inside of my cheeks, imagining the rounds it fired, eight thousand per minute. The flesh it tore, the holes made where no holes belong.

I stumble north and east, and looking down Kinzie, see what appears to be an L train car, derailed, lying in the street. It appears that this did not just recently happen. No one is running around, there are no emergency crews. Just a train car sitting in the street, crumpled on itself, like it belongs there. Like someone put it there.

I get to Hubbard and it looks clear in both directions, but I head east. East.

Walking down Hubbard, I notice something in the distance. Really it's more like a feeling; I can't see what it is from where I stand, but I know it's there, I know something is different. Something either new or so ancient as to be new again. Or still. It radiates, this feeling, from the lake. East. East. My sense is that I want to start walking west, to put as much distance as I can between myself and this . . . knowing? This presence? This shadow? Whatever this is, coming from the east. From the water. But my compulsion—ah, my compulsion—directs me east. East. Like there is unfinished business. Or I'm bound by honor, that I would shame myself by walking west. I have to investigate. I have to see.

Except that I don't have to. It is my choice what I do and where I go, the direction of my feet. People mistake oppression, coercion, manipulation, and intimidation as removing choice, but all they do is make certain choices harder. "You must do this, or else . . ." is more accurately, "You could do this, but then . . ."

Every man dies. Not every man truly lives. Who said that? Someone said that. Probably a president. Presidents don't say memorable things anymore. They don't need to, since they don't need to campaign or orate or get elected or really lead anymore. The president's only job these days is to go on TV and say, "Hey, we're going to war. Again. Or still." It could be in Iran, or Syria, or China, or Italy, or like three years ago in Pakistan, or like last year in Venezuela. He or she can say it however he or she wants, it still produces the same result. So at some point they stopped even trying to dress it up in a way that made it seem inspiring, or resolute, or patriotic, or necessary.

Also, we're bailing out the banks. Again. Or still.

Besides, it must have been tedious for presidents. All those years, those centuries spent trying to keep people convinced that they had a say and that someone was listening. That the nation had an identity. That we weren't destined to this. Whatever this is.

I, as an individual, do not have a say. But I do have a choice. Choices. They are numerous and full of branches, like a river (also, you can drown in them).

Without even understanding how I got here, I've ended up at the lake, the beach, staring out over the water. There is nothing there but water, but I can feel something. Else. Out there. And up. Something blocking light, reflecting heat, the impression of something enormous. It's as though I can sense a gigantic building that isn't there, like maybe it once was there or will at some time be there, but in the present, I'm able to feel it, to know of it. Or it's cloaked somehow, like that skyscraper in Seoul. In any case, like many things, it is both there and not there. Real and fake. It has a front door and stairs, it is asymmetrical and dark, it has no heating. There are no clouds in the sky, and as I stare up into the dull blue, it's almost as though I can see the wind turning, rocking, whipping around this structure, changing course. It is taller than the Willis Tower, and probably taller than One World Trade Center. Maybe even taller than the Burj Khalifa before it fell over. It terrifies me, knowing of such a height. Such a jagged height.

A plane is approaching. It looks military. I watch it come from the southwest, over the city and toward the lake. It's headed right for where the building would be. The plane, it is certainly not high enough. It is going to strike the building, the phantom building, the building that is there and not there. The pilots can't see it. I can see it, but they can't; they don't even know it's there, and so they can't even begin to avoid it. The feeling of a building will not show up on radar. The plane will crash into the building and there will be a fireball in the sky, alerting all of Chicago to the presence of a hidden tower in our lake. The plane will slam into the building and that will be it.

Only . . . no. It continues. Unimpeded. Unbroken. It crosses through the building. Where the building would be. It continues its eastbound course over Lake Michigan. You can find hundreds of videos of plane crashes online. Real and fake. They're extraordinarily popular. Lots of views. Lots of comments. Never read the comments. I lean over and vomit on the beach. Cockroaches crawl in and out of the sand.

Nearby, a man stands near the water's edge and cries, "HEEEEEEEEEEEEEEEEEEEEEEEEEEEEEEEEEEEEEEEEE
EEEEEEEEEEEEEEEEEEEEEEEEEEEEEEEEEEEEEEEEEE
EEEEEEEEEEEEEEEEEEEEEEEEEEEEEEEEEEEEEEEEEE
EEEEEEEEEEEEEEEEEEEEEEEEEEEEEEEEEEEEEEEEEE
EEEEEEEEEEEEEEEEEEEEEEEEEEEEEEEEEEEEEEEEEE
EEEEEEEEEEEEEEEEEEEEEEEEEEEEEEEEEEEEEEEEEE
EEEEEEEEEEEEEEEEEEEEEEEEEEEEEEEEEEEEEEEEEE
EEEEEEEEEEEEEEEEEEEEEEEEEEEEEEEEEEEEEEEEEE
EEEEEEEEEEEEEEEEEEEEEEEEEEEEEEEEEEEEEEEEEE
EEEEEEEEEEEEEEEEEEEEEEEEEEEEEEEEEEEEEEEEEE
EEEEEEEEEEEEEEEEEEEEEEEEEEEEEEEEEEEEEEEEEE
EEEEEEEEEEEEEEEEEEEEEEEEEEEEEEEEEEEEEEEEEE
EEEEEEEEEEEEEEEEEEEEEEEEEEEEEEEEEEEEEEEEEE
EEEEEEEEEEEEEEEEEEEEEEEEEEEEEEEEEEEEEEEEEE
EEEEEEEEEEEEEEEEEEEEEEEEEEEEEEEEEEEEEEEEEE
EEEEEEEEEEEEEEEEEEEEEEEEEEEEEEEEEEEEEEEEEE
EEEEEEEEEEEEEEEEEEEEEEEEEEEEEEEEEEEEEEEEEE
EEEEEEEEEEEEEEEEEEEEEEEEEEEEEEEEEEEEEEEEEE
EEEEEEEEEEEEEEEEEEEEEEEEEEEEEEEEEEEEEEEEEE
EEEEEEEEEEEEEEEEEEEEEEEEEEEEEEEEEEEEEEEEEE
EEEEEEEEEEEEEEEEEEEEEEEEEEEEEEEEEEEEEEEEEE
EEEEEEEEEEEEEEEEEEEEEEEEEEEEEEEEEEEEEEEEEE

EEEEEEEEEEEEEEEEEEEEEEEEEEEEEEEEEEEEEEEEEEEEE
EEEEEEEEEEEEEEEEEEEEEEEEEEEEEEEEEEEEEEEEEEEEE
EEEEEEEEEEEEEEEEEEEEEEEEEEEEEEEEEEEEEEEEEEEEE
EEEEEEEEEEEEEEEEEEEEEEEEEEEEEEEEEEEEEEEEEEEEE
EEEEEEEEEEEEEEEEEEEEEEEEEEEEEEEEEEEEEEEEEEEEE
EEEEEEEEEEEEEEEEEEEEEEEEEEEEEEEEEEEEEEEEEEEEE
EEEEEEEEEEEEEEEEEEEEEEEEEEEEEEEEEEEEEEEEEEEEE
EEEEEEEEEEEEEEEEEEEEEEEEEEEEEEEEEEEEEEEEEEEEE
EEEEEEEEEEEEEEEEEEEEEEEEEEEEEEEEEEEEEEEEEEEEE
EEEEEEEEEEEEEEEEEEEEEEEEEEEEEEEEEEEEEEEEEEEEE
EEEEEEEEEEEEEEEEEEEEEEEEEEEEEEEEEEEEEEEEEEEEE
EEEEEEEEEEEEEEEEEEEEEEEEEEEEEEEEEEEEEEEEEEEEE
EEEEEEEEEEEEEEEEEEEEEEEEEEEEEEEEEEEEEEEEEEEEE
EEEEEEEEEEEEEEEEEEEEEEEEEEEEEEEEEEEEEEEEEEEEE
EEEEEEEEEEEEEEEEEEEEEEEEEEEEEEEEEEEEEEEEEEEEE
EEEEEEEEEEEEEEEEEEEEEEEEEEEEEEEEEEEEEEEEEEEEE
EEEEEEEEEEEEEEEEEEEEEEEEEEEEEEEEEEEEEEEEEEEEE
EEEEEEEEEEEEEEEEEEEEEEEEEEEEEEEEEEEEEEEEEEEEE
EEEEEEEEEEEEEEEEEEEEEEEEEEEEEEEEEEEEEEEEEEEEE
EEEEEEEEEEEEEEEEEEEEEEEEEEEEEEEEEEEEEEEEEEEEE
EEEEEEEEEEEEEEEEEEEEEEEEEEEEEEEEEEEEEEEEEEEEE
EEEEEEEEEEEEEEEEEEEEEEEEEEEEEEEEEEEEEEEEEEEEE
EEEEEEEEEEEEEEEEEEEEEEEEEEEEEEEEEEEEEEEEEEEEE
EEEEEEEEEEEEEEEEEEEEEEEEEEEEEEEEEEEEEEEEEEEEE
EEEEEEEEEEEEEEEEEEEEEEEEEEEEEEEEEEEEEEEEEEEEE
EEEEEEEEEEEEEEEEEEEEEEEEEEEEEEEEEEEEEEEEEEEEE
EEEEEEEEEEEEEEEEEEEEEEEEEEEEEEEEEEEEEEEEEEEEE
EEEEEEEEEEEEEEEEEEEEEEEEEEEEEEEEEEEEEEEEEEEEE
EEEEEEEEEEEEEEEEEEEEEEEEEEEEEEEEEEEEEEEEEEEEE
EEEEEEEEEEEEEEEEEEEEEEEEEEEEEEEEEEEEEEEEEEEEE
EEEEEEEEEEEEEEEEEEEEEEEEEEEEEEEEEEEEEEEEEEEEE
EEEEEEEEEEEEEEEEEEEEEEEEEEEEEEEEEEEEEEEEEEEEE
EEEEEEEEEEEEEEEEEEEEEEEEEEEEEEEEEEEEEEEEEEEEE
EEEEEEEEEEEEEEEEEEEEEEEEEEEEEEEEEEEEEEEEEEEEE

EEEEEEEEEEEEEEEEEEEEEEEEEEEEEEEEEEEEEEEEEEEEE
EEEEEEEEEEEEEEEEEEEEEEEEEEEEEEEEEEEEEEEEEEEEE
EEEEEEEEEEEEEEEEEEEEEEEEEEEEEEEEEEEEEEEEEEEEE
EEEEEEEEEEEEEEEEEEEEEEEEEEEEEEEEEEEEEEEEEEEEE
EEEEEEEEEEEEEEEEEEEEEEEEEEEEEEEEEEEEEEEEEEEEE
EEEEEEEEEEEEEEEEEEEEEEEEEEEEEEEEEEEEEEEEEEEEE
EEEEEEEEEEEEEEEEEEEEEEEEEEEEEEEEEEEEEEEEEEEEE
EEEEEEEEEEEEEEEEEEEEEEEEEEEEEEEEEEEEEEEEEEEEE
EEEEEEEEEEEEEEEEEEEEEEEEEEEEEEEEEEEEEEEEEEEEE
EEEEEEEEEEEEEEEEEEEEEEEEEEEEEEEEEEEEEEEEEEEEE
EEEEEEEEEEEEEEEEEEEEEEEEEEEEEEEEEEEEEEEEEEEEE
EEEEEEEEEEEEEEEEEEEEEEEEEEEEEEEEEEEEEEEEEEEEE
EEEEEEEEEEEEEEEEEEEEEEEEEEEEEEEEEEEEEEEEEEEEE
EEEEEEEEEEEEEEEEEEEEEEEEEEEEEEEEEEEEEEEEEEEEE
EEEEEEEEEEEEEEEEEEEEEEEEEEEEEEEEEEEEEEEEEEEEE
EEEEEEEEEEEEEEEEEEEEEEEEEEEEEEEEEEEEEEEEEEEEE
EEEEEEEEEEEEEEEEEEEEEEEEEEEEEEEEEEEEEEEEEEEEE
EEEEEEEEEEEEEEEEEEEEEEEEEEEEEEEEEEEEEEEEEEEEE
EEEEEEEEEEEEEEEEEEEEEEEEEEEEEEEEELP."

I'd try to help him, but he doesn't want help from me.

I turn away from the lake and start walking back toward the city. As I cross the inner drive, I see two men on the corner of the sidewalk, both holding assault rifles across their chests like trophies. They each wear bulletproof vests. I keep my head down and my eyes forward. But as I walk past them, another man approaches, with a handgun drawn. He says something to the men with the assault rifles. I can't make it out, but it escalates quickly.

The popping sounds start. I feel an immense pressure on the side of my head, and I lose hearing in my right ear. I see a spray of blood. I hear someone running away, not sure which of those three guys it is, or if the other two are dead. I raise my hand to my left ear and things feel wet there.

My phone is broken.

"I need the hospital," I say, hoping someone can hear me. Someone. Anyone.

I get dizzy and the day darkens. It's not the first time I've been shot.

***

While unconscious I believe I hear sounds, but no visuals come to mind. No—I don't believe I hear sounds. I believe I am sounds. I am wind. I am screams. I am percussion. Blasts. Footfalls.

THIRTEEN

I come to in what looks like an all-white hotel room. There are beeping machines and lights, and the place smells of cleaners and regret. A hospital. I ended up in a hospital. Someone found me and helped me. Wow.

Outside my room there's a lot of activity, many people in a hurry. The side of my head is splitting, like someone is pressing into it with a dull meat cleaver. I try to lift my hand, but it is weighed down by tubes and plastic dealbobs. There are quite a lot of needles in me right now.

The Automat nurse affixed to the bedside "looks" at me with her long obsidian face and slender chrome fingers and says, "Good, Mr. Palazzo. You're awake. Let's check your vitals." She checks all my vitals at one time and reads them all to me. I ask her what's going on, to which she replies, in her completely human-sounding voice, "You sustained massive damage to your ear as well as a fractured skull."

"Was I targeted?"

"I don't follow. Could you rephrase the question?"

"The person who shot me, did they intend to shoot me, or was I just in the wrong place at the wrong time?"

"I understand. There's no record of that."

"No record of what?"

"There's no record of a person shooting you."

"How else did I get shot then?"

"That's a police matter. My job is to give you care. Please relax."

"Sure, yeah."

I look around and suddenly realize that Larry isn't here.

"Can you tell me where my cat is?"

"I don't follow. Could you rephrase the question?"

"I have a pet cat, and he was with me when I got shot. Did he end up here?"

"I understand. There's no record of that."

"Are you sure?"

"There's no record of an animal at the scene."

"So he just disappeared?"

"I'm sorry, Mr. Palazzo. I don't have any more information for you."

She takes some measurements, adjusts some tubes. I worry that I'm being watched in here. That I'm a person of interest. I feel a little woozy. I ask her, "Is there a drug in my IV?"

"There is. Something to manage your pain. You are recovering from surgery."

"Surgery? For what?"

"The injury resulted in the total loss of your left ear. You've been given a cybersynthetic replacement."

I reach up and feel my left ear. It's pliant like the old one but very clearly artificial. It had been a secret hope of mine to go through life without ever needing any of my body parts replaced. But then I got too close to a random argument. C'est la vie.

I run my fingers over the cybersynthetic ear, and the sensation is like touching an appendage that has fallen asleep. I can't feel it there, but still I hear with it. It isn't me. I don't trust it.

"Who made my ear?"

"I don't follow. Could you—"

"I assume my new ear was made on a 3-D printer, correct?"

"That is correct."

"Whose printer was it? Who's the manufacturer?"

"All of our biological 3-D printers are manufactured and distributed by Construct Bio-Technologies Limited, Madison, Wisconsin. The machine that printed your ear is model number—"

"What is the parent company of Construct Bio-Technologies?"

"OK. The parent company of Construct Bio-Technologies Limited is Pacific Liberty Healthcare Group, Seattle, Washington."

"What is the parent company of Pacific Liberty Healthcare Group?"

"OK. The parent company of Pacific Liberty Healthcare Group is Butler-Nova Incorporated, Charleston, South Caro—"

"What is the parent company of Butler-Nova?"

"OK. The parent company of Butler-Nova Incorporated is the Coalition of United Response Engineers, Philadelphia, Pennsylvania."

The room gets very quiet, as though someone just turned down the volume in my new ear. It's the final answer I expected, and yet still to hear her say it brings a deepening horror.

I can't just start unhooking all my monitors and tubes, because the nurse is those monitors and tubes. Maybe she'll just politely insist that I not do that, but for all I know she's guarding me and authorized to incapacitate; the thing with Automats is that you don't know what they're capable of or what they're armed with, and it's best not to chance it.

"Could I get up and use the restroom, please?" I ask.

"If you need to empty your bladder, I could provide you with a catheter."

"That's not . . . No, I'd rather not have that. Couldn't I just go, quickly?"

"OK. Please use the restroom in the suite. If you need assistance, press the call button."

That was easier than I expected. Maybe I'm not a person of interest after all. The nurse detaches from me, and I rush to the bathroom. I immediately start looking for an exit—a loose panel, a vent, anything. There's no exit. I'm in here for only about thirty seconds, though, before she starts asking after me.

"Are you all right in there? Do you need assistance?"

"I'm fine! Just a minute!"

I have no other ideas, so the one I run with is the stupidest idea I can come up with in this situation. I grab a towel. I leave the bathroom and act like I'm going to sit back down on the bed, but instead I throw the towel over the nurse's head.

"My view has become obstructed. Please remove the obstruction, or, if you are not able to remove it, please alert the attendant by pressing your call button."

She keeps going, but I'm already out of the room.

When I step into the hall, no one notices. I find a supply room and duck inside, thinking I might be able to find better clothes and maybe something else useful. I find both: a pair of scrubs, a doctor's coat, and a scalpel. When I pocket the scalpel and look up, I am face-to-face with an Automat nurse, but fortunately one that has been powered down. So she isn't "looking" at me, but she is still likely recording things, like changes in room temperature and sound signatures.

Near the supply closet, I find the elevator, and I take it down to the ground floor. The car descends slowly, and I vaguely remember hearing that security cameras can instantly recognize a person based on his or her cyber parts. There are certainly cameras on this elevator, but maybe my ear is too new to trigger any alarm. Off the elevator, I follow signs to the exit. I pass no one in the halls; the hospital is very quiet. When I locate the exit, I stop in my tracks. There's so much I don't know. And everything I don't know makes the exit seem miles away. I don't know who might be waiting for me by those double doors. I don't know if I'm on a list. I don't know if there are scanners in this hallway that will recognize me. I don't know what kind of defensive measures the hospital has in place that might keep me from escaping. Where technology is concerned, if you can imagine it, it might exist. And I have a good imagination.

And what if someone sees me? If I smile at someone, is that a dead giveaway? Is there a secret hospital handshake? Has the nurse already sent out some signal to lock me in the facility?

I stop thinking, and I do what needs to be done. I take a step toward the exit; but literally, that second—when I'd committed myself to that direction—the double doors open, and in walk two CURE sentries in their old gold and black with green boots. I can't change paths. Nothing draws the attention and general shittiness of CURE sentries as much as indecision. I grab a nearby phone and start saying nonsense into it as the sentries walk past. They don't look at me.

As I start again toward the exit, a woman on staff yells to me, "Doctor!" and again, "*Doctor?*" presumably to ask me something relevant to medicine. I turn to face her. She stares at me and does not ask me anything. She stares at me in a way I really don't like. I run out the door, and I'm immediately en route to the street where I was shot and lost track of Larry. It's not far away, just a few blocks. Larry's hopefully still there, cowering in a bush.

I get to the intersection where the shootout took place, and my blood still is fanned out on the sidewalk like a paint splat.

A woman who is not a sentry but appears to be an employee of CURE inspects some sort of organic material on the other side of the street, surely material that used to be inside one or more of those men. All the cockroaches in the area seem drawn to the crime scene.

The bag I was carrying is gone, meaning Larry and I have no remaining provisions. I whistle in a way that he'll recognize. I do it again. Nothing. From here I can hear the sounds of the water. There are no cars on the road.

From out over the lake, a bad sound. It's almost imperceptible, like a droning or a truck idling, far in the distance. A locomotive. A massive generator. It's a hum that seems to prick my skin, vibrate my bones, and slowly churn my blood. Listening to it is like falling. I have to close my eyes and crouch.

I wonder if it's my new ear. Maybe this sound, this hum, was always there. I'm just attuned to it now, I can pick it up. I don't know if this is a good thing, or if it's even a real thing. But the hum is incessant, and it is powerful. A new sound among so many other sounds of the city and of the world that cloud my head and remind me that I am not alone and I am not safe.

I feel something rough on my hand. I open my eyes, and though my head still spins and I'm groggy from whatever drugs they've given me, I see and recognize Larry, best fucking cat there ever was, licking my thumb. I pick him up and hold him to me, again closing my eyes. The sound of his purring drowns out the awful, awful hum.

When I feel stable enough to stand, I do. The woman in the CURE garb smiles at us, blood on her gloves.

I don't know where to go. I'd like to see my mother. I'd like to visit my brother's grave again. But I see no way of getting out of Chicago in the short term, let alone getting all the way to Plain City. And so I go to the only place in the city where I know we'll be safe and secluded.

I go to work.

***

Outside my building, there's a moment of doubt that my key-card will work. I don't know what it is. Something in the air. Something in my touch. Something in the asphalt. There seems to have been a shift. I don't expect this or anything else to work.

But it does.

And inside is like a cavern. There is a musty smell, and lots of roaches. It seems . . . it feels somehow as if no one has been in this building for months, even though I was just here a few days ago. Right? I was. I was.

Never in a million years would I take the elevator right now, so I take the stairs up. I stop at each floor and peek out of the stairwell, just to see. Every floor is deserted. I remind myself that it's a Sunday, and most, if not all, businesses in the building are closed on Sunday, but that doesn't make me feel any better. I don't know whom I expected to see. The building engineer? Other people who work in the building and were chased out of their neighborhoods by firefights?

I get up to my floor and feel compelled to make as little noise as possible. While I may have taken comfort in seeing someone on one of the lower floors, I absolutely do not expect to see anyone on my floor, as my firm rents the whole level. Unless one of my coworkers is here . . . but yeah, right.

I move very carefully, rolling my foot from heel to toe, not wanting to do anything too sudden. Not wanting to make too much noise. Just in case. The lobby of our office smells damp and mildewy, as though there's new water damage or mold. I move by the sunbeams coming in through the windows; I can't bring myself to turn on any lights.

Inside our office (or is it just my office now?) things feel very still. Even the cockroaches peppered across the walls and floor seem to be unmoving when I first enter the space. I feel uneasy here, but I always feel that way when I'm here on the weekend, like I shouldn't be here, like I'm doing something wrong being here. Intruding. I look around, and I'm surprised that there isn't a coating of dust on everything, even though I was just here a few days ago. Our cleaning crew comes on Saturday mornings, so I guess they were here. I guess they still get paid. I guess someone is taking care of all that.

I'm fairly certain we're alone here. I let Larry out of my shirt, but he sticks by me for now.

Out of habit, I check the messages. There are none. I look at the calendar. There are no clients scheduled for the week ahead. Or the following week. How had I not noticed that before now? I look in the minifridge. A block of cheese. I'm also elated to find that one of my (former? late?) colleagues left two unopened cans of tuna in here that Larry will scarf down.

I go into the coat closet and take all the garments off the hangers: coats, blazers, slacks, sweaters. We kept a lot of spare clothing in here in case we didn't want to dress for work before coming in or in case we spilled something on ourselves. Now it will all serve as my bed. I find a relatively roach-light area and create a makeshift mattress. There are more roaches here than in my apartment. Even though I know to expect them and I know what they feel like and I've studied them at length, I still can't ever get used to the feeling of their legs on me, and I doubt I ever will. Luckily, we happen to have some Maw-Gards on hand as well.

After getting my bed set up and opening a can of tuna for Larry, I eat two bites of cheese. Then I grab the first aid kit. I take out gauze and alcohol wipes. In our supply drawer I find a needle and thread. I go into the bathroom with the scalpel.

I look in the mirror, fully aware of what I must do, and yet fully unable to picture myself doing it. Perhaps I'm being paranoid, I don't know, but it seems possible and likely that CURE would place beacons or something in cybernetic body parts printed on their machines. The beacons might be nanobots that produce other nanobots that are already in my bloodstream, for all I know. I didn't want this ear. I didn't ask for this ear. This ear has to go.

I'm indelicate. With a few quick, forceful slashes I get most of my new ear off and throw it into the sink. I stare at it, marveling at how like an ear it looks while also acknowledging that it now resembles lunchmeat. Now comes the hard part: getting the rest of it. This will get messy.

I start cutting around what I believe is the edge of the ear, and it hurts only when I make contact with my own skin, which is unavoidable. Getting rid of the fake flesh takes a few minutes, but getting all the connecting fibers out of my skin takes hours. I have to take a few breaks from the pain—not the worst pain I've ever felt, but still a sharp thing in the side of my head. I wish that I had bourbon; carving out an unwanted, artificial body part is the kind of thing one does while slugging bourbon straight from the bottle. The sink gets very bloody during this; I run the water at intervals, to turn the red blood orange and then flush it away.

When I've exhausted the scalpel's effectiveness, I use tweezers to get the remaining fibers. Some of them are very stubborn.

At the point when I'm satisfied that I've extracted every last bit of that unnatural ear, I clean the wound around the opening to my ear canal. I take out the needle. I sterilize it with a lighter that Walt left behind. I crudely stitch up the whole mess. I'm bad at sewing.

I dress my earhole and wrap the bandage around my head to keep it in place. C'est la vie.

When I return to the office, I find Larry sleeping on the makeshift coat mattress. The roaches are leaving him alone. I look around the office, remembering as I look at all the functional furniture and neutral tones that the schedule is clear for weeks. It could be that no one is looking for this type of service anymore. That no one is looking for guidance. People have ceased wanting for better. I hope not. But in any case, this could be our new home for a while. I could be dismayed by that, but I tell myself there's no sense in being dismayed. It could be far worse.

After performing surgery on myself, I really don't think I can continue the day, so I darken the windows, curl up with Larry, and sleep as long as I need to.

FOURTEEN

NPR is still going strong, so each day, I stream the news from inside my office, eating tiny amounts of packaged snacks, feeding tuna out of the can to Larry. Riots in Canada. Argentina occupies much of South America. The Saudi royal family. I make one cautious trip to a convenience store on my third day down here, and don't go out afterward. It's mayhem outside right now. The Trump Presidential Tower looks from here to be covered on the outside with roaches. A Russian satellite fell into a residential area of Mexico, destroying four houses. China. Unemployment through the roof. Infrastructure crumbles, crumbles. Institutions vanish. War zones expand. North Korea. Warfwarf. North Korea.

All the wealthiest Americans abscond to fabricated libertarian islands in international waters. Massive tornadoes in Arkansas. Cockroach populations continue to explode, choking up roadways, overwhelming sewer systems, and, as I saw, coating buildings. Airports close as air travel halts entirely.

There are days during which Chicago's infamously eerie civil defense sirens sound off almost nonstop. The pitch of them is terribly creepy, as though the city is plaintively beckoning to some aquatic behemoth out in the middle of Lake Michigan somewhere, hiding. (Come out, come out.) On one occasion, I find myself listening to the odd dissonance in the sirens, listening for . . . I don't know. Patterns? Codes? The tones get worse as they go on. And on. And on. Even indoors they cut through the skull, and their disorienting warbles ebb and flow like madness, like grief. The sound fills me with a consuming sadness. At times the sirens seem to come not from the city, not from any one source, but rather from the air, from the fog, from the urban corridors, bouncing and echoing chaotically like the warning cries of a great invading evil. It's the music of aliens, these sirens, layers upon layers of wailing sounds designed to unnerve the populace, a hideous song impossible to ignore in its irregularity, and in it are voices calling to me and all with the message:

. . . *we are here . . . we do not come in peace . . . we mean you great harm . . .*

But that's just an assumption, because I only absorb the voices, I do not understand them. Get out of my head, I don't know your language. (And here, see, they've distracted me again.) I was saying: on one occasion I find that I've been sitting, staring, internalizing the sirens' call. At the time, I think that I've been listening to the sirens for a few minutes, but over two hours pass. I lose the time and start to forget where I am, forget where I could possibly be if not in my own nightmares. Where else could this cry exist? Why else?

A massive explosion devastates Los Angeles, all reports and details conflict with one another. No one knows.

Time passes.

The world changes.

I think.

About the wasteland.

About the bastion of cruelty.

About the Internet. Yes. Where society went to die. The Internet proliferated this feeling that nothing is real. Because online, that's true. Everything is a hoax. Even the hoaxes are hoaxes. If one was partial to conspiracies, one might think that the Internet was created by an oppressive regime to confuse us, crush our spirits, and drive us to despair. The Internet gives us unfettered access to limitless information, the vast majority of which is false.

There was a time when information was available only through a few narrow and trusted sources. The newspaper. The radio. Parents. Teachers. Perhaps your local government or your brand of clergy. And sure, you'd be lied to by these sources, but at least there was a single version of the truth most of the time, one story that was understood to be the accepted way of things. To overturn one of these truths was a big deal, it took a lot of effort and armies of support (or sometimes literal armies), a journalist, a whistleblower, some brave scientist to get enough people's attention and proclaim, "*What you've been told is wrong!*" risking scrutiny and exile and character assassination. For quite a long time, this was how it was. The Truth was the truth, or at least could be largely agreed upon.

Then came television, and with it footage, visual proof of horrors people hadn't allowed themselves to imagine. Now events would unfold live in motion, reporters' faces accompanying their voices while the storm raged behind them, bombs went off, scumbags caught in the act, tear gas resorted to, beheadings held in the town square. For those generations that grew up with live television, life progressed to the point where people were bombarded daily with tragedies, miseries, and strife. Warlords. Plague. Famine. Poverty. The Third World. War. When death and wrongs explode every day and night onto the receptors of your brain, they start to overwhelm them and turn the empathy off. The problems are too big. The suffering is too grand. There's nothing we can do. We can't grieve too strongly for the genocide in eastern Europe, because we suspected that all along. We've already grieved for eastern Europe. We can't be too shocked by the blast that destroyed the British Museum, because we always knew something like that would happen. We've already been shocked by the British Museum. I've heard old folks talk about the explosion of a shuttle called *Challenger*, something called the Branch Davidians, Nine-Eleven, an earthquake in Haiti, a tsunami in Indonesia, a tsunami in Japan, a tsunami in Portugal, how they watched it all happen live; and while they talk about these things, all I can think, all anyone my age can think, is "Yes, of course. These are the things that happen." And you can't care about all of it. One person can empathize with only so much, and when it's the world suffering, empathy is directionless and has nowhere to begin.

Three hundred held hostage. Wow. Scary.

Ten thousand dead. Oh. That.

The Internet came in and finished the job, like a filth-streaked raven snatching up a roach, flailing, backtrapped. The Internet slaughtered human empathy, perverted it, humiliated it, and turned it into something twisted and small, all while laughing and rising its own sea of devout worshippers. Because now, in the cloud, there are no human names or locations. Everyone is everywhere and nowhere. Uniquely faceless. A constant and unceasing avalanche of information, misinformation, disinformation, and fiction. No separating news from opinion, substance from commentary, fact from spin. The quantity won out—there is too much and it takes too much energy to take in even a minuscule fraction of it, so most people seek out only that which validates their worldview, making it harder and harder to nigh impossible to relate to, let alone empathize with, people of opposing or even slightly differing

stances. Our differences were entrenched, codified, encouraged. And here on the Internet, the worst of the brood are
at liberty to bash, slander, degrade, and threaten death upon
anyone who does anything—anything—and what place does
empathy have there? All creative endeavors, literary, scientific,
social, artistic, or otherwise, receive more scorn than they do
curiosity. The act of sharing one's self with the world is both
poison and elixir to the trolls. Give an interview? You deserve
to die. Publish a story? You deserve to die. Win a competition?
You deserve to die.

Don't make a film, especially not a documentary, and especially not if you're a woman, and especially not if you're pretty,
and especially not if you aren't.

Don't return home from the war, especially not that one.

Don't speak out against domestic violence. We'll punish
you.

Don't post a video of your child's first steps. We'll punish
him.

Don't run for office. Don't tell jokes. Don't open an ice
cream shop. If you do, you will receive death threats from
those who have only death threats left to give.

So then the question becomes, why do anything? The only
people who put anything out there anymore are the hoaxers,
and when everything is a hoax, we are asked—tempted—to
care about events that didn't actually happen.

And that's the last of it, the finishing move, the death
blow. What withering scraps of empathy the trolls leave are
devoured by the hoaxes. If we open our hearts and imagina-
tions to a story as it unfolds, we are almost certainly going to
be disappointed. We get excited about a new vaccine that isn't
real. We fear imaginary terrorists and the plans they are said
to have. We celebrate the finding of a lost child who is in reality still out there, alone. We become outraged at an injustice

that was fabricated in its entirety. (The White House stopped accepting petitions because too many were submitted under false pretenses.) We snarl at being tricked and fooled and say *"never again!"* but the information comes at us like candy, like salt, like needed warmth. We could wait for confirmation before we respond, but if we wait for the story to be confirmed, the moment has passed; we can never experience anything in the moment. Rather than allowing a torrent of woe to shut down our empathy, we instead accept that discerning what is real is impossible, and it renders our empathy hollow. Not to mention the fact that television and news editors are now doctoring every single photograph, video, and live feed we see so that we literally have no idea what we're looking at. It could be real, it could be invented in part or in full, the people seen on our screens may have, in fact, been nowhere near the event depicted, they may have been on the opposite end of the world, they may have been taken from other footage, or (as I learned from Emerald) they may be entirely invented people, not real in any sense, designed and constructed digitally, inserted into the real event to serve whatever purpose people on video serve. Or they could be real (they probably aren't). The media makers can make a bombing seem more dramatic, reduce gore, augment gore, make a person of interest more alien because it's scarier, or a celebrity look fatter because it's comforting, and they've gotten so good at all this that you can't trust anything you see, and you realize maybe you never could.

You hear a famous entertainer is dead. A guitarist named Scratch. A story is reported by a well-reputed news source that Scratch is dead. Floods of dismay and nostalgia. I'll always remember when Scratch . . . I first heard Scratch . . . Scratch made me the person . . . Never liked his music but one can't deny . . . Lost my virginity to . . . He was on when my . . . He'll be missed . . . Never be forgotten . . . We love you, Scratch . . .

Good-bye, Scratch. Later in the same day, a story is published by a less well-reputed but widely read news source, saying that Scratch is actually not dead. He's alive and well at his home in Washington. The death story was a hoax, we've all been had. Fans rejoice! He's even quoted in the story, addresses the reports of his death, has his typical dry humor, assures us he has many more years left. This story goes viral. You're a fool. You're so gullible. Read this. People don't just die, you fucking idiot. Why do you care so much, I used to like Scratch, too, but his music hasn't been that good for like fifteen years, so if he's dead who cares? Stop acting like you care. He's still a great guitarist, alive or dead. Then a third story. "Scratch Death Hoax the Actual Hoax, Guitarist Is Really Dead." Now an Internet search for "Scratch death" will return stories reporting his death, his not death, and his actually is death. People choose which story they accept, and the conversation becomes about who's lying, which source can be trusted, what's the real hoax, instead of, you know, that guy who's dead. Or not dead. We stop celebrating him, in the meantime. We aren't sure if we should be celebrating him, if he's alive we shouldn't mourn, we can't mourn until we know for sure can anyone prove he's alive I can I saw him at a cafe in Barcelona you're lying I saw his body he's dead no he isn't HES FUCKN DED AND MUSIC SUKSED ANEWAY YOU ALL DESREVE TO DIIIIE god I hope it's a hoax we can't lose him not now I can attest Scratch is still quite alive who are you I'm Scratch actually you can't be Scratch because Scratch is dead WAT R U GOEST DUDE you idiot ghosts aren't real I never died I mean I'm here NOT COOL DICK SCRATCH WAS MY FAV LOST AN AGNEL 2NITE ghosts are real I have proof ghosts aren't real click here it's not nice to play with people's emotions don't get hopes up let them be RIP SCRATCH hugs xoxo I'm not dead please stop perpetuating this story it's very bothersome to me and my family I hope you die.

The Internet will be made flesh and the hoaxes will walk among us.

The apocalypse appears on the front page of the *New York Times*. Bloody bodies in the streets, widespread destruction, an entire country's population wiped out. Just kidding, it's only marketing for a zombie-themed resort. But seriously, folks, twelve hundred dead in Egypt.

The trolls rose. The trolls ran for office. The trolls were elected.

And I start to wonder if I'm the crazy one. Maybe it isn't the world. Maybe it's me. Maybe I'm crazy for not seeing the glory of violence, the virtue of narcissism, the comfort of the abyss. Maybe I'm just an insane clown. I look around and nothing makes sense. Tragedy is weathered so easily, blame assigned so recklessly, humanity mocked so openly. I hear a news report about a nursing home shooting in Florida. Forty-one dead. The reporter covering the story says at one point that "at least two gunmen stormed into the nursing home and took a couple dozen lives." And I get angry, unaccountably angry at this. I throw everything I can get my hands on at the walls. Larry flees the room. I'm saying words but they aren't even real words. They're sounds, gasps, cries, coming out of me involuntarily. I hear the words "a couple dozen" and it just sets me off. A couple dozen. But it isn't that forty-one residents, caretakers, nurses, staff, and CURE sentries are dead that makes me angry—no. There's nothing to be done about such carnage, that's been made plain. The fury comes from the phrase "a couple dozen." Those are words that mean something. "Couple" means two. Not two-ish. Not two maybe. Not three or four, or eight. "Couple," the word "couple," means two. "Dozen" means twelve. "Couple" means two and "dozen" means twelve. "A couple dozen" means twenty-four. There is nothing else that "a couple dozen" means, and yet, here this man has said "a couple dozen" to mean forty-one. Like it's nothing. Like there's no difference. But there is a difference. The difference between the Truth and the reporter's convenient phrasing is exactly *exactly* seventeen lives. Seventeen lives that, somewhere in that instant, are not real. They are between existing and not existing. Real and fake. They are lives that are lost but that are not worth counting. And why? Because language doesn't matter. Language doesn't matter when laziness is easier. Language doesn't matter when hyperbole sells. Language doesn't matter when disaster is normal. Language doesn't matter when a civilian cruise ship is sunk by a botched military drill and hundreds die and the incident is described using the same words used to describe a poor fashion choice. Language doesn't matter when a professional football player assaults a referee and is shot dead by another official right in the middle of the game, and it's all shown on live TV even though they could have not shown it but of course they show it over and over, and the game continues, and the next day there's an earnest discussion about whether the incident disrupted "the flow of the game," and if the official who shot the player deserves any punishment, or if he's a hero, and how the dead player's team's postseason chances will be affected by his "absence." Language doesn't matter when the police raid the wrong house and throw a flash grenade into a baby's crib and in the media coverage there's more discussion about the word "flash" than about the words "grenade" or "baby." Language doesn't matter when chaos is entertainment and it is imminent and it is everywhere. Language doesn't matter when you forget whether yesterday's mass shooting was a mall shooting, or a college shooting, or an office shooting, or a bus terminal shooting, or a government building shooting, or a theatre shooting, or a church shooting, or a mosque

shooting, or a synagogue shooting, or a national park shooting, or a supermarket shooting, or a *quinceañera* shooting, or a
museum shooting, or a hospital shooting, or a zoo shooting, or
a stadium shooting, or a shooting at a Waffle House or a Burger
King or a Mother's Day parade, because really, does it matter what noun comes before "shooting" anymore? Language
doesn't matter when your country is at war with itself. And it
definitely doesn't matter when the rest of the world finds that
funny. Language doesn't matter when freedom becomes a trap,
a rusty umbrella for idiocy and arrogance. For meanness and
greed. Systems fall apart, roads crumble, governments dis-
solve, servers crash, all email is spam, all contracts are void,
calls are never answered, and no one believes us anyway.

Language doesn't matter because we don't want it to matter. We're afraid of what might happen if it does.

FIFTEEN

It isn't until the fifth time the phone rings that I allow myself to believe it isn't a mistake. The first time makes me jump, like it's some alarm I can't remember how to turn off. The second time, I panic that it's a raider of some kind, someone looking to loot the place. The third time, I worry that it is someone in trouble or desperate for a safe place, and that I'd like to help him or her or them but hesitate because I also don't want him or her or them coming up here and taking over. The fourth time, I'm too distracted by the inconceivable reality that the phone still works to answer it. But the fifth ring convinces me that whoever it is down there, ringing up from the call box in the lobby, does intend to be here and does intend to come in. If it was a looter or a squatter, they'd just break the front door down. It wouldn't take much, and no one would notice—the other tenants in this building have long since closed up shop.

I don't pick up on the fifth ring either. It's been such a long time since I spoke to anyone friendly, and I can't imagine that this is the person who will break that streak. I stand by the phone, staring at it. Five is a good number. A reasonable number of times to try something before giving up. The other rings had come at pretty regular intervals. The ring would stop, then twenty seconds or so, then it'd ring again. But as I stand here, at least forty or fifty seconds go by, and no ring. I know because I watch the clock. The second hand slowly drags itself forward. If it hits a minute, there's no way it will ring again, I'm certain of this. The next ten seconds go on for hours, but then I remember my difficulties with relative time even though I'm staring at a clock, and it should be easy for me to track time when staring at a device that tracks time, and we cross a minute.

Then, at the sixty-three-second mark, the phone rings. I feel a sense of betrayal. I answer, incredulous.

"That was long," I say, incoherently, my voice almost not working.

"What?" says the voice on the other end, frustrated and female.

"I mean, um . . . yes? Hello?"

"I have an appointment."

"You what?"

"Have. An. A-point-ment," the voice says, clearly articulating each syllable.

"You do?"

"Uh, yeah, I do. I made it like eight months ago."

"You have an appointment for . . ."

"Coaching. Guide me. Whatever the hell."

"Oh. Well that's . . ."

"I paid a deposit, man."

I pull up the calendar and leaf through the utterly vacant weeks and months that have passed by. Sure enough, when I reach today's date, there's a name shouting at me. *9am: Blank (F).*

"What's your name?"

"Madison Blank."

My heart leaps into my throat. *F* stands for "full evaluation," which is an all-day affair. I really don't have it in me. I cannot believe, whoever she is, that she kept this appointment.

"OK, yeah, I see your . . . appointment. Um . . . come on up." I hit the button to let her up. It is winter in Chicago, and a bad one. It is snowing. Last time I looked out the window there was a lot of snow on the ground, and a glance at the sky suggested more on the way.

Seeing nothing else to do, I go to the front door of the suite and open it. Immediately upon doing so, I see this Madison Blank, and she has her gun drawn. She's got it trained on me, and there's nothing in her face that tells me she won't use it. I don't put my hands up.

"You work here?"

"Uh . . . yes. Yeah. I do."

"You look like shit."

"OK."

"Rough morning or what?"

"A lot of 'em, actually. Yeah."

"Got some ID or something?"

"ID?"

"You don't look like what I expected."

"What'd you expect?"

"I don't know. Someone clean, dressed up, at least maybe a suit. Older."

"I haven't had a client in, I don't know, months. I kind of thought we weren't in business anymore."

"But you keep showing up?"

I don't answer. I don't want to tell her I live here.

"See an ID and a card?" she says.

"An ID and a card. OK."

"Yeah, show me that and I'll take this off you. Don't try anything. I'm a vet, man. I know a threat when I see it. You go back and grab a weapon and I'll put you down, believe that."

"I believe you." We stand there for a few tense moments, establishing a weird sort of trust. In this moment she keeps her gun on me, but I am certain enough that she is not going to kill me with it just yet, and she is certain enough that this isn't going to get stupid. Still, she needs to see the requested proofs. I back into the office and grab my wallet and a business card. I walk back out, with each plainly visible in my hands. I place the card in the billfold and toss it to her. She reads the name on my ID and on my business card, sees they match, then looks at my face and laughs.

"*Dude.* You really look like shit. You didn't even know I was coming."

"I guess I lost track of . . . the weeks, I guess."

"Yeah, well . . . this is the only day I got. Can't come back, so let's go."

"There's . . . you still . . . ?"

"Yeah, man, come on, I need direction. It's actually my uncle who wanted me to do this, highly recommended, said to find my path."

"I can't evaluate you."

"Can't? The fuck not?"

"I haven't . . . seen anyone in . . ."

"What? Fifty years? You said it's been a couple months, you forgot your entire job in a couple months?"

This takes me a moment. Could I have forgotten? Will I ever forget? When you do something so many times, it becomes as fluid as thought. But people forget things. People forget who they're married to. I sometimes forget my address. I don't have an address anymore. I remember my job, though.

"No, I guess I didn't."

"Then let's do this. Unless you're just too lazy, but I'll tell you what, man, if you turn me away because you're too lazy we're gonna have a problem."

"I really don't know, I mean . . ." I trail off awkwardly and stare at her. Glazed and dumb. I really can't come up with a good reason not to do my job today.

She asks, "You wanna get cleaned up or something?"

"Yeah, yeah, I think I will."

"I'll just wait here, right?" she asks, taking her outer coat off and throwing it down on a chair.

I go into my office and grab a toothbrush and a comb out of my drawer. I don't have any deodorant, which is too bad for Madison. I look around and it's a disgrace. It hasn't been cleaned in months. I flick the switch to my overhead light, and it doesn't work, but there's a decent amount of natural light coming in through the windows. Before heading back out, I decide to check my boss's office, thinking we can use it if it's in better shape than mine. I stand outside the door, and inside I can sense something. A sound like a light wind, or sandpaper being dragged across wood, forever shaving it down. I press my ear against the door, and it sounds almost like breath, gasping over and over. I place my hand on the knob and turn it.

When I open the door, it's like looking into another dimension. There are roaches literally covering every surface like dust. They're on the ceiling, the desk, the shelves. They fill every square inch with their writhing bodies. The windows are two gleaming amber rectangles that offer no view of the outside world, but that give off the quality of early light traveling through a tree's leaves in autumn. It's a peaceful image, conveyed by the most disgusting of things, and the disconnect makes me queasy. I mourn the room, as no one will ever set foot in here again. It is a dead space. And the roaches, they aren't leaving; when I open the door, hundreds of roaches don't pour out, but rather all the roaches in the hallway start making to get in. I peer into the skitter-scuttling madness for only a split second, but in that split second, I feel that I have glimpsed something I shouldn't have. Something of hell. I go to brush my teeth.

Before I go into the bathroom, I give Madison some paper-work to fill out. This is merely a formality, just something to keep her busy, because no one is ever going to look at it. When I give it to her, she says something about it being forever since she held a pen. She gets comfortable in a waiting room chair and gestures toward the bathroom. Now that her gun isn't in my face, I actually see her. She's probably about my age, possibly a little older. Ambiguous race, hair pulled back into a bun. Her physique substantiates her claim of being ex-military. I fill a cup at the water cooler so I won't have to use sink water.

When I finally see myself in the mirror, it's pretty frightful. I do look like shit. I don't have to describe it.

I brush my teeth and comb my hair. I splash the water from the cooler on my face. I empty my bladder. When I emerge, I am dismayed to see that Madison is already almost finished with her paperwork. I go back into my office and start pull-ing materials together. Personality assessments. Ability tests. Questionnaires. All of it meant to provide Ms. Blank with a satisfying career path that suits her. I take an empty binder and brush a few roaches off the desk. Her voice comes from right behind me, startling me.

"I'm done with this. Wow, I really scared you. Chill."

"I just didn't hear you."

"You don't really need my email, do you? I don't want to get a bunch of spam."

"I don't. And you wouldn't, but I don't."

"Cool, I'm gonna use the ladies' room real quick, b'right back."

She hands me her paperwork and disappears. The form tells me that her first name is actually spelled with two *y*'s.

Madysyn. Oof.

She ignored most of the other fields on the form; other than her name, all she filled in was her date of birth and job history. Her most recent job is listed as "UNITED STATES ARMY," and the nature of work reads "KILL BAD DUDES." In parentheses she's added "haha." Before that she was a nanny.

I could just leave. Right now. I don't have much here with me. I could gather it up in thirty seconds, toss Larry in a backpack, and go, maybe make my way back toward the old neighborhood and see if things have calmed down. Or go in a new direction entirely. Hell, I could just wander around for a few hours and come back later, and surely Madysyn will have left by then. (Right?) Another possibility would be to lock her out. I could lock the door, slide two hundred dollars under it as a refund of her deposit, hunker down in here, and hope that she doesn't go berserk and force her way back in. But then, I don't have two hundred dollars. And she definitely would go berserk, somehow that's a given. The thought crosses my mind that Madysyn might kill Larry. I have no idea why she'd do that, but I also don't know all the reasons why she wouldn't. I hope he stays out of sight, in any case. Knowing Larry, he will.

She returns.

"Guess I can just leave this door open? We're the only ones here, right?"

"Eh . . . close it," I say. No reason to buck procedure. Madysyn Blank sits in the chair across from me, and just as I start to speak to her, she fidgets and then pulls two guns out from somewhere on her person and lays them off to the side. I recognize one as being the one she pointed at me in the lobby. The other is somewhat bigger and has a laser sight. She puts them down so that the barrels are not facing me. A simple gesture that is incredibly meaningful and endears her to me in an unexpected way. Now she's comfortable, I'm comfortable, she exhales and nods.

"OK. Let's get started."

***

We begin with an interview. I'm not as sharp as I normally would be, though I'm not sure whether she perceives this. She doesn't know what I'm supposed to say, how this goes. I'm usually great at drawing people out and getting them to talk about themselves, their education, their experience, their goals. I listen and learn. Madysyn Blank is a unique specimen, though. She seems put off by (and skeptical of) most questions, even the most innocuous ones.

"Have you had any civilian jobs other than nanny?"

"Nanny's not enough? That's a hard job."

"I wasn't . . . I just want to know about the experience you have."

"I took care of a family's kids, and then I joined the army."

"In the army, what kind of skills did you acquire? Anything related to technology? Or problem solving? Executive leadership?"

Madysyn laughs as though I've told a dirty joke. I take this to mean that my question was either absurdly far off and she did nothing like that, or that it was absurdly reductive and she did nothing but that. She doesn't elaborate.

"Did you graduate high school?"

"Yeah, I graduated, I'm not stupid."

"Even if you hadn't, it wouldn't mean you're stupid. School's not for everyone."

"Yeah, I get it. No judgment, right? Everyone gets a hug and there are no bad choices? I graduated high school."

This goes on for a while; I try to get anything out of her that might help me do this job that I desperately don't want to do—that for whatever reason she's making me do—and yet she won't give me anything that would help me do it decently well.

After chatting pretty casually, all things considered, about how fucked-up the world is at present, thank you, and how bleak Ms. Blank's prospects are—her words, not mine—I decide to move forward with some personality tests. I start with a few of the less prying ones in my arsenal, the types of tests that get at work and environment preferences, introversion versus extroversion, and so forth. I'm not ready to ask her the more intense ones just yet, the questions like whether she gets squeamish at the sight of blood, or whether she values "justice" over "mercy." Maybe later.

I give her some skill tests. Typing skills, filing skills, computer skills. She refuses a composition test. She performs reasonably well at the tests she agrees to. Nothing extraordinary; she's competent. I'm shocked, however, when she agrees to take a vocabulary test. When I suggest it, she blows a raspberry but then says, "Sure, what the hell." As she starts in on it, I get up from the desk.

"Where you goin'?" she asks.

"I was just gonna give you privacy while you . . . do that."

"I'll keep my pants on."

"Oh, uh . . ."

"Least I can do."

"I'm just um . . . gonna get some water then."

"All right. You're coming back, right?"

"Of course."

"'Cause I got abandonment issues."

"OK. That's—"

"I'm faster than you."

"I'm not going anywhere."

She nods and then goes back to her test. I go out to the water cooler, get a drink. I stand in our lobby and just listen to the building. The lights flicker, like a giggle. It's quiet. I haven't heard the shrill tone of police activity in a while. Haven't heard gunshots outside. I refill my cup and head back into the common office. While I wait for Ms. Blank to finish her test, I pull up a news site. Drone strikes. Drone strikes in retaliation of drone strikes. Drones killing drones. I find a video posted from a source in the Russian Empire, a motorist's dashboard camera footage of a huge pack of deer seemingly committing mass suicide. They're all standing on an overpass, blocking the highway. Dozens of them. They stand about serenely, and there are no sounds in the video other than wind whipping, then a few sentences spoken by a few off-camera voices, in Russian. There are no subtitles, so I don't know what they are saying (a few commenters on the video claim to be "Russian language experts," "translators," and even "native speakers" and provide transcripts of what is said, all of which are wildly different, even from one "native speaker" to the next). The video is a solid three minutes of mostly motionless deer, who seem to be without a care in the world. A couple of bold motorists walk up to the deer and make gestures with their hands like "Shoo, shoo." One guy lifts his arms over his head and waves them around. Somewhere on the other side of the deer horde, someone lays on a car horn for about twenty seconds. Then silence returns. Again, the deer seem unperturbed. Then, without any warning, with no visible or audible provocation, one of the deer jumps off the overpass. Many of the people on the scene gasp. Some murmuring, concerned exchanges. Then a second jumps over, then a third. The position and angle of the camera makes the ground below the overpass invisible, but it's clear from the shouts and protestations of the people on the scene that the deer are most certainly jumping to their deaths. A fourth jumps, a fifth, a sixth. Now they're just following each other over, but not in any sort of rush or panic. Nothing seemed to startle them. It's like they're just walking up to a fence separating one pasture from another, and then hopping over. Easy. Now there's a steady flow going over the edge, and others just wait their turn. The camera zooms in on one of the deer waiting for his moment, and the video lingers on this close-up for quite some time. The look in his eye is something I'll never forget. A look of . . . certainty. The camera zooms in closer, and I see a reflection in the eye of the deer. A reflection of a person. I hope like hell that it isn't me, though somehow I feel that it is me. I am in the video. The deer is reflected in my eye, too. We see each other, in this moment before he jumps. We will always see each other just before he jumps. All around me I hear debris falling, the building settling, the humming of heavy machinery outside. I pause the video, staring at the deer eye. The cold, wet, black. Behind those eyes is a complex being waiting its turn to intentionally die. Before those eyes is everything else. I look closer.

"Hey." Madysyn Blank's voice comes at me from the doorway. "I'm finished with that."

I bite back disappointment that I now don't have time to watch the end of the video. (Or do I? No, I don't. Is that disappointment? I'll call it that.) There are other videos of the same incident, lots of them, taken from other cars' dashboard cameras, side-view cameras, bumper cameras.

I ask her, "How was it?"

"Fuckin' hard. Apparently, English not so much. What was the point of that?"

"To, um . . . see how developed your vocabulary is."

"OK, and so, why?"

"It's . . . important?"

"How so?"

"It's . . . useful . . . to have a command of language."

"Pfft," Madysyn says, "Language doesn't matter."

***

We get into some ability testing. This is where things have the potential to get ugly. Ability tests frustrate even the most composed people, because they aren't tests of skill or knowledge. You can either figure out how to do them and do them quickly, or you can't. They're like puzzles, deceptively simple but actually quite challenging. I hold a lot of tension in my body as I work up to this, fearing that if a test doesn't go well, Madysyn may very well reach for her gun, and I have no real clue as to where she'd point it. I check the corners of the room for Larry, but he's still hiding.

We start with some short-term memory tests, which she bombs. At one point she just starts to laugh. (Even her laugh says "Fuck this.")

Next we move on to some reasoning tests. Her performance on these tests really alarms me, making me simultaneously sad and terrified. On one of the tests she's presented with an assortment of ideas and concepts, and she has to arrange them in a logical progression. She can't get even the simplest ones. For example, there's one in which she's presented with tiles that say *cake, chicken, eggs, farm*. The correct order is *farm, chicken, eggs, cake*. (A farm comes first, on which a chicken is raised, the chicken lays eggs, eggs are an ingredient in cake.) The test gets much more difficult than that, but Madysyn Blank is hung up here, placing *chicken* and *cake* next to each other and hollering, "Chickens love cake!" She then places *eggs* and *farm* next to each other on the far side of the desk and mutters, "I don't know, it's an egg farm." When I tell her it isn't right, she says, "Well, fuck, I got nothin'." I encourage her to think about it, think through the problem, to which she picks up all four tiles and tosses them over her shoulder, stating, "That's done." She has this incomprehensible smirk she wears, impish eyes that make it impossible to know whether or not she's fucking with me, and if so, am I in on the joke? A few more tests yield similar results, and then we get to a relatively hard one. The tiles are *artist, brush, canvas, frame, gallery, inspiration, paint.* She puts *paint* first, saying something about paintball. She follows that up with *gallery: paint, gallery.* She stares at it as though it's the only thing she can come up with, glancing at the other tiles, breathing heavily. I cannot even imagine what's going on in her head. She chews her nails, brushes a roach off the desk. Finally she exhales loudly and picks up one of the tiles and holds it up so I can see it: *inspiration.* She says, "No idea what this is."

I test her numerical and spatial reasoning abilities. Both performances are quite poor. She struggles to get one single answer correct, even on the practice items. One of the spatial tests is a sort of 3-D puzzle that Madysyn cannot complete; in fact, she barely tries. But watching her attempt it is one of the most stressful things I've ever witnessed. She tries the same things over and over. She starts sweating and swearing. She stands up at the desk and piles the pieces into a haphazard clump that bears no resemblance whatsoever to the form I showed her at the start, saying, "That's not it?" She proceeds to throw the puzzle into the wall about nine minutes in, causing roaches to scatter. So she has virtually no ability to organize concepts, see patterns in numbers, or to visualize three-dimensional spaces. Memory is low. Vocabulary is low.

We move on to a test of inductive acuity, in which the tester has to determine a rule or common element that connects disparate observations. The ability is useful for diagnostics, investigation, troubleshooting, and research. She is presented with images and ideas, some of which have a connection to each other and some of which don't. She has to suss out what's connected from what isn't. I assume, given her military background, that this may be an area of strength for Madysyn. My assumption is wrong, though. Way wrong. Most of the time, it seems like she's guessing; there are items on which she states the connection she sees, and they are mostly far off. She stares at the test items as though they were pictures of tragedies, solemn events immortalized. She gets hung up on one. She stares and stares, leans in and scrutinizes each picture. At length she says, "Nothing's connected."

The only ability that Madysyn shows an exceptional aptitude for is one of the musical abilities: pitch distinction. In fact, she's off the charts on that.

We take a break for lunch. During the break I hop online and find that many sites aren't loading. At first I think maybe there's something wrong with my Internet connection; only, no, some sites do work, and quickly. Others are just . . . not there.

I can't stream NPR; its entire site seems to be down. I try to load a different page. Nothing happens. Another. And another. And another. The Internet connection has finally, it seems, been shut off. Dead roaches everywhere.

It is snowing.

SIXTEEN

I hold up a thick folder of papers for Madysyn to see. "Got some test results here."

"Let me guess, failed 'em all, can't do anything?"

"No, uh, that last bunch was ability tests, strength assessments; you can't fail tests like that. Just looking to isolate your talents."

"See what I'm good at."

"See what comes easily."

"Yeah, OK, got it."

"Madysyn, we're here to talk about what kind of work might be a good fit for you in civilian life, so we've got to think about the whole package. Skill, knowledge, experience, personality, interest, and this piece here: aptitude."

"Right. So how'd I do?"

"Just to be clear, this is only an indication of innate ability, not a measure of what you've learned. I have no doubt that you picked up some very valuable skills during your service, and when—"

"How'd I do, man?"

"You scored very low on most of them."

"Aw, fuck this."

"Now, that's *not* a bad thing, it's not. It's just different than, say—"

"If I was good at something."

"You are good at things."

"Other than killing people."

"It doesn't mean you aren't good at things, all it means is that—"

"I have no talent."

"No. Not true. There was one test that . . . well, there was one that you scored very highly on."

"No shit?"

"Yes, and that . . . well, it's . . ."

"What?"

"It's just . . . well, you don't strike me as a musician."

"OK."

"And you . . . um . . . it's just, I say that because one of your auditory abilities is pretty remarkable."

"My *what* abilities is *what?*"

"Auditory."

"Which is?"

"Basically, your hearing."

"Hearing."

"Yeah."

"Why'd you say, what'd you say about a musician?"

"You don't strike me as a musician."

"I'm not a musician."

"That's what I'm saying."

"You're not making any fucking sense. Who's a musician?"

"You have an amazing auditory ability, I mean."

"Which is hearing."

"Yes. Well, in a sense it is."

"I hear good."

"Your hearing is very sensitive."

"OK. Awesome. And I should be a musician?"

"The musician comment was . . . let's move past that, I was being glib."

"Glib?"

"I wasn't being serious. Or, I was—"

"I shouldn't be a musician?"

"I was oversimplifying."

"I don't have good hearing?"

"No, you do. You have a heightened ability. To recognize differences in sounds."

"Like . . . a musician."

"Well, sure. That's somebody who—"

"I sucked at piano. *Fuckin'* sucked, I mean really."

"Do you like music?"

"Do I like? No man, I hate music. Yeah, who doesn't like music?"

"OK, let's start over. What I should have said was this: you scored very high, perfect as a matter of fact, on the test called Pitch Distinction—"

"Which means?"

"That's what I'm—I'm trying to tell you. Pitch distinction is an ability to recognize very fine differences in the pitch qualities of sounds, noises, or voices. So yes, musicians would score highly but . . . OK, OK, let's say . . . I assume in the army you occasionally worked on machines?"

"What kind of machines?"

"Did you? Trucks? Tanks? I don't know, jeeps?"

"Jeeps?"

"I don't know. Did you work on anything like that?"

"Sure."

"I'll bet you could tell what was wrong with something by the sound it was making."

"Well, yeah, when something's fucked-up, you fix it, it's not hard."

"But I'm saying you could probably tell based on its sound."

"You listen to it and yeah, you hear something, and then you fix it."

"Not everyone can do that."

"Do what? Hear things?"

"Everyone can hear, not everyone can—"

"Deaf people can't hear."

"Right . . . well, actually a lot of them can, they just can't hear very much. But you, Madysyn. You hear more than even someone with normal hearing, is the point."

"Like it's freakish?"

"It's not weird, it's, it's special."

"Special's what they call retards."

"Oh, come on."

"Fuck you, man! Should I be a musician or shouldn't I?"

"Look, you have a peerless ability to hear differences in all types of sounds. You could use that. You should use that."

"Really."

"Yes. In sound engineering, podcasting, languages. You could use it in voice recognition."

"Voice recognition. Like for spying?"

"Sure, or whatever. When you have this, you literally hear more than other people do."

"I hear more than other people?"

"Think about it. Are you very sensitive to sound? Like changes in environmental sound, do they bother you? A buzzing light, noise from outside, train wheels are screeching and it's all you can hear? People with this ability find it can cause some distraction when—"

"You mean everyone can't hear them?"

For the first time, Madysyn Blank's guard seems to drop. She seemed to ask the question almost by accident. But she doesn't retract it. There's a change in her eyes, a curiosity sprung. When the words fall out of her mouth, it's like seeing a ghost. The hairs on my neck and arms stand up. I'm pretty sure I know which "them" she's referring to. I have this ability, too.

"No. Everyone can't. Most people can't."

"Can you?"

"Sometimes."

"I hear them all the time. I sometimes, man, I sometimes think I hear them, and I don't even see them. Like maybe they're hiding. I always just thought I was crazy."

"Yeah, I get that."

"There are a lot of them in this building."

"I know."

"Like, a lot. Like, more than other places. It's kind of driving me nuts, hearing them. Especially when we stop talking, like, man, taking those tests and shit when you weren't talking, that shit was the worst 'cause then I just hear them."

"Yeah."

"Like . . . I look at the walls and I think they move. Like . . . there's so many inside the walls they make the walls creep."

"What else do you hear?"

"I hear everything, man, I hear shit underground, I hear the wind, like how it's moving. I hear electricity, you know? Sometimes I think I'm hearing screaming, but there's no one around and it seems like . . . I mean you'll think this is like fucked-up or something, like I'm a dumbass and whatever, but I swear it sounds like the sky is screaming."

"I don't think that's fucked-up."

"You don't?"

"I mean, I do. It is fucked-up. But . . . you, I mean I don't think you're—"

"There's this day I remember all the time." She sniffs loudly. Takes a deep breath. "Two years ago, we're going door-to-door in this little Ukraini town, piece of shit, like no one there, we're looking for this guy. He's . . . well, never mind who he is, we're just looking for him, and we have orders to kill, just bang, on sight. And we're going door-to-door and you know, like, the locals hate that, so we're getting a lot of, like, little old women yelling at us and probably like putting fucking curses on us or something, lots of doors closed in our faces, lots of us trying like hell to speak to them in their language, and everyone's accent sucked except mine, so they kept making me talk to these fucking idiots. And everywhere we go, I'm asking, 'Did you see him? Did you see him?' and they're all, 'No, go away.' 'Did you see him?' and they're like, 'No one's here.' 'Did you see him?' 'Fuck you, devil,' and, like, yeah, I get it, if I was them, I'd say the same shit to me. But then there was this one house. We go to it and knock on the door, and this bitch opens it up and is all like, 'You're evil spirit' in her accent, and I'm like fuck this, you know? Like we're just looking for this guy, I have an order, I'm looking for him. And she says some Ukraini shit to me with this ugly-ass face like I know she's insulting me, and I say, 'Ma'am, if you aren't going to be helpful then go fuck yourself,' and this was, like, for her own good; like, if we didn't find this guy, they woulda sent drones in to bomb out the whole place, so really I'm trying to do something good here. But she starts trying to grab me, and her nails are long and dirty, and she's looking at me with these eyes that are just, like, sad and angry and kind of empty but also full of, like, I don't know, history, I guess. And I ask, 'Did you see him?' Nothing. 'Did you see him?' And that's when I hear him. It just kind of scrapes my ear, this sound, like a scratching, a rustling. Or not even, it's like a, like a, like a wave, I guess. No one else even noticed it probably. But I did. And I just know he's there. To my left. About twenty, thirty yards away. He's trying to slip out of the next house, knowing we'll be there next. And I turn, I put my weapon on him, and I tell him to get down on the ground. And he doesn't, of course, motherfucker, he takes off running because, yeah. Gets about a football field away from me when *pop!* Hit him in the heart. Or maybe like, near the heart. Anyway, he goes down. But even from a hundred yards away I could hear it. I could hear the exact moment. His breathing changed, weaker, wetter, his lungs stopped filling, his blood like in some places it sped up, in others it slowed way down, and that was—and his heart, whoo, his heart, that thing was going up, like, all out of rhythm. And, like, yeah, I shot him, so of course all that's happening, but it wasn't just that. I didn't know he was dead because that's what happens when you shoot someone in the heart. I knew he was dead because I heard it. I heard the last moment of his life. It hit my eardrums and I knew. And that was the first time I noticed it. The sound of death. Now I hear that shit everywhere."

"Everywhere?"

"Everywhere."

"You mean . . ."

"I can hear you dying right now."

In the pause that follows, Madysyn holds my eyes with her own, and I'm shaken by the sound of billions of legs and feet scuttling on rotting wood, on rusting metal, on each other. In this room. In the next room. In every next room. Everywhere.

Raising her eyebrows, she asks, "You hear that?"

"Yeah."

"You can hear them talking to each other."

"Talking to each other?"

"Yeah, well I mean not fucking English, no, but they talk to each other. You can hear it in the way they flick their little wavers."

"Their antennae?"

"Yeah."

"You can hear their antennae waving?"

"I can hear what's being sent."

"Sent . . . they're sending signals?"

"Uh-huh."

"I hear their legs. I hear movement."

"You gotta listen in between that."

"In between?"

"Yeah, OK, look. Look at me. We're both gonna be uncomfortable with this, but it's not like we have to hold hands. Look me in the face."

"Just like . . . make eye contact?"

"Fuckin' look at me. And listen. And concentrate. You're gonna have to block them out, just try to hear me."

We stare at each other. The roaches get a little quieter. Then a little quieter. Then Madysyn continues. "*All energy bounces and flows*," she says, softly.

"What energy do you mean?" I ask.

Madysyn smiles and shakes her head. "That's what I'm talking about."

"Huh?"

She laughs. Very clearly *at* me, not with me.

"Dude," she says, "I didn't say shit."

"When?"

"Just now."

"Sure you did. Or . . . what . . . you're saying you're telepathic?"

"I don't know what that is, but no."

"I just heard you."

"Did you see my mouth move?"

"I don't know. You're a ventriloquist then?"

"Don't be dumb. There was energy, I sent it, and you picked it up."

"You mean you thought something and I . . . heard some interpretation of it . . . in my head?"

"Look, I'm not here to explain it to you, especially because you already know what I'm talking about. I'm just saying they do something like that. They transmit. And they do it fucking constantly, like it's all I can hear sometimes."

She removes her jacket, revealing that one of her arms is cybernetic from shoulder to wrist. She takes a small tool out of her pocket and makes some adjustment to the machinery in her arm.

"That must have—"

"What?"

"Losing your arm."

"Hey, you know. Arm falls off. Just like anything else."

"I can't imagine—"

She points her gun at me. It feels different than the other time.

"You want a robot part?" she asks. There is feeling in her voice. In this moment she loves me. "I can shoot you in the knee, they'll give you a robot knee. I could shoot you . . . Ooh, I could shoot you in the eye. If you do the angle right, it won't even touch your brain. You could have a robot eye."

"I don't want a robot eye. I had a robot ear once, briefly, that was enough."

"Oh yeah. One ear. Look at that. Pfft. Never woulda noticed."

She lowers the gun.

"Are we almost done here?" she asks.

"Yeah, uh . . . yes, I guess we are. I, um . . . I'm sorry, can we talk about what just happened?"

"What just happened?"

"You read my mind . . . or you made me read . . . you have a gift—"

"No, man, I can't be in here anymore, that sound's driving me crazy. I need to go."

"Wait. I just . . . I need to go into the other room and . . . print out all the reports, the supporting literature."

"I don't need any of that shit. I just came here because my family was on my ass. And I learned I should be a musician or a spy, I get it. And I'm not creative and don't really like being in front of people, so music's out. And I'm sure the NSA can use some more spies, or CURE maybe, so I think I have a pretty clear path."

"Please don't be a spy for CURE."

"Easy for you to say, man. You got a job."

Got me there.

I heard that.

"It will only take a couple minutes for me to put everything together. Even if you don't want it right now, you might someday. And it's already been paid for, so—"

"Fine, sure. I need to wait in the lobby, though, there's too many of them in here."

As soon as Madysyn finishes that sentence, the lights go out. Not just in my office, but everywhere. Looking out the window, I can see no artificial lights on anywhere, in any other building. There is still sunlight but it's indirect (my office gets pretty dark just now). Madysyn reacts to the outage by grabbing her gun and turning toward the door. Clearly she thinks we're under attack. And maybe we are.

It rains. Lightning. Thunder.

The civil defense sirens come on. Hearing them, in all their disquieting strangeness, while standing in this dark room, ten feet from an unpredictable vet who's keyed up and ready to fight, I feel the sirens to be ever more pregnant. Harbingeresque.

"The fuck is this? Tornado?" she asks.

She steps on a cockroach and its instant death echoes in the room. She steps on another. She's got great boots for crushing cockroaches. There's a clatter from the next room. Madysyn flinches but in a way that isn't visible; rather, she pushes her energy into her legs and feet, grounding herself, and I feel the charge in the floor.

"Someone out there?"

I'm afraid to say anything, afraid to speak to her. I'm also afraid that the "someone" she hears is Larry. But I'm also afraid that it might not be Larry. It might be *someone*. And if it is *someone*, I must say it comforts me to be with Madysyn Blank. I surprise myself in feeling so. She puts me at ease. But it is not because she is armed, it is because she is aggressive, and decisive, and brave. It is not because she is armed. There are other reasons she makes me feel safe. It is not because she is armed.

Madysyn Blank looks me square in the eyes.

You hear that? You hear that? She's not talking about the interloper, she's talking about something else, something bigger, something Out There. She asks again, *You hear that?* I realize she isn't actually speaking aloud.

"I don't know."

She whispers, "Sometimes I can hear, fuckin', like, a breath, a rush, like a real deep breath comin' out of the whole world and it always happens right before . . ."

A woman screams. Outside. And up. Above us. Around us. Madysyn runs to the window and looks out and up, still in attack mode. I stand frozen. There are vibrations in the room.

She looks at me, wide-eyed. "It's not the sky, it's some fuckin' weapon I think; that's what it is, some scream weapon, meant to make you go apeshit."

"Well, don't go apeshit."

"This is fucked-up, man. Why'd the lights go out?"

"It's nothing. I think that everyone at my company is gone, but all of the accounting systems were automated so people still got paid, and bills. Maybe the money just ran out."

You don't think there are, like, Nigerians?

"I doubt there's anyone here."

As I say that, there is another sound, a thump from the next room. Madysyn trains her gun on the door.

"Make me, motherfuckers," she says—in fact, she keeps saying that. Over and over. "Make me, motherfuckers." *Make me, motherfuckers.*

"Madysyn?"

She turns on me, aiming the gun right at me. My heart, probably. Maybe my lungs.

"I think . . . I think it's . . . probably just my cat."

"Huh?"

"I think it's probably just my cat—"

"Who?"

"I have a pet cat. He spends a lot of time in the office over there. He probably just knocked something over."

"Well, one of us has to check."

I don't want to go out there alone. I want to follow her out there. I want to stand in her wake, be guided by her. But I'm legitimately afraid that she'll kill Larry on sight. So I must go.

"I'll go. I'll find him. I'll bring him back here."

"You don't carry? What if it's not your cat?"

"Guess I'll find out."

"I don't fuckin' understand people like you."

"I'll be quick," I say, to which she gives me a flawlessly indecipherable nonsmile. I don't know why I said it, "I'll be quick," as though I need to reassure her. I don't. First of all, nothing on earth will reassure Madysyn Blank, and second of all, if anything could, it would be nothing I could provide. So it's just something I say. For myself, much more so than for her. I'll be quick.

The interior spaces here are much darker than in my office. Much less natural light. Inky. I step into the hallway, until I cannot see anymore, until the dark swallows the light. Cockroaches flit about the boundary of the light and the dark, expressing themselves as a living edge to the shadow. I crouch.

I call to Larry. Not by name; I flick air through my teeth, producing a hissing half whistle. I repeat. I click my tongue. There is no response, no further clatter, no movement, no meow. I pat the side of my leg. Nothing.

I take a step, and then another into the darkness. The rain picks up, its force loud on the windows, filling the room with a sickening white noise. And the sirens cry on, that melancholy, mechanical keening.

This is the end. Don't look up. This is the end. Don't look up.

I bump into furniture, even though I've walked through this room thousands of times. I should know it, but its layout seems somehow different, the angles have changed, the dimensions of the desks and tables, the corners stab out, the floor sags. There is lightning. In between the lightning and the thunder, the lights in the office flicker. Under one of the desks I see what I believe is Larry's tail. I move toward him, listening for him. Is he crying? Is he OK? Whether it's the sirens or the rain or the sounds of the building humming all around us, Larry does not hear me when I approach. He does not look my way.

Another flash of lightning, and again the lights flicker, and what I see—it must be a trick. For a moment, it looks as though Larry has six legs.

I reach under the desk and grab him. He jumps out of his skin from the surprise, scratches me on the arms before settling the fuck down. I hold him close, and I can feel his rapid heartbeat. I stand with him and turn toward the room, and I get that nervous, charged feeling you get when you feel like you've been followed. A little ticklish in the face. Lightning fills the room again. There's no one here. I look back toward my office, where Madysyn Blank awaits. It's so close, I marvel at how close it is; on the way in here I felt I had traveled a mile in the dark. A mile, easily.

When I get just outside the doorway to my office, I see Madysyn. I don't know what's happened to her in the few minutes I've been gone (Or was it longer? How long has she been like this?), but she sits on the floor with her back against the wall. She stares straight ahead as she tears at the machinery in her cybernetic arm. She pulls at wires, she pries at joints, she yanks at its pieces violently. The wreckage is already strewn about, parts and connections scattered around her. Her hand is bloody from her give-no-fucks approach to the disassembly.

I want to ask her what's happening, I want to ask her if she's OK, I want to ask her why she's doing that and if it hurts and if it's the siren making her do it, but I don't ask her anything, because I've managed to spend the entire day with Madysyn Blank without setting her off, and I feel that my luck has run out. There's nothing I can say to her. But just then, she looks at me, her expression just as impossible to read as the girl in the blue coat's. She opens her mouth as if to say something, and I realize she's looking over my shoulder. I hear a growling noise. My body shakes and I lose all strength. Before I hit the ground, I see the CURE insignia out of the corner of my eye. Black. Old gold. Green boots. I know what it is: I've been shocked by a Growler. I'd heard of them, these CURE weapons that growl like a giant dog before delivering a debilitating burst of energy. Larry, too, is paralyzed; he can make no feline attempt to scurry away.

Madysyn looks me in the eye again as I lie on the floor. Her eyes are brown.

. . . nothing to see here . . . nothing to see . . .

My head is covered by a dark sack.

Another growl. I feel no pain, but I see flashes of light, wonderful shapes on the inside of the dark sack, and my head feels cloudy and numb. Before passing out I have a sublime moment of clarity in which I am able to appreciate the comedy in the number of times I have been knocked unconscious in the past year. I taste blood in my mouth.

***

I'm walking down Lake Shore Drive. The Outer Drive. It is snowing. There are cars abandoned all along the road. There is no one to be seen. I hear a cry from underneath one of the cars. I crouch down and there's Larry. I try to call to him, but his name doesn't come out right. He looks at me with suspicion. I make enticing sounds. He looks away. I move toward him, to pick him up, and he avoids me. He runs into the middle of the road, stopping and looking back at me in alarm. I take a step toward him, and he runs ten more yards down the road. I feel panicked that we're in the open, and if he wants to get away, he will. I try to edge toward him without scaring him, when I catch something in my periphery. Out over the lake, a storm approaches. A gargantuan black cloud rolls toward the shore, a green light glowing from within. I stare at it as it comes, and it seems to take the shape of a face. A long, gaunt face, with a thin nose, squinting eyes, stringy hair, its mouth gaping. The face cloud gets clearer, more recognizable, becomes sharper. A deep rumbling.

Then, closer, I hear a faint click, like a balled-up sheet of paper hitting the pavement. I look over and see a single cockroach, on its back, kicking its legs. Within the dream, I am aware that someone is watching me. Maybe the face in the sky. Maybe CURE. Maybe my parents. Maybe Jack. This someone who is watching me is watching me watch this cockroach. It is snowing. I am filled with dream-logic anxiety, as I understand that I am expected to pick this cockroach up and what? Put it in my pocket? Eat it? I walk slowly toward the roach as large, frigid Lake Michigan waves crash on the embankment. I stoop to get a closer look. I consider the imaginary lines drawn by the insect's six angry legs. I consider righting it. I consider stepping on it. Then, just behind me and to the right, I hear something else hit the ground with that same papery click. A few feet away. Another roach. The strange thing is that these roaches seemed to have fallen from above, and where I'm standing, there's nowhere for them to fall from. Unless . . .

A third, fourth, fifth, sixth, seventh, eighth, ninth, tenth, and eleventh cockroach fall from the sky. It is snowing. And that's when it begins in earnest.

Roaches.

Like rain, roaches.

By the thousands.

Falling. Falling.

The asphalt is covered in snow.

The snow is covered in roaches.

Skittering. Scuttling.

They get deeper.

Like water, roaches.

They rise and flow.

Before I know what I'm doing, I run down Lake Shore Drive as the roaches splash and skid off my shoulders.

I get into a parked car, to get away from them. Of course, they're everywhere in here, too. They tumble down the windshield. They patter on the roof. It's not much better. There's an umbrella on the passenger seat. They're in the folds of the umbrella. It is snowing.

Back outside, I open the umbrella and watch (and listen) as countless horrific insects sleet down on the vinyl, running off the umbrella and onto the ground. I head toward downtown, wading and kicking my way through a marsh of roaches crawling all over each other.

Then suddenly, all stops. The roaches stop. The snow stops. The sky darkens.

I look up and see the face, which seems to have twisted, but is still giving off an eerie light. The light grows. I hear a scream. That scream I've heard before. (I picture . . . nothing. This is a dream and I can't picture anything in my dreams. That fails. The dream picture of myself attempts to picture nothing and he both succeeds and fails. That, too, fails.) The scream goes on and on, and I'm crippled by it, held fast by it. I can't move until it stops. I stand there with my umbrella, as though an umbrella can protect me from anything.

When the scream ends, the dream gets worse.

When the scream ends, there is a penetrating silence that I feel like ice on my flesh. Then, in perfect unison, all the cockroaches spread their wings.

Sprinting, pitched forward, out of control, hurtling toward the lake in a dust storm of wings and legs and windblown snow, my own terrified moans sounding far away and like someone else's voice. This is the last I recall before plunging into the freezing water, and waking.

PART IV
After losing my job

SEVENTEEN

A cramp in my leg. I suck air through my teeth and rub my calf. I open my eyes and all I see is black, though I realize after a few seconds that I'm still wearing the dark sack over my head. I remove it, and see that I'm on the floor of what looks like a disused conference room. I have a roaring headache, that strange scream still echoing between my ears, clouding the edges of things. The ceiling tiles are water damaged. I prop myself up on my elbows. A water bottle sits next to me, unopened, but with a roach on it (on the side, not the cap, but still). The room's main feature is a large rectangular table, with mismatched chairs along its perimeter. I'm still wearing the same clothes, lying on a deflated air mattress. There are large windows, but most of the outside world is obscured by what looks like twisted scrap metal and rotting wood. The room smells like smoke and rust. The only sound I can hear is the buzzing of the fluorescent lights and an occasional structural groan that, if I didn't know better, might make me think I was in the bowels of a pirate ship.

The room has two doors. One of them creaks open, and a large black man in a too-small suit pokes his head in. Half of his head appears to be cybernetic.

"You're awake," he says. "Are you ready for your interview?"

"Um. Where am I? Where is—"

"We're ready for you whenever, so . . ."

"Did you say interview?"

"Uh. Yeah."

"Interview for . . . what interview?"

"The job."

"Where am I?"

"Bathroom's right out here in the hall."

"I'm . . . not . . . what's happening?"

To someone just outside the room, the man says, "Oh, you're here . . . I think he's good."

"Warfwarf?" says the person in the hall. The big man laughs and stands aside. A white woman in business casual walks in, a wide lanyard around her neck bearing a familiar seal.

She sits in a chair near my end of the table, a grimly vacant smile on her face. In her eyes I see nothing. She has a small scar on her chin. We stare at each other for a moment, and then she gestures to the seat at the end of the table.

I get up with difficulty, the cramp in my calf causing my leg to buckle. My knees and back pop like bubble wrap, and I shakily walk the three or four steps to the conference table. I sit in the seat, and dust leaps from it, floating all around me. I try not to inhale any of it, unsure of its composition.

She's middle-aged with an obnoxiously overstyled haircut. I can see from her lanyard that her name is Mary Kay Sutton. She looks at me with an awful smirk, patient, like she wants me to speak first. I realize at this moment that I must have terrible breath.

I don't speak first.

"Tell me something about yourself," she finally says.

"Tell you something?"

"Yep. Ready for ya."

"Like what?"

"Something surprising. Something I wouldn't guess."

"I'm sorry, what's going on here?"

"I'm from HR."

"I'm being interviewed for a job?"

"Yes."

"With CURE?"

"We call it the Coalition around here, but you got it."

"Why?"

"Hard to say, maybe people think 'CURE' sounds too—"

"No, I don't . . . Why am I interviewing for a job at CURE?"

I hear the skitter-scuttle of cockroaches. There's one peeking around from the back of her neck. She leans ever so slightly forward.

"Because we're hiring."

A knock at the door. The big man pokes his head in.

"Need anything? Water?" As he says this he sees my unopened water bottle, points at it, gives a thumbs-up. "MK?"

"I'm fine, Daryl. No, actually, Daryl. Daryl? An energy drink."

"No ice, right?"

"That's right." The door closes, and Ms. Sutton pulls out a briefcase, which unnerves me because I didn't notice her carrying a briefcase when she walked in. She opens it and pulls out a single sheet of paper. My résumé.

"We tried to call your references, but no one answered the phone when we called. All three. Are those organizations still operational?"

"How'd you get my résumé?"

"It was in our system."

"I'm not interested in working for CURE, ma'am, really—"

"Call me Mary Kay. Or MK, if you're feeling snazzy. I'm your team advocate, not your schoolteacher, so I won't answer to 'ma'am.' *Capiche?*"

"Where's Larry?"

"Larry? You met Larry? When were you in IT?"

"No, not . . . I mean Larry my cat, I have a cat named Larry."

"No pets in the Lookout, long-standing policy, not even any service animals. If you're blind, tough luck." She laughs a mean, impish little laugh. "Seriously, though, no pets; it can get pretty ugly, with the buggers I mean, you should see it."

"But what happened to him?"

"To who?"

"Larry. My cat."

"No pets."

"I understand that. I want to know where he is."

"I can ask around."

I imagine Larry snapped up in some cage somewhere in whatever building this is. "The Lookout," she said. What the hell is that?

Daryl returns with Mary Kay's room-temperature energy drink, and now that I see him fully, I see that his entire neck is cybernetic. A man who had his life saved by a 3-D printer. Who knows how much of his body is machine? (Maybe that's why his suit fits so poorly.) He places the energy drink on the table with reverence and walks out. The drink is called Be Free ("Be" being the brand, "Free" denoting its advertised sugar content). The can bears the CURE insignia. Mary Kay takes a long pull and swallows loudly.

I can't help my curiosity and I ask, "What's the open position?"

"Consultant."

"That's pretty vague."

"Highly specialized."

"Consultant on what?"

"R&D."

"I have a bachelor's in sociology."

"Perfect."

"What could I contribute to R&D at CURE? Don't you want an engineer or someone with a tech background or—"

"I'm gonna stop you right there. We have all the engineers we need; heck, it's right in the name of the place! It's what the *E* stands for!"

"Yeah, OK. While we're talking about the company name, actually, I've always been curious about something. Maybe you can clear it up for me."

"Fire away."

"Why is it called CURE?"

"C-U-R-E is an acronym."

"I know that. Coalition of United Response Engineers."

"Sharp guy. What's the question?"

"Is it engineers of a united response, or is it response engineers who are united?"

"That's the beauty of it. Works either way."

"Sure but . . . there's no such thing as a 'response engineer.' So it seems like maybe it was an invented term. So that CURE could be the name of the place."

"The name of the place?"

"They needed something to fit with those letters. Like the acronym came first, then the name."

"I'm not sure I follow."

"There's no deeper meaning to the name CURE?"

"CURE, it's shorthand for—"

"The simplest cure for anything is a bullet in the head."

At this Mary Kay freezes up, her lips tighten ever so slightly, tiny creases around her mouth deepen. She waits for me to continue.

I pause.

I pause.

I continue: "That's a quote from . . . oh, I can't remember who said it now, some lobbyist, maybe CURE's CEO, someone who says things like that. Anyway, I thought maybe that's why the company was called CURE. You know, because of how your sentries solve problems."

Mary Kay sniffs and stares at me, smiling. There's a little bit of panic I detect in this smile, a plea for me to stop being this way, for crying out loud. I expect the interview to end, but a moment later it goes on.

"What we're lacking right now is a certain type of person, someone who's autonomous but loves working in groups. Someone who's big picture but obsessed with detail. Open-minded and creative but craves systems and convention. A deliberate thinker who makes snap judgments."

"That's a lot of conflicting traits."

"We're looking for a dynamic candidate."

"And that's me?"

"Tell me about a time you had to make a really tough decision, and then—a follow-up—do you think you made the right decision, looking back?"

"I'm not really interested in answering your questions."

Mary Kay pulls out a preposterous handgun and places it on the table. I look at it, then back at her.

"I've seen a gun before, yeah."

"Rock and roll," she says, nodding. She turns the gun around so the handle faces me. I don't look at it. She goes on, "You can't work for the Coalition and not be armed, son."

"Lucky me," I say. It takes Mary Kay an unreasonably long time to process that I'm not going to pick up the gun.

"If it were up to me," she says, "everyone would have a gun. Not just at the Coalition but everyone, everywhere. No exceptions, you know? No option."

"What about people without arms?"

"That's what I'm saying. Make them get arms. Pass a law."

"I don't mean without guns, I mean without arms. Literal, like, arms. What if someone doesn't have arms, they can't hold a weapon?"

"Why wouldn't someone have arms? That's ridiculous."

"They lost them. In an accident. In a war."

"Then they get cyber arms."

"What if they don't want cyber arms?"

"You can't go through life without arms."

"I mean, you could."

"The technology we have now, there's no excuse not to have arms."

"So even if someone doesn't want new arms, you'd mandate that they get new arms."

"I would. It's an issue of public safety."

"So you'd require everyone have arms so they can be armed. In your America it would be illegal to be unarmed?"

"Yes, it would."

"And also to not carry a gun?"

She hesitates. She is not amused. She nods at the gun on the table.

"That's for you."

"No it isn't."

"It is, I've got all the paperwork."

"I'm saying I don't want it."

"It's a fine weapon."

"I won't carry a gun."

"Everyone who works for the Coalition—"

"I understand that."

"You're not gonna take it?"

"No."

"You're just gonna let it sit there?"

"Definitely."

"All right. Well. You will have to fill out some forms. No exceptions on that. I'll need a W-9, NDA, couple other things." She passes me a folder full of papers. "We'll have to try your references again, run a background check. You affiliated with any groups? Any antistate subversives? Friends with artists, or—?"

I just shrug at her.

"Ah, never mind, I'm sure it'll all check out. Welcome aboard."

Mary Kay puts a yellow slip of paper in front of me with a smile, then gets up from the table and trots out. The top of the slip of paper reads:

*****NEW EMPLOYEE IDENTIFICATION AUTHORIZATION*****

Daryl leans back in and smiles hugely. He appears to be sweating. "Come on," he says, "I'll take you up there." Daryl's got several cockroaches on him, like brown brooches. One crawls in and out of the machinery in his neck, which nauseates me, and my mouth fills with saliva. I consider swallowing it, but then I remember where I am and decide to spit it all over the wall instead. I then smile at Daryl, without bothering to wipe my chin, and I say, "Sounds great."

***

We head up toward the IT department; the whole way Daryl takes on the role of de facto tour guide. He keeps stopping at

odd times and pointing at corners and spots on the wall as
though he's trying to remember something to tell me about
that spot, and oh man, it's funny, it's a really good story, man,
if he could just remember it, smiling and pointing. But then he
remembers that he doesn't remember and we continue on. At
no point does he refer to a break room, or a bathroom, or an
exit. The hallways in this place twist and bend at sharp angles
like some hyperdesigned murder house.

We get on an elevator. At least that's what I assume it is. It
feels like we're moving up, but also a little sideways . . . maybe
diagonally. Daryl plucks a cockroach off of his chest and holds
it up, looks at it quizzically, tosses it aside.

"You're gonna have to have a weapon, you know?"

"Excuse me?"

"A weapon. Mary Kay said you refused your company firearm, and that's really not gonna fly around here."

"I disagree."

"You disagree? Everyone has one. Coalition policy."

"I'm aware."

"I'm saying you wouldn't want to be the only one. You
wanna fit in I mean, don't you?"

"You have no idea who you're talking to."

And I have no idea what I mean by it, exactly. I don't know
if he believes there's weight behind my pseudothreat (chances
are he doesn't). All I know is that it achieves my objective,
which was to get cyber-necked Daryl to stop talking to me.

The doors open, and we walk down another hallway. We
walk through an uncanny labyrinth of office space, all of which
seems warped or distorted, as though it's an office in a hallu-
cination. We go through so many doors, walk down so many
corridors, that at each new corner it seems impossible that we
have not yet arrived at our destination. Finally, down a short
flight of stairs, through a door to the right, up another short

flight, through a storage room, and down a ladder, we come to IT.

IT is one translucent pale white guy with a beaming smile. His name tag says *Lawrence*. On the desk in front of him, right next to a pile of lanyards, is what's known as a Woodpecker, a tiny, formerly banned automatic handgun that's designed to rattle off fifty rounds in half a second. It became a weapon of choice among suicides, and an ironic favorite among the anti-home-invasion set. (Ironic because, a few years ago, more people were killed in their own home by their own Woodpeckers than by any other gun. They were banned because too many people found it to be too easy to get fifty bullets into his or her spouse before realizing he or she was not, in fact, a burglar. But that ban was abolished because fuck bans.)

"New guy, huh?" says Larry, visible sweat on his forehead. "What department?"

"Good question," I reply.

"Leave it blank for now," says Daryl.

"Well that's an odd request, isn't it?" asks Larry. "Not protocol."

"It would be a personal favor to Mary Kay Sutton."

"MKS. All right. All right. I can make that happen. Tell her to stop down and see me."

"Later. For now, could you—"

"Yeah, yeah, sure, no problem, don't worry about it, it's all good, you name it. What's your name, chief?"

I tell him. He gets me an ID in about fifteen seconds, and I'm really not sure when my picture was taken or when I was smiling, but apparently both things happened because there I am, smiling in the picture. Although, of course, such things as smiles can be easily faked.

Daryl then takes me to an office space somewhere in the bowels of this place they call the Lookout, a windowless, humorless space. On my desk is an antique phone. By the wall is a filing cabinet. I walk over to the cabinet and grasp the handle.

"I wouldn't do that," Daryl warns, adjusting some mechanical part in his neck. There's a sound of pressure being released, like steam.

"What is this?"

"It's your office. Well, workspace."

"I still have no idea what's going on."

"You're working for us now."

"I never agreed to that."

"You either work for us here or you work for us out there."

"I don't want to work for CURE, period."

"Well, if you want to work at all, you will."

"Why was I brought here?"

"Not my role. They don't tell me that. I assume you're creative, or shrewd, or well connected or something. Smart, maybe. You have potential, I guess."

"Where is everyone?"

"They're around. It's a big building, so everyone's spread out. You can go an entire day without seeing anyone if you don't want to."

"Where is this, anyway?"

"The Lookout. Actually Coalition Tower Two, but everyone calls it—"

"I know, but I mean where is the Lookout?"

"Chicago, Illinois."

"But where? Where in the city?"

"The lake."

"Lake Shore Drive?"

"No, the lake."

"The lake . . ."

"Lake Michigan."

"What do you mean, 'the lake'?"

"I mean the tower is built several hundred yards out into Lake Michigan."

"I've never seen it before."

"It's pretty new."

"It doesn't look new."

"Best we got."

"In the middle of Lake Michigan . . ."

"Well, not the middle, that'd be ridiculous."

"What the hell is this place?"

"I think you should just get to work."

"I don't even know what job I'm expected to do."

"Someone will call you on that phone there, most likely. Oh, and sorry about the buggers. They're uh . . . plentiful down here."

Daryl leaves. I lift the phone and two roaches shoot from underneath. Man, they're fast. The phone is disconnected, or seems to be; when I take the handset off the hook, there's no dial tone. I look around the space, and there's really nothing to it. The kind of place someone goes to die.

All the offices are empty. In that way, it reminds me of my old job. Four walls and a door. Some don't have a door. Most are completely empty save some debris. In one room there's an old desk. In another, there's a broken chair lying on its side. Two legs are broken, and another looks splintered and ruined. My desk is out in a fishbowl kind of area surrounded by these empty rooms. There's no paperwork or anything left for me, no task list. No computer. Water drips.

I sit at the desk. I start to think about Larry and I wonder if he's OK. I wonder what chance a cat has in a world like this.

I ponder unfairness. Cruelty. I stare. Time passes. In the end, the phone rings, a sad, meaningless sound. I consider not answering it, but then, what the fuck else am I here for? I pick up the phone, and I say:

"No."

"No, what?"

"Whatever it is."

"Who is this?"

"I was about to ask you the same thing."

"You're that new guy down in the mail room, aren't you? Palermo or something? Plashenko? Boring down there, huh? We don't really get any mail."

"It doesn't look like a mail room."

"Well, right, we don't have a real mail room. Who sends anything in the mail? No one."

"So why have a mail room?"

"What company doesn't have a mail room? Gotta have a mail room."

"I thought I was supposed to be in R&D or something."

"That's right, there's just a lot going on right now, big re-org, lots of . . . You know what, I hate talking on the phone, I'm coming down there."

Whoever it was hangs up. I hang up. I go to the filing cabinet. The one Daryl warned me away from. I can't imagine why I'm not supposed to touch it or open it or whatever. If it's so special, its contents so sensitive, why on earth would they toss me in here with it? Why leave it sitting around? Are there honestly paper files in there? He might have just been messing with me. I reach out for the handle of the filing cabinet, and as my fingers touch the metal, a cockroach lands on the back of my hand. I jump back and flick it away.

Someone approaches.

"Hey."

It seems ludicrous to me that such an inane, casual word could be uttered in a setting such as this. As though everything is fine. I'm looking at a small man of mixed race, very well dressed.

"They give you anything to do?"

"Not even a little."

"Did you open the cabinet?"

"Um . . . no."

"Yeah, that's probably better anyway. Who did your onboarding?"

"What?"

"Was it Mary Kay? She's something, isn't she?"

"Who are you?"

"I'm Kevin."

"Oh, sure. Kevin. Why not?"

"What's your name again?"

"It's Palermo. Or, like, Plashenko or something."

"Palazzo. That Mediterranean?"

"Listen, Kevin, I have no idea who you are or what this place is or what I'm doing here, but I woke up here and nothing's making any fucking sense, and I know that's the world now, but I wish someone would just tell me what CURE wants with me and where my cat is, my fucking cat, his name is Larry and I don't know where he is and I don't know if Madysyn was killed or if she was just left in my office but I'm sick of this shit, I'm sick of everyone I meet being killed or fuckin' spirited away or whatever the fuck is happening to them, and being lied to about everything, and Daryl said something about the building being out in the middle of the lake and I have no idea what the fuck that means, and besides all this *I don't want to work for a company I hate.* I don't know how I can make that any clearer, but no one cares, I'm just supposed to work for a company I hate because I'm here and you're here and there's an opening and I'm just supposed to take it and be glad that they'll have me, and that's fucked-up, and are we seriously in the middle of the fucking lake?"

"Yeah, we're in the middle of Lake Michigan in a tower made of gunmetal—pretty sweet, right?"

"Fucking what?"

"The Coalition built this tower out of repurposed gunmetal. It's way better for the environment than just throwing them in a landfill somewhere."

"The building is made of guns?"

"The exterior is, anyway. I have no idea how it was put together or who the architect was or anything. I know, right? Bad Chicagoan. I should know the architect. The whole enterprise kinda sprang up overnight. Like the Look wasn't here, and then it's as if the Coalition thought, 'I need a new headquarters,' and boom, up went the Look. I've heard somewhere that the building was made with a giant 3-D printer."

"That was creepy."

"What was?"

"You referred to CURE as an 'I.'"

"Oh, that's just easier than, well, you know. Anyway, yeah, pretty incredible structure. I heard it broke records for, like, speed of construction and it's now the tallest building in North America."

"Huh?"

"Yeah. It went up so fast that a lot of people thought it was, like, some kind of weird act of God or something. Actually, if you're on one of the higher floors and you look toward the beach, you can see just, like, hundreds or maybe thousands of people gathered to, like, worship or bask or whatever, it's crazy. They, like, march around and chant. Really odd, but I try not to judge."

"Who are you?"

"Kevin; I told you that. Kevin Grimmy. I work up in Marketing."

"What do you do, exactly?"

"Oh, you know, it's what you'd expect. I provide support and solutions for our international clients. I speak nine languages."

When he says this, his eyes momentarily look like a snake's.

"'Support and solutions'? What does that mean?"

"They didn't give you anything to do down here? Just dumped you off and said 'good luck'?"

"No one said 'good luck.'"

"Well, we've got a spot open in Marketing. You should follow me up there."

"I think I'm supposed to be in R&D."

"Yeah, thing is, there's a new director of R&D, and it might be a little while before they get their shit together; and in the meantime they'll just leave you rotting down here, might not even feed you. Anyone show you to your apartment yet?"

"My what?"

"Well, yeah, you'll have a living space out here. Everyone does."

"I can't . . . go back to shore? I'm stuck here?"

"There's no reason to go to shore, and be with those crazies? Everything you need is here. And then the commute is super short. Isn't that what everyone wants? To wake up and already be at work?"

"Absolutely not. No."

"Well, I'll take you up to the Residences, we'll figure it out for ya. And then we'll go to Marketing and you can settle in there until R&D figures out some way to use you. Whenever that is. Come on."

I look around the room, and the cockroach population in here has grown since I arrived. They're crawling all over each other everywhere the floor meets the wall, the wall meets the ceiling, the walls meet the walls, the walls meet the walls. I have no real choice but to go with him.

"I won't be in trouble, for leaving here?"

"Ha! Trouble? No way. No one really needs to be down here. Mary Kay just puts people down here when she's not sure where else to put them. She's not very creative that way. New guy? Mail room. Just a knee-jerk thing. Really, we can find a much better place for you."

I follow Kevin. He takes me up many floors. He shows me the marketing department, which is him and roughly forty other people. Everywhere I go in the Lookout, I expect to see thousands of people. CURE's reach is society-wide. Worldwide. CURE seems to have its fingers in every industry. Seems to influence every aspect of daily life. So I always assumed it had thousands upon thousands, maybe millions of employees.

After introducing me to many people who have dubious job responsibilities, Kevin takes me to the housing office to get information about my apartment and get a key-card. There we talk to a guy named Lawrence. (But it's not the same Lawrence as in IT. This is a different Lawrence. Lawrence is a common name.) Kevin then takes me to the Residences.

The Residences are where the entire staff of CURE lives. The floor he takes me to is basically a long hallway dotted with doors every few yards. We get to my apartment, and Kevin slides the key-card in the door for me. He tells me to go ahead and drop my stuff inside, even though I'm empty-handed. Maybe he is joking. I'm not sure anyone in the Lookout has a sense of humor, is the thing.

The apartment can't be more than four or five hundred square feet. It's almost like a carpeted and minimally furnished jail cell. He mentions that no one has yet lived in this unit, though you'd never think that from the look of it. The room is dingy and discolored, though surprisingly roach-free. The

size of the bathroom is comical. Kevin remarks that not everyone has his own bathroom; there are some floors that share a
bathroom. I'm lucky, in other words. I'm very lucky. I should
be thankful.

Kevin tells me I should just take the rest of the day off and
go ahead and settle into my new living situation. "Explore your
new domicile," he says.

"I have a question for you," I start, as he leaves.

"What's that?"

"I had a cat. When I was brought here, I had a cat. I haven't
seen him. Do you have any idea where he'd be? Is there an animal control office or anything? A vet?"

"Sorry, buddy. Can't help you there. Never heard of an animal in the Look. Other than, you know. But they don't count."
Kevin leaves.

I sit down on the bed. And this is a moment. It's one of
those moments in my life in which I feel like I want to cry,
but then I realize crying would be superfluous. From the room
(or the residence) below me I hear a hammering, like someone
driving nails into their ceiling/my floor.

As night falls, I hear a faintly melodic drone through my
window, coming up off the water. The chanting. I don't sleep;
instead, I listen. Outside, I can hear the wind singing and gulls
calling. I can hear Lake Michigan lapping at the tower's gunmetal exterior. I can hear the sun setting and the clouds as
they move across the atmosphere. I hear the sighing of night
approaching, and the imaginary sound of now-absent airplanes. I can hear the cockroaches in the building; I can tell
there are a great many, an uncountable sum, especially in the
lower levels, as though they, too, make up the building's structure. As though they, too, are of the foundation on which freedom, as we know it, is built. And I hear pain. In the chanting
voices. In the sky. In the water. I hear pain. I keep listening in

the hallway for the sound of Larry's claws clicking on the floor, but I never hear them.

In the morning, the sounds of imaginary planes become the sounds of real planes. Fighter jets. I wander out of my residence and find Kevin Grimmy. I ask him if he heard the jets (there was no way to miss them) and if he knows what's going on. He says, "Oh, it's the Air and Water Show."

It's hard to believe the Air and Water Show still happens, but Kevin tells me something I didn't realize, which is that CURE is a silent partner of the Air and Water Show, and has been for years. I kind of can't believe I hadn't assumed that; the Air and Water Show is an obscene demonstration of military prowess, weaponized engineering, pyrotechnics, and boastful showmanship, which puts it right in line with CURE's values.

"Wait . . . the Air and Water Show?"

"Yeah."

"This time of year?"

"Sure, why not?"

The jets screech past, their sound like the air itself ripping apart, peeling back. They roar the same as they would over a war zone, because planes aren't emotional. They sound like missiles. They sound like doom.

Kevin walks me up to a small cafeteria of sorts. There's no staff or kitchen or anything, just vending machines. He says, "It's all free," and I want to remind him that nothing is free, *nothing is free*, but I don't. I notice that CURE's insignia appears on the packaging of all the food and drink that comes out of the machines.

"They even got special labels, huh?"

"Well yeah, but that's not just a label. This stuff's all made by the Coalition."

"CURE makes food?"

"The Coalition makes a lot of food. A lot of the stuff you buy at the grocery store comes from Coalition farms."

"CURE farms?"

"You didn't know the Coalition ran farms? Seriously?"

"How would I know that?"

"Just figured it was something people knew."

Kevin lives here. He knows things. I can learn things from him. He never leaves. No one who lives here ever leaves. I live here now. I'm never leaving.

Maybe I'm being dramatic. Maybe I'll be able to leave. Maybe I can refuse to work and get thrown out into the lake. Maybe I'll find my cat. The thing is, while I'm in a place that absolutely freaks me out, my curiosity is too great to consider escape. Plus, if I try to escape, they'll kill me. I'm probably far safer in here than I am out there.

Kevin is now talking about CURE's various operations: law enforcement, homeland security, defense and private security, agriculture, aquaculture, healthcare, pharmaceuticals, energy, the financial sector, education, science and technology, urban planning, transportation, textiles, emergency services, entertainment, and, of course, public policy and jurisprudence. Kevin adds that "those last two are areas where the Coalition operates, but they aren't really industries, of course." I laugh, perceiving this to be a joke. But he isn't joking. Kevin then just starts listing corporations in all sectors, as well as brands, products, services, firms, and municipalities that are owned and operated by CURE. If I take him at his word, the scope of this knowledge is terrifying, and yet not surprising; still, I don't know if I can entirely believe him.

He leans closer and grins as he says, "You wanna know the real kicker? I bet you didn't know this: The Coalition is technically a not-for-profit. Isn't that great? One of the wealthiest, most powerful organizations in the world, and we're tax-exempt. What a country!"

He takes me up to Marketing. The energy is low, the lighting is dim. There aren't a whole lot of people here, fewer than yesterday. He says he has to make a couple of calls, but in the meantime he gives me a task to complete. He wants me to explore video content sites and search for videos that don't contain any "Coalition points," meaning he wants me to find videos in which there appears no image, no signage, no word or mention of any CURE product or subsidiary. (I'm provided with a sprawling list of every CURE product and subsidiary to check against.) If I find any, I'm to bookmark them and keep a register as I go. "You won't find many," he says, at which I scoff, because there's no way I'm going to do work while I'm here. But after I sit idly for a minute or two, my incredulity takes over. What he said can't be right, there's measureless content online—surely most of it doesn't reference CURE. So I decide to look.

And he's right.

In every video I watch, at least one Coalition point appears. In this video of a cat, there's a can of cola in the background made by a CURE company. In this how-to gardening video, the gardener is wearing an apron with the logo of a CURE company. In this video of a deadly car crash in France, there is a billboard in the distance advertising a CURE product. In this video of little kids dancing in their yard, the car parked in the driveway behind them is a CURE-made model. In this video of a beached whale dead on the coast of California, there is a wrapper of a candy bar made by CURE. In this video of a police chief giving a statement about an incident in which one of his officers shot an entire unarmed family, seemingly without provocation, and then that officer was cleared of any wrongdoing, and there was a great deal of outrage in the community, and so the chief is giving a statement to try to quell the situation before it erupts in violence, there is a woman standing behind him holding a bottle of water carrying a CURE brand. Oh, also his gun is CURE.

I pull up the video of the kids exploring the Polish sanatorium. CURE brands are all over it, on nearly every supply they have.

I realize after I've been doing this for some time that I don't actually know why they're having me do it. Do they just want to track how omnipresent they are? If there is a video in which a Coalition point does not appear, do they somehow modify it? Or suppress it? Do they hire trolls to flame it? I'm at a loss as to the point of this.

I do, however, start to worry that Kevin Grimmy is going to come back and I'm going to have nothing to show him. He's walking toward me now. So I pull up the one video I can think of in which no products of any kind appear. The girl in the blue coat.

"Hey man, find anything good?"

"You're right, I couldn't find much, just this one." I show him the girl in the blue coat, I don't mention that the video was completely fabricated by Emerald's friend Pedro and that her hair took weeks to animate. Kevin nods and says, "Yeah, that one's pretty clear, except for one thing."

"What's that?"

"Her coat."

"What about her coat?"

"It's Liberty Blue."

"Oh, what, that's the brand name?"

"No, that's the color."

"That color is called Liberty Blue?"

"Yep."

"OK, so what?"

"The Coalition owns it."

"Owns what?"

"Liberty Blue."

"CURE owns that color blue?"

"Sure does. Good job, though. They might want to have another look at this." I don't get to ask what that means.

Kevin walks away and doesn't instruct me to continue that same task, so instead I just start reading the news. This is, of course, a mistake. Giant wasps. Civil war in Spain. Hurricanes pummeling Australia and New Zealand. Reptilian flu. Riots in Montreal. Massive flooding in Mexico City. The Academy Awards are next week. Ebola. Superstrep. Cockroaches overrun a subway system in Japan. Medical clinics sacked and destroyed by warlords in West Africa. Twenty-one nuclear weapons "misplaced" by Israel. I stop reading the news.

Kevin comes back and launches into a rant about one of his accounts, some financial consulting something or other. I can't even tell what his client does, let alone what Kevin does for it (or therefore, what CURE does for it, or if this is a company that CURE owns or what). Blah blah blah's not how it's done. Blah blah blah's the bottom line, ya know?

His rant somehow takes him to Portland, Oregon, which I guess is something of a dirty word around here because Portland is one of the only major cities in the country (the biggest city, certainly) where CURE has not managed to become the dominant law enforcement. They rely on "standard police" he says, with a bitter face. I comment reflexively that I get it, that I understand why people would want their local police instead of CURE. This was the wrong thing to say. Kevin looks at me as though I just told him his baby is ugly, and then he lays into me:

"The police? You trust the police? Do you even know what you're saying? The police? The Coalition is the police. Haven't you heard anything I've said? What used to be called 'the police' in every city, town, and village in the US is now operated by the Coalition. What you call the police now, who you call the police—they're practically volunteers. Hall monitors. They have no real authority, you need to get that."

"But CURE is a private corporation."

"Yes, and?"

"And paramilitary."

"Your point?"

"The police are neither."

"OK. That's . . . I understand what you're saying. Or what you think you're saying. But it's a fantasy, OK? You're thinking of the old 'serve and protect,' but that's a throwback. The real police became a combat outfit a long time ago. The people you're talking about, in their blues with their pathetic excuses for guns and ancient codes and protocols, you think they can protect you? You think they can do anything? They're practically ceremonial. Empty vests. The DoD and Homeland Security turned all of the real police into soldiers, just supplied them and trained them up. Long time ago, actually, so the people who are 'police' now are all replacements, and shoddy ones, mostly. Who you call 'CURE,' the sentries, those guys armed to the gills, flexing on top of tanks, gassing crowds, shooting anything that moves—those badasses? They're the police. The true police. They just go by a different name now."

Everything that he's saying makes sense, though I don't want it to. I don't respond or interject, because as he's been talking, his fingers ever so lovingly graze his own handgun, holstered there on his hip. Kevin Grimmy has been nice up until now, but I don't think I should challenge him.

But then I think: Fuck that. I should challenge him. So I don't even think too hard about it, I just say the first thing that comes into my head, which is:

"CURE sentries are the worst human beings on earth."

Kevin looks genuinely shocked. "Whoa. You can't say shit like that, man."

"I did say it, and it's true. They're the worst people. They're actually hardly even people. They're really more like vomit. But only if the vomit doesn't have anything good in it."

"Shut the fuck up, man, someone will hear you. I can hear you."

"Actually, CURE sentries are like cancer. They'll either kill you or someone you know. And everyone hates them."

This gets the gun drawn.

"Get the fuck out of here saying that shit."

"Where should I go?"

"I don't care, you piece of shit. That's what I get for investing in you. Shoulda known you were fuckin' crazy."

I leave Marketing as Kevin holds me at gunpoint, repeatedly calling me an asshole and a fucker. He shoves me into the hall and slams the door behind me. That got bad fast.

. . . nothing to see here . . . move it along now . . .

In the hallway, there is a powerful draft, as though a gaping hole has opened in the side of the building. There's no one in the halls. I start walking in the direction of the draft. I pass several office suites, most of which appear to be empty. None of them have signs indicating what kind of corporate activity might have been done within when they were occupied, if they ever were. One room has a big pile of cybernetic parts in the middle of the floor.

Jets scream past, shaking the building. I wonder if the tower worshipers on the beach pause their chanting to watch the Air and Water Show, or if they just chant right under it. I find a window and spot the jets, flying in formation over the beach. I feel almost certain that one of the jets is going to lose control and crash into the beach. One doesn't, but I felt almost certain one would. And that's not nothing.

The jets fly off far to the north, and the skies quiet. There, in the new silence, I hear an unmistakable sound. The mew of a cat. I look around, having definitely heard it, but I can't quite place where it came from.

Again. It comes from a narrow corridor to my left. I go. I hurry.

The corridor is long and unbroken. No doors, no turns. As I trot down the corridor, I hear the mewing twice more. I'm going the right way. At the end of the corridor, expecting to find Larry or maybe a room of some sort that I could search, I instead find a freight elevator. I open the heavy doors and step into the carriage, surrounded now by thick air that reeks of gunpowder and body odor. I close the doors. I hear the mewing again; it seems to come from below. There's only one possible destination, reachable by the pressing of a large yellow button. I push it with my thumb, needing to use all my weight to depress it. There is a brief, abrasive siren coupled with a loud and immediate thrumming, the entire thing shakes and vibrates miserably. Then, slowly, as though having first to remind itself how to work, the elevator starts to descend.

The descent feels quite long. Quite long. Far longer than any elevator ride should be. I wonder if it will ever end.

When the elevator stops, I can hear activity on the other side before the doors open. It sounds like an industrial plant, like countless machines at work, pounding, ringing, rattling, whirring. When the doors actually do open, I'm met with a sight much worse than any factory.

Cockroaches. And I won't even try to describe the number. This is certainly a case in which language doesn't matter. It not only doesn't matter, it's useless. There is no number I could guess at, no metaphor I could use, no astronomical term that could possibly describe it. They defy quantity, they are count-less. Literally countless. Any attempt to count them would be futile in perpetuity. Because, as panicked as it makes me to acknowledge, they are not regular cockroaches. They are the cockroaches you see anywhere and everywhere, but they are not regular cockroaches. They are duplicates. And they are duplicating. In this room, the cockroaches are replicating themselves on what appear to be thousands of 3-D printers. Only, I can't quite tell, as my overwhelmed eyes try to take in this horrid facility, if the printers are mechanical or if they are somehow . . . organic. They seem to be made out of roaches. Roach parts. The sound of the many, many, many, many legs is deafening, like standing by a waterfall. That fails. Like staring down an avalanche. That, too.

They are infinite. The printers never stop. Each one can put out a new roach every few seconds. Times the number of sec-onds in a minute, minutes in an hour, hours in a day . . . they're probably making new printers, too.

I watch one of them make eight or ten roaches from start to finish. They look like plastic pieces at first, then, in an effi-cient frenzy, they are bent and twisted into a fully and imme-diately functioning arthropod. They stream forth from the mouths of the printers at revolting speed, antennae waving, skitter-scuttling.

I remember what Madysyn said, about the way they com-municate with each other. The energy they send, its bounce and flow. I hear it in my mind. Like shouting. Like hissing. Like crying.

I sneeze.

When I sneeze, for just a second, all the roaches in the place stop moving. Somewhere, at the far end of the massive space, I hear it again. The mewing. I can't be sure that it's Larry.

But I can't be sure, either, that it isn't. I stay on the elevator, unable to move.

The carriage shakes and rattles and the heavy doors slam shut on their own. It starts to rise. I see now that dozens of cockroaches got in while the doors were open. Suddenly, *dozens* of cockroaches seems quaint. Manageable, when compared with infinite. The trip back up seems much shorter. When the doors open again, a young, small-of-stature Asian American woman stands there with a clipboard and a bewildered look.

"What the—?"

"Oh . . . hi."

"Who are you?"

"I'm from . . . the mail room."

"What's your name?" She grabs my lanyard. "Palazzo. Oh! Hey! You're the new guy! You were supposed to start yesterday."

"I technically did start yesterday."

"Aren't you supposed to be in R&D? I was told we had a new guy with a weird name, that's you, right? I can take you, but, um—what the heck were you doing down there? You're not supposed to be down there!"

"What was that place?"

"I'll explain on the way, you dope. You could get in giant trouble down there. Like, *huge.*"

She closes the doors of the freight elevator and turns to go.

"Oh. You mean you don't need to go down there?" I ask.

"No, God no. I was just walking past and I saw the elevator was out of position so I called it up. You're really lucky actually, that I came by when I did, and also that it wasn't someone else. I won't tell on you, but most people probably would. That place is super off-limits."

"I heard my cat down there."

"I can pretty much guarantee you didn't. Also, you have a cat? Since when can we have pets? Did you have to negotiate that?"

We start along a completely illogical and serpentine route, similar to the one I followed Daryl on yesterday (that was yesterday?). I can't believe that anyone can get around this place. It seems as though its layout spontaneously changes. I ask her what her name is.

"One of my names is Shea. The other is Flannery. I'll let you ponder which is first and which is last."

I do ponder it, silently and briefly. I ask her some other questions, and learn that she is twenty-three years old, and that she works in R&D with a division called Silent Weapons. She makes several more references to how lucky I am that she retrieved me from the lower level when she did. She has a funny little nervous laugh. Finally, as we enter a long hallway, she elaborates:

"That used to be R&D down there. But we had to move out. The Coalition developed a cockroach that was part organic, part synthetic, and would behave like a normal cockroach but could be programmed, or given a job. They were intended to be used for surveillance, reconnaissance, delivery of pathogens and other bio-badness. They're incredibly versatile creatures, and very, *very* smart; we were coming up with amazing possibilities of how they could be used, but then, something unexpected happened. They started replicating, like, whoa—"

"They started printing themselves."

"Yeah, you saw, right? Insane stuff. Still completely beyond our grasp how they did it, how they developed the technology, if you can call it that. Our nanotechnologists were flipping out, all excited and, like, super, super scared. They kept talking about the end of the world and *grey goo*"—she waves her arms dramatically as she says it—"and they started just generally coming apart at the seams. But, so now, the buggers are just down there, multiplying away. And I'm sure they'll be there well after this building falls out of use. A few researchers have gone down there to see if they can study what's happening down there or, like, understand it, but none of them came back. The buggers get defensive if you start looking too closely."

"Defensive?"

"Aggressive."

"Do they get out? Like, out of the tower and into the world?"

"Oh yeah. They get everywhere. They're cockroaches. There are actually tunnels that go from that room into the floor of the lake and over to the shore so they have a place to go."

"I mean . . . is that the reason there are so many cockroaches now?"

Shea or Flannery laughs. "Oh, hell no. That's been going on since way before. What you saw downstairs is just making it worse. Way worse. You've heard what they say? If you see one, there are thousands? Those roaches down there? They're the 'one.' The 'thousands' were already here."

"Can that be true? There were so many down there."

"It's just one room. One room in the world."

At last, we arrive at a glass door with a security pad beside it.

"Is this it?"

"This is it," she says with a smile, as she contorts her hand oddly to touch the security pad in the correct way. She breathes into a tube. As the door opens she gestures toward the room with her head. "This is where the nerds live."

***

My life has been many things. At times it's been fun. At times it's been interesting. It's felt full of promise. It's been lonely. It's been comfortable. It's been dark. And it's been strange, and complicated, and quiet, and quick. And it's been scary. There are small things that scare me and big things that scare me, and sometimes my fears are broad and unfocused, seemingly everywhere, and sometimes they are specific and narrow, seemingly this and only this. Sleeping scares me. Leaving my house scares me. Reading the news scares me. And the cockroaches . . . I never got used to them, and while I see much to admire in them, while I've tried to convince myself of their sublimity, their perfection, while I collected them and spent hours and hours observing them in the hopes of understanding how and why they live, they still fill me with anxiety and loathing and dread. And when cockroaches scare you, everything scares you, because they are the world. The world scares me.

Even so, nothing could have prepared me for CURE R&D. Shea or Flannery leads me into the scariest room I've ever been inside my whole life, and I just walked out of a warehouse teeming with cockroaches. While the rest of the Lookout seems to be as empty as outer space, R&D is packed wall to wall with scientists, engineers, technicians, and designers. The room seems to go on forever like some mad convention center and everywhere you look there are weapons being tested, isolated roomettes housing chemical experiments, think tanks and breakout groups and teams upon teams upon teams. If you see one, there are thousands.

After two minutes in this place, I can surmise that it is populated with a great number of extremely intelligent people who are more in the habit of imagining what they can do than questioning what they should do. Which is exactly what their employer wants.

A sign hangs above that reads *be creative. be safe. be free.* Shea or Flannery walks me around and introduces me to some people, all of whom are wearing gas masks or body armor, many of whom hold ridiculous experimental weapons, which they talk about entirely in the abstract. They gloat, gleefully cite capabilities, various features and benefits; they tweaked this beam cannon so it could fire a more concentrated charge; they modified this virus so that it would be more lethal and easily spread by the tiniest drones you've ever seen (or not seen); they improved the SID so that its radius is longer and the fuel burns hotter and yet more slowly; and they flash excited smiles as they talk because science is fun!—not connecting the dots that those features and benefits will be used by Coalition sentries *to kill people*. Shea or Flannery mentions, offhand, that all these people graduated top of their class, mostly from "elite schools."

There are thick clear walls that separate us from the testing "cells," to protect against shrapnel, chemical splatter, contamination, fire. At the far end of the room are a small number of cells that are specifically for tests on "actuals." That is to say, live humans. We approach a cell in use, surrounded by a crowd of scientists and engineers buzzing with anticipation. The actual in the cell, I see, is Madysyn Blank. She looks insane, scarred, bruised, defeated, as though she's been tortured for months. She is restrained. She wears a green tank top and matching pants. There is no life in her eyes.

Shea or Flannery says, "Ooh, we're just in time, they're testing a new and improved version of diamond dust." Madysyn briefly makes eye contact with me, and in my head I hear her, she says something to me. I can't tell you what she says.

One technician aims a small hose at Madysyn; the hose is connected to a tank on his back. Another technician says, "Under way! In three! Two! One!" A harsh siren sounds off, and the armed technician engages the weapon. In looks like the blast from a fire extinguisher. But the moment the edge of the cloud touches Madysyn, she purges her demons. That does not fail. It is the only way to describe the sound she makes, to describe her suffering. After a few horrendous seconds, during which I scream but no one hears me (or no one cares), the cloud clears and Madysyn is an unrecognizable wet, red mannequin. The only part of her that is not red is her cybernetic arm, and that has clearly been damaged by the diamond dust. The armed technician checks his shoulder and hollers, "Should I hit her again?" and thankfully, oh fucking God, thankfully, the other technician says, "Negative."

Negative.

Two technicians come in and take Madysyn away. Of all the things I wish, one thing I can say with all honesty is that I wish, and deeply so, that this would not have been the last time that I saw Madysyn Blank. I had hoped we'd have another meeting, that I could help her, save her, that I could be an ear for her, she could tell me of her pain, the injustice she's faced, serving in a foreign war and then returning to a society in which she is only a test subject. Only a point of data. A one. A zero. A scratch more than nothing. I could listen to her cries, listen to her words, her bald honesty, her anger. I wanted that. I still want that.

But it was. It was the last time I saw her.

I pitch forward, end up on my knees, holding myself off the ground with one hand while throwing up into the other. I really am a coward.

Shea or Flannery misunderstands my nausea, telling me I'll "get used to it," while seeming genuinely concerned for me. She then points to a man about twenty yards away and says, "That's Mike, he's the guy you want to talk to."

And that's impossible. Mike. His name should be Judge. Or Rock. Or, like, Reaper. Not Mike. Seriously? Mike? I don't go to Mike. Instead, Shea or Flannery calls out to Mike, and he comes over to us. Mike has shark eyes.

He shakes my hand, then immediately starts grilling me about my knowledge, trying to figure out where I'll be most useful. I don't have any scientific acumen, no knowledge of engineering, was terrible at math. There's no contribution I can make to anything technological or tactical that they're working on, nor would I want to if I could. I've always thought of myself as relatively imaginative, inventive, creative—but the last thing I want to do is lend that to weapons research. I tell him, in no uncertain terms, that I have no real measurable skills or any specific aptitude that I'm aware of. So, by default, he leads me to a room marked *POLICY*.

There are several other people in this room, men and women, all older than me, staring at and reading off tablets. Mike tells me their function is to think up policy initiatives that will further the interests of CURE and its stakeholders. (I still have no idea who sits in the C suites of CURE. That should be public knowledge, this being a nonprofit and all, but alas. Or maybe CURE runs itself. Like self-replicating cockroaches, perhaps CURE, too, as a corporation, has found a way to perpetuate its own existence, reliant only on its own machinations and not on the output of any select humans. That is to say, maybe CURE has no leader.) The group begins discussing a policy initiative that will expand CURE sentries' legal abilities to shoot civilians if those civilians can be deemed "hostile to the Coalition, its agents, and their purposes in any fashion," even if those civilians are unarmed. They are the most uncritical critical thinkers I've ever encountered. Just hearing them talk for a few minutes, their lack of perspective, their pathological lack of human decency, makes me wonder if they've spent their entire lives around this table. As a way of breaking the ice, I start smashing their tablets, grabbing them and throwing them across the room. Some of them protest, stare at me with wide eyes, but no one gets up and stops me. No one draws a weapon. If you act crazy enough, people will assume you know what you're doing.

When I'm done, and I have the attention of the room, I say, "That's it. This office is closed. This division of R&D is closed. Go home."

There's a collective "*huunnh?*"

"No more. Stop thinking. You've all done . . . *so well* . . . that CURE—I mean, the Coalition—officially has enough influence. No more policy needed. Go home."

One of them asks, "Who are you?"

And it hits me. I know just what to do.

I furrow my brow and say, "Uh. I'm the new policy director."

"You?"

"Yes, me. What's your problem? Who's currently the policy director?"

"We don't have a director."

"They told me I was taking over for someone."

"But we don't have a director."

"Huh. Well, no wonder they brought me on."

"Oh."

"Yeah, oh. Now go home, all of you."

"Go home?"

"Leave. We're done for today. Actually, stay gone until you hear otherwise. I'll be in touch when it's time to come back."

With an almost palpable sense of relief, everyone at the table gets up and goes. Disappears. I sit in the room by myself and just wait for something, anything, to happen. Someone to come in and reprimand me. Someone to come in and ask me to do something, to demand something of me, to hold me accountable. Someone to come in and ask me my name. Anything. Nothing.

I sit and sit. I expect the phone to ring, before realizing there is no phone.

A cockroach skitter-scuttles across the desk. I take off my shoe and *I obliterate that fucking cockroach into paste.* Of course, there are trillions more. That fails. Quintillions more. That, too, fails. But this one is dead.

The door opens. Mary Kay Sutton peeks in. She gives me a cheesy little salute and asks, "Settling in?" and then she's gone. My ear aches. The ear that isn't there.

***

Days go by. Each day, I show up to the CURE R&D policy center or whatever the fuck. I sit in this office and I do nothing. Absolutely nothing. I research nothing. I develop nothing. I make no recommendations.

But it doesn't last. Eventually, leaders from other departments start coming to me and asking what I think about this or that. How existing policy might prohibit, restrict, or otherwise affect the use of this or that weapon, this or that special tactic, this or that offensive. These people's boundless creativity, coupled with their unflinching lack of empathy. And so thrilled are they, to have a job they can do well, so thankful to have any job at all in this economy, any employer that cares enough to pay them for their talent, that they'll develop the nastiest, most insidious technologies known to man. Gladly, they do this. Bonnie Shale was right when she said CURE was the great antagonist of our time. These people don't care that their brilliance is exploited to inflict unimaginable pain. CURE monopolizes everything. CURE bought out and brought down the electoral system. CURE systematically reduced our once great language to meaningless sound bites and slogans. CURE steals information from everyone and uses the histories or nude photos or writings or tax filings for blackmail. CURE molded the world in its own paranoid, egomaniacal, ultraviolent image. An image that is, like all bad people, fundamentally pathetic.

Whenever other employees stop in and ask me questions, I treat them horribly. I sneer and bark. I call them names. I'm willfully ignorant. I abuse them. I throw things. I just want them to leave me alone. A few times, some of the original members of the department show up, confused, bewildered, wanting to work, but I send them away. No, sorry, I forcefully drive them away. I incentivize them to never return. I surprise myself with my viciousness. Unfortunately, what I realize is that this only increases people's collective desire to please me. C'est la vie.

Over time, the department of R&D starts to look like the rest of the Lookout. There are cutbacks. Redundancies are identified. Managers are fired. Layoffs. Automation. Already impressed that I've streamlined my department's operations, I keep getting asked if I can absorb the responsibilities of other departmental directors as they're dismissed. There's a lot of "If it isn't too much to ask" and "If it wouldn't be a burden" and "If it would suit you to do so." And each time I'm like, "Fuck it, why not?" Better me than someone who will actually do it. Strangely, nothing changes in my day-to-day life. I suck up new titles like a vacuum, yet somehow I never do more.

I have a lot of time to think while I'm sitting in this little room doing nothing, avoiding any work that might manage to make the world a badder place.

One week, I am told that the director of the silent weapons division has been laid off, and would I mind overseeing that department as well? I am also asked if there are any silent weapons I wish to have developed.

And I realize: this is power. The ability to make immense decisions arbitrarily. I know nothing about silent weapons. I don't know how they work or even what they do. Shea or Flannery tells me that they are any variety of nonballistic weapons that either change the environment or affect their targets psychologically or neurologically, in many cases, doing so with no aural signature detectable by humans, hence "silent weapons." She tells me, "You've seen what a silent weapon can do."

"I have?"

"Diamond dust. Diamond dust is a silent weapon. Diamond dust is a *baller* silent weapon."

"Oh. Sure."

"Not all of them work so well. A lot of times they're backed by a great idea, but the execution just never comes together."

"You know I was put in charge of the silent weapons division?"

"Yes. I also heard you . . . saved my job. That you . . . that you said my name." Tears reach her eyes. "You asked for me by name. Thank you."

"No problem."

In this moment, Shea or Flannery and I are people who like each other. People who have no desire to kill each other. I wonder how I could get all people to not want to kill each other. What would it take? We have empathy. Empathy is real and it is powerful and we all have it. All of us. Even the worst among us, at one point, knew empathy. They still have it somewhere within. Is it too late to recover what little we have left? What will we be if we lose it entirely? If we snuff it out willingly? If we kill it?

I ask Shea or Flannery, "So, I could ask you, the silent weapons division, I mean, to investigate an exploratory neurological weapon?"

"Well, yeah. Totally. Honestly, we've tested so many that whatever you want, we probably already have some research on it."

"Interesting."

"What do you want it to do?"

***

I have Shea or Flannery, along with some other science types pilfered (salvaged?) from other departments develop something that I'm calling the Light of Empathy. It's a work in progress. As Shea or Flannery suggested, there was indeed some applicable research in this area already; CURE had wanted to find a way to provoke powerful emotional responses in targets, specifically, fear, anxiety, and grief. What I want is slightly different from that.

In essence, the Light of Empathy unlocks neural pathways that control empathetic responses and associates them with memory; it allows—forces—a person to recall moments from his or her life when he or she made another person feel a strong emotion, be that a positive or negative emotion, and to experience those moments from the other person's perspective. That is to say, someone blasted (I prefer the term "bathed") with the Light feels anything they've ever made another person feel. Anger, guilt, love. Anything.

It was something Madysyn said that made me think of it. About energy, how it bounces and flows. When we make another person feel something, we know it—we know it because we feel it, too. The energy comes back at us in waves. I sought to harness that. The erosion of empathy is what's sickened the world. Something else Bonnie Shale was right about. Her speech that night runs through my head constantly. Empathy has been lost, forgotten. It used to be the exceptions who lacked it. The *ones.* Now, it's the *millions.* The best weapon against a cruel, embittered world is one that forces it to feel again.

I originally describe the Light of Empathy to the developers as a silent weapon with the capability to target specific memories and times, and to use the imprint of those memories against the target. I meet no resistance, only eagerness and brainstorming. Questions of excitement, questions meant to clarify rather than confront. They praise my vision. They get right to work.

Initially they fail to achieve my original intent, but instead something very, very serendipitous occurs. What they bring back to me cannot target individual memories; what it can do instead is more, shall we say, broad. The person bathed in the Light would feel everything. Years' and years' worth of emotional responses, everything he or she ever made another person feel, every relationship, every enemy, every great romance, every betrayal, intimidation, and joy. Felt all at once and immediately.

I have it tested on two sentries, and my observation is that one of them had done a great deal more good than bad in his life; the other one had done more bad than good. Consequently, their responses to the Light are very different from one another's, but it is safe to say that each is now changed.

To be honest, I believe both of them are now quite mad as a result. Like I said, it was a work in progress.

Once the technology is far enough along, I have to think more about the problem of mass delivery. I have Development make two huge Lights and attach them like beacons to the spires on top of the Lookout, one that can be directed and focused, as well as one that glows like the sun. Ultimately, while I can see this being the most practical short-term solution, I'm afraid it doesn't reach enough people, just those in Chicagoland, and even people in the area might learn to avoid it. That being the case, maybe I could do a live feed of the Light. (I wonder if a video of the Light would have the same effect as the Light itself. I test it, and while it takes a bit longer than direct exposure, it does eventually—and completely—succeed.)

I worry that, in effect, I'm weaponizing empathy. I'm not killing anyone, though, so aren't you being a little dramatic? Does one die of joy? Of grief? I guess we'll see. Anything's possible.

You could argue, if you were so inclined, if you were the argumentative type, that I'm making people's lives worse by forcing them to feel things they might otherwise suppress or avoid. I guess it is a pretty nasty business. But it punishes most those who cared least. Empathy is a good thing. It is a force for good. Take a moment to think of the families that died in this year's tsunamis. Last year's civil wars. Today's train wreck. Take a moment to care about them. All of them. Doesn't that feel good? It doesn't? Why not? Aren't you a human being?

Empathy is volatile, I admit. Difficult to control. It spurs some people to great kindnesses, others to manipulation, and others yet to suicide. Something so unpredictable is scary. Maybe that's why all the cruelty: it's a fear reaction. We're afraid if we don't steel ourselves against caring that it could consume us. That it will turn on us.

Shea or Flannery comes to me and delivers bad news. More cutbacks. The company is more profitable than ever, but none of the profits are being diverted to worker pay. Very little is coming to R&D. This gives me a great deal of satisfaction. I want this department to be defunded, I absolutely want that. On the other hand, I like to finish what I start, and the Light of Empathy still needs time in the incubator. But time is something we do not have. Time is running low. It won't be long before CURE eliminates the human employees entirely, and then all that's left in Coalition Tower Two will be empty offices and a cockroach farm.

I need to devise a way, in the immediate future, to push the Light out to the masses that's more efficient than what we've been doing. We've been thinking too small, just hitting the locals. We need to take this national, but then that depends on video feeds and Internet connections, and those things can slow down, be interrupted, be ignored. Windows can be closed. There has to be another way, another strategy.

I hear a voice in my head. A mocking voice, so I think it's Madysyn's. She says *The Truth is all around.* I don't know what that means, but it sounds nice.

I step out into the R&D warehouse, this giant facility that not too long ago was packed with smarties devising ever more ingenious ways to kill people. Where is everybody? Doesn't anyone work in this place anymore? Why is this always happening to me?

I wander the halls of the Lookout, thinking. I think about a lot of things, and among those, I think of Larry. It breaks my heart to think that I was knocked unconscious, again, and didn't even get to say good-bye to him. And now I have no idea where he is or if he's alive, and the not knowing darkens me like a shadow and dulls me in a way that's hard to describe accurately, so I'll call it despair.

I walk past Marketing, and it looks like no one is within. I can hear what sounds like a circular saw cutting through metal. Or trying to. I step inside, and some of the lights are flashing, some are out entirely.

And then there's the wall. I look at the wall and there are roaches, and I don't know what they're doing exactly, but they seem to have arranged themselves in a pattern, a pattern that looks a bit like a brain. Brain activity, I should say. Neurons. Or like galaxies.

The Truth is all around.

It's the roaches. The roaches are all around, they are in everything, their feet have touched everything. They are the key to knowledge, all the earth's secrets, all human experience, all ecosystems, all history. Cockroaches are knowledge. Hideous knowledge. There is nothing that anyone could want to know that couldn't be learned from a cockroach. The information they've collected over the millennia, it may almost be complete, be total, and growing each second, like an endless sea, or like space. And it all comes here.

If you see one, there are thousands. Trillions upon trillions.

I follow a line of roaches from the brain pattern out into the hallway, and find—now that I see—that I can trace them. They lead me. I follow them down the hall. I follow them to an elevator. It goes up. So I go up. Up, up, up, to the top of the Lookout. My ears pop.

The elevator opens to an observation deck, one of those rooms that on the wrong day would be shrouded in low clouds, but on the right day, like today, allows you to see forever. I can see forever. If this were a normal company, in a normal country, in a normal world, this is the kind of room that might serve as an executive suite or, perhaps, a fancy meeting room. But here, this company, this country, this world, what I find instead is a mostly empty room with a pedestal made of gunmetal. Something on top of it glitters. I approach, and when I see what it is on the pedestal, I think that I must be hallucinating, as I've never seen anything like it. What I see on the pedestal is a single albino cockroach, with extremely long antennae, sitting patiently like a sage. And it's beautiful.

There is the sound of a woman screaming, as if from the sky, though from up here, the scream is coming from all around me. And I realize it's not a scream at all. That is the sound of the transfer. The armies of roaches worldwide take their knowledge, their observations, their surveys, everything they've touched and recorded, and they funnel it here, through an ever-expanding and ever more sophisticated network. The scream is the delivery, the scheduled upload of that information, en masse. It's not a scream at all. It's an arrival.

I'm standing on top of a tall, tall building. The city doesn't look like Chicago, but I know it's supposed to be Chicago from the civil defense sirens. Fighter jets buzz the city, weaving in between buildings. Maybe it's the Air and Water Show weekend again. Or still. I feel energy in my hands, as though they are electric, but no, that description is inadequate, it is beyond electric, it is volcanic, it is oceanic. These fail, too. I can't describe it, but I don't need to describe it, because language doesn't matter.

Language can't matter.

I understand that now that I'm here, I can't descend. This is somehow where I was meant to be, where I was meant to come, where I belong. Seeing no other possible course, seeing that it was here for me to find, I step toward the albino roach. I can see it considering me, waving its pale antennae. I can't hear any noise from the roach, but I do feel that it is speaking to me, sending me energy. I know what it wants me to do, and the thought is so jarring that, upon hearing it, I strongly consider crushing the albino cockroach with my fist, or brushing it to the floor and grinding it under my heel. But no, it assures me, this is what you want.

This is what you want.
This is what you want.
And it's right.

I look at the world and I see a psychopath. It is said one of the defining characteristics of psychopathy is the absence of empathy. It's not only lack of empathy, though; psychopaths are marked by unreliability, insincerity, lack of remorse, lack of shame, unmotivated violence, egocentricity, inability to learn from past failures and mistakes, a chilling and wholly artificial charm, and at times, a seemingly bottomless capacity for cruelty. If there's a better description of society, I can't imagine what it is.

It used to be that empathy was what separated us from the warlords, from the terrorists, from the school shooters, from the rampagers. Empathy was our great difference, what made us and kept us human in the face of monsters. But empathy is hard to wield, it turns out. We got tired of empathy, tired of trying to understand the things we fear, the persons we loathe, tired of trying to make sense out of madness. So we became the madness. We became the shooters. We killed our empathy and found that we preferred it this way.

In the corner of the room, I hear a rumble, like a rolling thunder. No, that fails. Like an earthquake. Fails. I look over and see a great black hound. Her. She lies on her belly holding what looks like a heart made on a 3-D printer in her paws, gnawing on it like a cybersynthetic bone. I look at her, and for a moment she pauses in her chewing and looks back at me. I hear voices in my head. Deceptive voices. Dark voices. I already knew that she was unlike other hounds, but in this moment I notice that she is unlike other hounds, in part, because she has six legs. She returns to her snack, and I try to forget that she's there. As if I could ever forget her. As if she's ever been forgotten.

Curled up and sleeping beside her, as comfortable as can be, is Larry. Precious Larry. He's alive. He's here with me. There are pets in the Lookout, if you climb high enough.

The albino roach sits patiently, ready to deliver me access to every bit of information collected by the feet, eyes, and antennae of every cockroach on the planet. Because this is what I want. To receive this information is to know everything. Cockroaches have traversed every path, gotten into every corner, squeezed through every crack. They've been on every person, heard every conversation. Energy bounces and flows—so they've heard every human thought.

This albino cockroach has infinite knowledge. It is a masterwork. A 3-D-printed living motherboard, a six-legged power source that CURE has been using, presumably, to spy on the world. Or maybe the albino roach has been using CURE to police the world. It's hard to say. But with it, I can know everything. Every inch of the planet, every person in every country, all their private thoughts and issues and problems and ideas. All fed into countless cockroaches' feet and feelers. And consolidated here. No errors. No redundancies. A single version of the truth.

I put my hand down by the roach, and it waves its antennae. I can't grab it, I know that to be true. I have to wait, to be accepted by it. It's going to consider me first. I don't know what it is in me that it's looking for, if it's reading my mind, my brain waves, looking for clues. I worry it may walk away from me, refuse me, but then I see instead that it opens its wings. It doesn't fly; rather, under its wings I see a universe. Energy leaping and exploding like supernovas, strands of light. Information.

Then I hear a voice in my head, but not a human voice, not the voice of any person speaking to me, nor are they really words that I hear. The best way I can describe it is language I feel in my mind (though that fails), language asking me, in its way, what it is I plan to do if I have what I want.

And without answering, without needing to answer, I respond that what I would do with the albino roach's power, the reach and scope of its connections, its pathway into the consciousness of every living human being on the planet, some nine billion people, all told, what I would do, what I would make them do, is simple, and I hold it in my head as the little white bug lifts its legs and skitter-scuttles onto my hand.

I will make them feel.

Feel. Not only my pain, but also my joy. My anguish. My love. My despair. My hope. I would solve the world's empathy problem by making them all feel what I feel. If I smile, the world understands why it is that I smile, and it, too, smiles. If the world fills me with agony and anger, so, too, will everyone know and experience that heat, that frustration, that bitter rage. If I stub my toe, all people will stub their toes. If I cut my hand, it's nine billion cuts.

The world will know my memories, my fears, my failings and insecurities. People will understand my shame because it will be laid bare for them in their hearts, and they, too, will know it, it will be their shame, and in time they will understand why.

The world will miss my brother, as I have missed him. Jack. He will be their brother. They will all suffer the loss, they will cry at his grave, they will not blame him for his own slaying, swift and senseless as it was. When they think of him they will want to drink, because when I think of him I want to drink.

The world will cry for my mother. The world will answer for my father.

The world will understand my loathing of roaches. Even as I use them, speak through them, I cannot escape how they make me feel. And everyone will know how paralyzing it can be; everyone will understand my sadness, understand my confusion that such a thing exists and how I've always questioned the existence of a divine being because of them, for why would anyone intentionally create something like cockroaches? They are the proof to me that God either doesn't exist, or does exist but is completely indifferent toward us. What a terrible creator made, CURE perfected. I hold that perfection in my hand.

The world will deeply and intimately understand at least one person—universally—and that person will be me. I use the roaches to transmit myself, my consciousness, to everyone.

After a few months, I start to wonder if this is effective enough, though. After all, I'm just some guy in a building that might be invisible, in the middle of a lake. There's not much happening to me that is all that relatable or would provoke the deepest of empathies. Though I did have a brother and his name was Jack. He was killed by an impatient man. I have parents whom I'll never see again. I believed in a girl in a blue coat, who turned out to be nothing but numbers. I have lost friends. I have seen tragedy. I start with these ideas because I figure if people can empathize with the things that have made me sad, then maybe they won't be so quick to threaten death upon others, that they'll consider who else might be sad, that they'll try to relate. The roaches report back to me, and their reports indicate that what I'm doing is making an impact, but it's not nearly enough. I'm relying on wells of empathy that may have long since dried up. I can deliver my thoughts to the world. I can't make them care.

I page Shea or Flannery but get no reply.

I move from thinking about sad things to thinking about scary things, so everyone can know and appreciate fears rather than mocking them. I think about things that make me anxious. I dwell on things that I dread. I step on a cockroach and grind it with my foot, making that awful crunch. I spend some time thinking about the ways roaches are superior to us, hoping that it will instill in everyone across the globe a certain humility, and ability to understand that we are not in charge anymore, if we ever were. I find a window that looks out over Lake Michigan (hahahaha, that's all of them), and I stand a foot or two away from it and then lean forward, pressing my forehead against the glass, so now everyone understands acrophobia and will not belittle others for their fear of heights. I find a small cabinet under a sink and I crawl into it, so now everyone understands claustrophobia and will stop ridiculing those who feel terrified in elevators. In my mind, I cue up blasts, dust, the smell of chemicals, the scream of low-flying jets, the uncertainty in distant percussion, so that everyone knows what it's like to live in a war-torn country and stops acting like it can't be all that bad. I lie in the dark and conjure up the image of demons, real and false, and those who would come to violate us in the night. I spend a lot of time on fears, as much in the world will be better if people can relate to each other's fears instead of diminishing them, ignoring them, shaming them. We are, all of us, afraid. Each day, old fears are validated, latent fears awaken, and unnamed fears we never even knew we could have overwhelm us. Each day, even if we are lucky enough to return to our beds unscathed, there are things that we could not ignore, even if we wanted to. Videos of killings and disasters. Images of blasts and crash sites and structural failures. Things we never wanted to see, we are forced to behold. We have no choice in the matter. We all have PTSD from being alive.

I do spend time on joy as well. Things that give me joy, like Larry, and the taste of cold beer, and language that is intentional and precise and makes sense. And kindnesses large and small. Seeing people hug each other. Hearing the word "yes." Joy is one of those things that, for some reason, people decide they can't comfortably relate to, so when they see joy, they demean it, attack it. I want everyone to understand joy and let joy be joy. Joy is needed, now more than ever.

Somewhere along the line, though, there's another change in my thinking. I've arranged it so that everyone knows me, that everyone can empathize with me, understand me. But can they empathize with each other? The answer is likely no, sadly. In fact, the roaches sending in their reports confirm this: there are still wild conflicts, still persecution, still corruption, still rampant disinformation and hate-mongering and trolling on the Internet. So I decide to shut down the Internet. There. That's done.

Then, I concentrate.

The idea is to expand the work. It's not enough that they empathize with me. They must empathize with each other. Everybody must empathize with everybody. Everybody must understand everybody else. Empathy will be universal. All pain will be shared. All circumstances known. All the invective and callousness will crumble into dust. No one will be able to do anything or feel anything without everyone else on the planet feeling that same thing.

And I have the means to do it. I have the Light of Empathy. The Light has the power to make someone feel what he or she has made others feel. But I can take it a step further. I can tweak the Light so that it makes everyone feel anything that anyone has ever felt. I ask the albino to locate the knowledge I need from the collective brain of science and engineering, and it takes nanoseconds to find it. I have what I need.

Energy bounces and flows. Just as the roaches have transmitted my consciousness, so, too, may they transmit the Light of Empathy. All it would take is a little adjustment. I try it. It works. The Light can now be sent anywhere and at the speed of thought.

The Light reaches every dark pocket of the earth. Anyone who sees a cockroach sees the Light, bathes in it. And everyone feels everything. A side effect of this is widespread madness, but it is a madness that is uniform. To teach empathy to a psychopath is to destroy him. And so it goes with society. You can't just take something that is unfeeling and cold, something that has spent ages and ages refining its cruelty and suddenly, in one moment on one blustery day, open its heart to everything it should have been feeling: all the panic, all the wonder, all the remorse, all the love. But that's precisely what I've done. And it's what I wanted.

This is what you want.

The albino roach rests on the back of my hand. Or maybe it's embedded itself. In any case, we are one.

We are the one who took a monster and gave it a heart. We are the one who administered this aggressive, necessary treatment. It will take time for society to heal, but when it does heal, it will be far, far better off. In the end. People will be fair to each other. People will stop tormenting the others. They'll stop killing children. Stop laughing at suffering. Stop denigrating all that does not please them. Stop authorizing the use of force. People will see each other as people. They will see each other as life.

But that's all in the future. That may be long after I'm dead. I know that. But I am hopeful. The Coalition of United Response Engineers has served its purpose. It has discovered the ultimate weapon, and that weapon is feeling. From my perch atop this Lookout—a perch built on misery, quickly and under budget—I can feel them, the billions and billions touched by the Light. I feel them all. I know them all.

Their heavy postures.

Their stares of awe.

Their quaking smiles.

Their gibbering.
Their wavering.
Their screaming.
Their catharsis.
Their song.
This is what it is to be human.
I understand them.
They understand me.
It is snowing.
And I am happy.

ABOUT THE AUTHOR

Photo © 2011 Braden Moran

Scott T. Barsotti is a playwright, author, and horror fan, tracing his love of the genre back to childhood readings of *Scary Stories to Tell in the Dark*. *Single Version* is his first novel. Scott spent over a decade in Chicago making theatre, in particular with WildClaw, producers of horror theatre and the annual *Deathscribe* radio play festival. His dramatic work includes the plays *Jet Black Chevrolet*, *Kill Me*, *The Revenants*, and *Brewed*. Scott received a master of fine arts in writing from the School of the Art Institute of Chicago. He now lives in Pittsburgh. Visit his website at http://scottbarsotti.wordpress.com.

LIST OF PATRONS

This book was made possible in part by the following grand patrons who preordered the book on inkshares.com. Thank you.

Abbie Speer
Adam and Carey Barsotti
Aly Renee Amidei
Amy Le Donne Dixon
Anna Brenner
Barry Brunetti
Benjamin Macaluso
Bill Schildnecht
Carrie L. Tancraitor
Casey Cunningham
Charles N. Benson
Chris Skerrett
Christopher Oscar Pena
Craig Cunningham
Dave Barrett
Debbie Strecker
Dustin Pettegrew
Eleanor Matelan

Eric Silvera
Evann873
Ezra Smith
Jean Boster
Jocelyn Steele
Katie McLean Hainsworth
Leanne Phillips
Mark D. Steele
Mark Raymond Moller
Morgan C. Conrad
Newell M. Grant
Randy Steinmeyer
Robert Cappelletto
Robert Kruse
Ryan Hoadley
Sarah Espinoza
Steve and Marisa Barsotti
Tom Katzenmeyer

Quill

Quill is an imprint of Inkshares, a crowdfunded book publisher. We democratize publishing by having readers select the books we publish—we edit, design, print, distribute, and market any book that meets a pre-order threshold.

Interested in making a book idea come to life? Visit inkshares.com to find new book projects or to start your own.

CPSIA information can be obtained
at www.ICGtesting.com
Printed in the USA
FSOW02n2255080916
24734FS